Alex Christofi was born and grew up in Dorset. After reading English at the University of Oxford, he moved to London to work in publishing. He has written a number of short pieces for theatre, and blogs about arts and culture for *Prospect* magazine. *Glass* is his first novel.

'Günter Glass, with his flaws and his limitations, and his belief in the better part of human nature, is a great pleasure to spend time with. I was moved and amused and ultimately comforted by Günter's sky-reaching spirit and his quest for deeper meaning in a world of transparencies' Stephen Kelman, author of *Pigeon English*

'*Glass* was such a pleasure to read, funny, beautiful and perceptive. I found Günter a gentle endearing hero, a unique little fish in an extremely moving *bildungsroman*. It struck a deep note about the fleeting nature of existence' Sara Crowe, author of *Campari for Breakfast*

'*Glass* is a brilliant novel with a first-person narrative voice that's so natural and understated, I found myself re-reading passages in order to relive emotional experiences that were happening as a result of the gentle, but Nabokovian precision of Alex Christofi's prose' Simon Van Booy, author of *The Illusion of Separateness*

ALEX CHRISTOFI

GLASS

A NOVEL

SERPENT'S TAIL

First published in 2015 by Serpent's Tail, an imprint of Profile Books Ltd 3 Holford Yard Bevin Way London WC1X 9HD www.serpentstail.com

ISBN 978 1 84668 967 3 eISBN 978 1 78283 024 5

Designed and typeset by Crow Books

Printed in Great Britain by Clays Ltd, St Ives plc

10 9 8 7 6 5 4 3 2 1

FSC
www.fsc.org
MIX
Paper from
responsible sources
FSC® C018072

Someone taught that temples are for fanatics only and took away the temples and promised there was no need for temples. And now there is no shelter. And no map for finding the shelter of a temple. And you all stumble about in the dark, this confusion of permissions. The without-end pursuit of a happiness of which someone let you forget the old things which made happiness possible. How is it you say: '*Anything is going*'?

David Foster Wallace, *Infinite Jest*

Foreword

I am well aware that you probably do not consider glass to be crucial to the success of the human race. Let me assure you, it is as essential to the story of humanity as light, or water, and has a quality of character unsurpassed in any other substance. It appears pure and clear though, like the pearl, it is a purity composed of dirt. There is nothing like glass to catch the various accretions of the world on its surface, though we create it for its opposite quality: that of transparency.

Glass is a cipher. It can be sharp, or soft. It can stop sound; it can make the blind see. It can bend light itself with the dexterity of water; it can focus light into a cutting laser, or disperse it in a thousand droplets. Glass can even form mirrors to turn light back on itself, and show us what we are. Without glass, there would be no civilisation, any more than there might be without fire. It was glass that brought light into our homes; that reeled in the whole wide universe, so that we might better scrutinise it. Without glass, we would live in a windowless, flat world, unshaven, blind, thirsty, sullenly groping at our faces to discern what shape they made.

One man is responsible for my deep awe of glass. I met him in Salisbury, at the Cathedral where I work. He is dead now, sadly – his family has a tradition of jumping the queue to meet their

Maker – and as one of few who might understand his hidden motivations, I have taken it upon myself to tell the story that he now cannot. I have gleaned what particulars I can from newspaper and police reports, and from those who knew him.

You wouldn't believe the truth if I told it to you, so I am taking the liberty of couching it in my own brand of picaresque. Above all else, it amuses me. But if I deviate from the reality, or invent a character here and there, I do so only to separate out the various truths, just as a prism shows white light to be composed of a number of distinct and brilliant colours. I am convinced it is the only way to proceed: he was a very great man, composed of many contradictions, and I do not propose staring at the sun.

Of course, I do not know whether Günter would have approved of my rendering him in a work of fiction. I rather think that he might cry out, like Jesus before him, 'Woman, what have I to do with thee? Mine hour is not yet come.'[1]

Dean Angela Winterbottom, Salisbury, 2 May 2012

---

1 John 2:4. DW: I know one is not really supposed to use the King James Version in this day and age, but it's a damn sight more poetic than that awful New International Version.

I

An Introduction to Glass

As it happens, my name is Glass. My mother cut a deal with my father: if I was to get his surname, she would pick my forename. Perhaps yearning for the abandoned country of her birth, she decided on a solid German name, a hero's name. And so they called me Günter.

I have come to wonder whether I will make it through my twenty-third year. In the nine months since my mother died, I started a new job, which led me to meet a number of new people, one of whom I killed in a misunderstanding. But other things happened in the first twenty-two years that I should explain first.

My first years, as you might imagine, were unremarkable. I went through all the usual phases: vegetable (0–1), animal (1–4), memorable (4+). I look down on my early childhood as a time when I didn't know many words and couldn't put things in categories. The benefit of this was that almost everything came as an epiphany. A gloopy substance! It tasted nice! Light changed colour through it! It was sticky! It stuck to the cat! The downside was that I had to formulate rules for behaviour, such as 'one is only allowed honey sometimes (when?)' and 'do not pour honey on the cat'. It seems to me now, though it wasn't apparent at the time, that growing up is the forfeit of one's pure experience in return for the comfort and reliability of rules.

I would say that we had a happy family. I mean, Dad's not the sort of person to actually say that he is happy, and obviously, if you picked a day at random, the strong likelihood was that there would be some kind of disturbance or argument, but the important thing was that it was always replaced by a different one the next day, so that it didn't develop into a feud. Apparently there weren't any arguments before Max was born, but that was only a year after I was born, so I can't remember. I can't think that I would have caused any.

I should explain something about my brother. People assume that, because he's deaf, he can't be a bad person. But his being deaf is completely unrelated to the fact that he's a total bastard. Whenever it gets too much I close my eyes and think to myself, *you'll never hear music*,[2] and then I feel bad for him, and I suspect that other people do something similar and this is why he gets away with being such a bastard. But I know what you're thinking: surely he wasn't always such a bastard. Maybe there was an event in his childhood that made him lash out at the people who cared about him, and maybe before this event there existed a pre-bastard Max.

Let's have a look at the evidence. When I was four and he was three, he managed to get hold of some scissors and cut my comfort blanket up into neat confetti. When I was five and he was four, he put Lego under my sheets and in my empty shoes and everywhere he thought they might cause me discomfort. When I was nine and he was eight, he woke up early and unscrewed the inside door-handle of our shared bedroom before shutting me in. I thought I was stuck in some inescapable nightmare and, needing the toilet very badly, resorted to

---

2 DW: Some deaf people can't hear music at all. They are called 'profoundly deaf', their ears being about as much good as if they were submerged under a hundred tonnes of water. Max can, in fact, hear music, but it's the difference between a live orchestra and a touch-screen phone.

escaping through the (ground floor) window, only to find that he'd also locked the back door. The cat appeared, staring at my bare feet and pyjamas, as if to say, *you too?*

In return for these human rights abuses, I had the privilege of sitting with Mum every time we took a family trip to the hospital. Dad would go in with Max, and Mum would sit with me in the waiting room, where there was an abacus and some other toys that I was too old for. When we arrived, there was always a gang of two or three children playing with them who would tell me to go away. Once, I remember distinctly, I was called 'fatty fats McNugget'. I suppose I didn't really mind being outlawed, though, if my mum was there. I would sit on her lap and help with her wordsearch. Mum explained that a wordsearch was easier than a crossword because you didn't need to know what the word meant, but she always did know, and she would always tell me. I thought of wordsearch like battleships. The big boat might look bigger and therefore nastier, but it was the easiest to hit. So if there was a word like 'sesquipedalian', it wouldn't be hiding in the corners. When we first started playing, Mum would read the words to me; later, she would try to make me read them to her. She took great pleasure in pronouncing long words with me. German has lots of long words because you can join two words together to make a new one.[3]

The fact that it was always my mother who looked after me during these long waits confirmed my instinct that my mother and I got on the best. Though the rules weren't stated, we wouldn't speak sign in the waiting room, and we would not talk about Max.

Lots of people love their mothers, but I think it's fair to say I loved mine more than you love yours. When I was very young, it

3 DW: I can't find any record that Günter spoke German, even later, in London. His mother seems never to have taught him, perhaps because she had spent so long convincing herself she was English.

felt as if we were still one person, as if my every need were pre-
empted by her. Nestled in close, I could hold her and have her
arms surround me and almost feel she still carried me through
the world. We had been separated, of course, but I was still a
part of her. If I ventured out into the world at all, it was on her
behalf, as an extension of her, and I would always report back
on the things I had seen and done, the knowledge I had collected
to share with her. Sometimes, to help me in my job of bring-
ing the world to her, she would tell me things that she already
knew, things that would help me understand what I was seeing
and doing. And even though I got things wrong, and I never
knew the right thing to say, and I sometimes forgot to put socks
between my feet and my shoes, she loved me.

She wasn't pretending, either. She liked to look at me. She
thought my jokes were funny, even or especially if they didn't
make sense. As we grew older I wanted to reach a balance point
in our relationship where I might also look after her. But I never
got that far. Even in the end, I had no way to comfort her as she
had comforted me.

2

Salad Days

When I was seven, my father took me to discover glass. Mum had a shift on the checkouts at Sainsbury's, and there wasn't space to hide me under the till, so I had to go on Dad's business trip. Dad was a salesman. What he sold changed regularly, so the only constant was that he was always selling something. He never excelled, which means he probably didn't cheat anyone out of their money, but when other children asked me what my dad did, I got a bit confused and mumbled something about him wearing a tie.

My father has always been a straightforward man. You wouldn't catch him using two words when one would do. You'd never catch him using words when a nod would do, though this did not make him good at sign language. He was always an advocate of just getting on with it, eating what was put in front of him, putting one foot in front of the other, drinking in moderation, almost hitting targets, making ends meet, walking before jogging, but he would never tell you this because he kept himself to himself. He has not, until recently, been the kind to share his thoughts or feelings, so I used to think of him as a kind of anti-philosopher, capable of doing many things unthinkingly that others might question.

On this particular day, my father had to take a trip to Dudley. He couldn't very well have taken me into his meeting, as I liked to pull out long strings of questions which, if left unchecked, would unravel the very jumper of the universe. I might have ruined the meeting, and cost Dad his reputation, or worse, his job, and then there wouldn't be any money for food or the mortgage. To have allowed that to happen would have been irresponsible. So he did something that would no longer be considered Good Parenting: he found the nearest museum, put me in it, and told me not to leave the building.[4]

At first I wandered around peering at and through the pieces on display, marvelling at how they chewed up the world and spat it back out in swirls and strange perspectives. It was very like a liquid, but frozen, so when a kindly old man told me that glass was in fact a very slow liquid, I could see for myself that he must be right. And yet how very like a solid it behaved, how very like ice. I had just learnt about solids and liquids and gases, and it definitely looked like a solid. It was exciting to see something breaking the rules.

I learnt that glass was one of the first materials that man made; that scientists found glass very useful because it could hold almost any chemical; glass was made of the same stuff as sand; glass was the reason Galileo saw the stars.

I imagined that my family were the royalty of glass. I was Günter, Prince of Glass, and people could see straight through me, and they came to me to ask about the stars and I gave them all the answers. As I wandered towards the end of the hall, I wondered what my father, King of Glass, was up to. He was probably magicking sand into crystal palaces for the people of Dudley. That must be why he travelled so much, because Salisbury didn't really have any sand. And he went on a trip to Bournemouth once, and there was lots of sand there.

---

4 DW: It's called The Broadfield House Glass Museum. It's still there, if you're ever stuck for childcare.

Thinking about my dad made me feel lonely. I looked around and there were some adults standing still and looking at things and holding their chins, but they all looked very stern, and I was hungry, and my dad had left me all alone. I began to well up. If Dad was making castles he had to show me how for when I was king, and it was very mean of him not to take me along. Instead I was alone in this stupid place, and he'd been gone for – I looked at the clock – thirty-seven minutes! I started to cry in earnest.

The old man who had told me about glass being a liquid came over and knelt down beside me.

'Now then, where's your daddy?'

'I don't know,' I said angrily. I'd thought that much was obvious.

'Deary me,' he said. 'Would you like to come and sit with me behind the desk?'

I nodded, still a bit angry.

'Come on then,' he said. I took his hand, which felt like sugar paper.

We sat behind the desk in the foyer, and I took the money from people and gave it to him to put in the register. He gave me one of his liver sausage sandwiches. When he chewed, his moustache wriggled.

'Your moustache is lovely,' I told him. He laughed.

'Thank you,' he said. 'Where's your moustache?'

'I left it at home,' I said. 'My moustache is made of glass.'

'Is it now?'

'Yes, it was a present from the Queen of Sweden,' I said. I instantly regretted saying the last bit. It had been quite believable up to then. Now he probably knew I was fibbing. I wasn't very good at telling lies.

But he didn't seem to notice, and after a few minutes another man came up to us and said hello. He was wearing a short-sleeved T-shirt with thick, tight sleeves over his forearms like black bandages.

'Would you like to see how we make glass?' said the moustache man. I nodded vigorously, sandwich rattling round in my head. 'This is my friend Daz. What's your name, son?'

'Günter.'

The other man shook my hand with thumb and fingers. 'Nice to meet you, Günter.' I left moustache man at the desk and followed T-shirt man through a door to a workshop.

I watched, mesmerised, as he took a long metal rod about his height from the corner, and walked over to a big thing on the back wall that looked like a cupboard. He opened a little door to reveal a circular hole, belching heat and glowing orange. It looked like a rising sun. My face got hot.

He dipped the rod into the middle of the sun, and then pulled it back out again, a gloopy mass of sun-honey glowing on its tip. He twirled the rod in his fingers quickly, blowing into the end so that the sun-honey blew up into a balloon. He was a sorcerer, a priest. I decided then that I would live here, in this room, sleeping under the work bench and living off liver sausage sandwiches, and I would learn how to make glass birds and castles and moustaches. The sorcerer rolled the glass around on a metal table surface, shaping it into a perfect oval and always keeping it moving before it dripped out of shape. I was enraptured.

I heard shouting from behind me. Only in crescendos did I hear the words '—WOULD YOU LET HIM—' and '—YOU BLOODY—' and I realised that my father had come to take me back. Could he not see I had made a life for myself here?

The door opened to reveal the moustache man, red in the face, and my father, redder. The T-shirt man had to keep the glass moving while it was still cooling. I walked over to say hello, sensing that this was what the situation required, and Dad pushed me out of the room with a big hand on the back of my head.

'You shouldn't have let him in here with all the equipment,' my dad continued, his face gradually returning to its normal colour. 'He has some funny ideas. Not much going on up there,' he said, patting my head.

'He was as good as gold,' said the moustache man. And then, with the apologetic tone of the defeated, 'Mind you, you shouldn't have left him on his own like that.'

I personally thought there was a lot going on in my head, but I decided that my dad wouldn't understand. I decided that it was really other people who were stupid and not nearly as interesting as things like sun-honey. When I grew up, I didn't want to be a man with an angry face and a tie, I wanted to make beautiful things and have a moustache.

We didn't say much in the car on the way home. I only interrupted the silence for really important questions, like, 'Is glass where our name comes from?'

'No.'

'It sounds the same.'

'The word is German. The name is Welsh.'

'Mum's German.'

He didn't reply to that, so I assumed my line of reasoning was correct. How wrong we can be when all we have is logic.

But I wasn't stupid. I didn't care if Dad thought I was. People could think of me whatever they wanted. I knew what was interesting, and that was what mattered. My classmates all had boring ambitions. If they didn't want to be in the emergency services, they were going to follow their parents into the army or onto a farm, or they wanted to stay in school as a teacher. At a push, they could conceive of breaking news to people as a lawyer or a doctor. Not one person ever claimed they wanted to be a magician, a spy or a ship's captain. There were a million jobs out there, and half of my classmates wouldn't even end up in one of the jobs they said they wanted – they'd end up wearing a tie and farming invisible fruit. Not me. I didn't know what it was yet, but I was going to find something different.

3

A Death in the Family

The week that my mother died was eventful for many reasons. Dad had his last day at work, and after decades on the road, I think he was secretly looking forward to staying in one place for a bit. It was my twenty-second birthday. Max had just got a job, which was a massive step for him. Though no one ever officially discriminated against him, he would always receive a carefully worded letter describing a 'more able candidate' or someone whose CV 'better reflected the qualifications they were looking for'. That was the thing about discrimination that was never mentioned: it was the passive option, the coward's way out. *You don't have any legs? Well, we do have stairs ... Although in the interests of fairness, looking at your CV, I think we can find a more able candidate.* One company even had the gall to tell him that the position had already been filled, while they continued to advertise the vacancy.

So the circle of life continued: Max was gainfully employed and my dad was given a crystal whisky tumbler and a bottle of Laphroaig for his long service to the company. It has always amazed me, looking back, how easily trivial events make an impact on people's lives. If I'd told him, at the start of that week, that he'd soon discard the tumbler in favour of drinking straight from the bottle, he probably would have replied that he didn't often drink whisky, and point to the novelty gift on the wall, which had appeared one Christmas under the tree, with no named sender or addressee. It was mocked up to look like a fire alarm. It said IN CASE OF EMERGENCY, BREAK GLASS. Behind the little clear plastic barrier, there was a minibar-sized bottle of whisky. 'That's been there for, what, nine years,' he'd have said.

My parents were fussing around the kitchen, having just returned from an anniversary break to Rotterdam. Mum was getting some lunch together and Dad was fiddling with the new DAB radio that he'd bought.

'Can you pass the red pepper, Günter?' asked Mum.

'Yes of course.'

What is this button? signed Dad.

That's to save the channel as a favourite, signed Max.

'Try one of these,' my mum said.

And this one? signed Dad.

'What is it?' I asked.

That's to switch back to FM, signed Max.

'It's a Dutch waffle,' said my mum. 'Try it.' I bit into it. 'It's mostly syrup. Don't eat them all, we've got lunch ready in half an hour.'

'Ishhamazhin,' I said through a mouthful. 'Whatshitcall?'

'Stroopwafel.⁵ I tell you what though, those Dutch, they never eat any veg. I didn't see a carrot the whole time we were there. They won't touch a vegetable unless it's pickled.'

'Sounds like German food,' I said.

She rubbed my back affectionately. Mum was always a touchy-feely person, which I miss. Dad's more of a get-drunk-and-punch-a-wall person now.

We all sat down for lunch and passed each other dishes, and we all ate healthily, and the food was delicious in a way that I

5 DW: Günter only ever called them Dutch waffles.

took for granted at the time. It never occurred to me that cooking might go wrong, because Mum made it look easy.

'Shall we all go out for a celebratory dinner tonight?' asked Mum, as she cut up a spinach and ricotta filo pastry. She put down the spatula. *Celebrate? Max has a job now, Günter is turning twenty-two and your father's finally going to have a rest.*

'I told you I don't mind working,' said Dad irritably. 'I've been working all my life, another year won't kill me.'

'It's not your choice to make, dear. You're getting older, you have to retire. Simple as that.'

Me and Günter will help, signed Max. *Well I will, and Günter can when he finds a job.* Ha! He never lifted a finger round the house. Mum did everything for him, washed his clothes, practically bathed him. He lived off her guilt. I had always tried to tell her that Max's deafness wasn't her fault. She was convinced that it was something she'd eaten during her pregnancy, but I told her it wasn't that simple. I'd even printed out a page from Wikipedia to show her the week before but she had refused to read it.

'What's the point in reading it if some idiot can come along and write any old rubbish?' she'd asked.

'It's not like that, Mum. The people who write this thing, they're participating in something higher, they're idealists. There's an article on basically anything that's ever existed.'

She didn't say anything, but I could tell she was impressed.

Later that night, after we had decided to go out for a meal at the Seafood and Steakhouse, she picked up the conversation again.

'So this encyclopaedia.'

'Wikipedia.'

'Yes. Can you learn about any topic on there?'

'You can learn about pretty well anything, I suppose.'

'You should brush up, then. One day, someone's going to ask you about Napoleon or, or, trigonometry, and you're going to feel very silly.'

I stared at the menu guiltily. The three men in the family ordered steak, and Mum went for seabass. We all shared a bottle of wine, since it was a special occasion, and we held our glasses silently to the centre of the table. A waiter arrived, carrying four plates using only two arms.

'Who ordered the steak tartare?'

Did he say T-A-R-T-A-R-E? signed Max to Mum.

Yes, I signed. 'It's my brother's.'

The waiter looked at Max nervously.

'I wish I could learn sign language,' he said as he put the plate down.

'Is there a court injunction preventing you?' asked my mum with an encouraging smile.

'And who ordered the seabass?' he cut in.

'That would be me,' she replied.

'There you are. And two steak frites.'

He gave a perfunctory smile and made a hasty getaway.

We ate, and Max talked about all the things he wanted to buy with his new salary.

Because I'm retiring, signed Dad gracelessly, *I might try painting.*

Max and I both stifled a laugh, Max making his small glottal noises, and Mum coughed on a mouthful of seabass.

But you've never liked art. You always used to say that art was for people who didn't have jobs, I signed.

But I don't have a job, signed Dad. *It might be good. I need to stay busy or I get glum.*

Mum was still coughing on her food, and threw back a mouthful of water.

'You okay my love?' asked Dad. 'Pat on the back?'

Mum shook her head. Her eyes were filling up.

Bread, she signed.

The waiter was studiously ignoring our table so I got up and asked for some bread, as Dad tried to pat her on the back. She put her hand into her mouth, which was the moment that I realised something must really be wrong. My mother always had impeccable manners. She winced. Then she tried to drink more water, but couldn't. Around us, everyone chatted amicably, murmuring and knocking sonorous cutlery together. Mum had closed her lips but her mouth looked unnatural, like she was harbouring a golf ball. She rooted around in her handbag, pushed her plate away and emptied the handbag's contents onto the tabletop, finding a compact mirror. She opened her mouth again to inspect, but by now she was quite red in the face. I stood up and cleared my throat.

'Is there a doctor in the building?' I said loudly, not knowing quite where to look.

'Günter . . .' began my dad, who hated to make a fuss.

'She's choking!' I hissed.

One woman in the corner had wiped her mouth with a napkin and excused herself from the woman that she was dining with. She had a dark bob and almond eyes. Everybody was looking at us, though they pretended to continue their discussions.

The doctor led Mum off to the bathroom, picking up tweezers from the spilled contents of the handbag on the table. We shifted in our chairs. Max prodded at his yolk, which burst and dribbled down the side of the mince, pooling at the bottom and mingling with the blood.

'I should go and check on her,' I said.

'She's in the ladies',' Dad replied.

Max grinned at me. *Don't let it stop you.*

This isn't funny, I signed back.

It's only a fish bone, he replied.

All I could think was whether Mum's last word would be *Bread*.

She came back out, eventually, and insisted that the doctor join us for a glass of wine. The doctor, in turn, insisted that she couldn't leave her friend alone, so her friend joined us, and we spent an awkward twenty minutes trying to make conversation, with Max looking at the time on his phone and asking me to translate the odd comment that he couldn't catch.

The next morning, I brought her a cup of tea but she didn't drink it. She made throaty noises with each inhalation and I didn't know what to do, other than to phone for an ambulance. As we sat waiting in the lounge, a small bird flew into the patio doors, its beak hitting the window like a hailstone. It dropped to the floor and remained there. Our elderly cat appeared and began to inspect it for vital signs with its paw.

The paramedics wanted to take her to hospital, so I sat in the ambulance with her. She gave me a wan smile.

'I'll be fine,' she whispered.

'Of course you will,' I said.

We hit a little bump.

'I didn't bring any make-up,' she whispered, as if it was the only thing on her mind.

'It's okay. We'll be out in no time.' I squeezed her hand. It felt horrible, lying to each other like this. I wanted to say something true.

They didn't think that she was in immediate danger, so she sat up in a bed amongst many others and waited for the doctor to come round to her. I asked if there was anything she wanted. I hated hospitals. I was hoping she wanted something outside.

'You know what I would love?' she rasped, smiling like a dame at a ball, 'A glass of water.'

There were only useless little cones at the water cooler down the corridor, so I went into several wards and asked around until a kindly nurse offered to get me one from the staff kitchen. She brought it to me full past the brim, so at first it looked empty. The water level was above the top of the glass, held together only by a strange physics. I took a sip and carried it back to my mother's ward slowly and carefully. As I reached Mum's place, I found her looking a little off colour, her skin shining like a waxwork. The index finger on her right hand was extended, as if pointing outside – at the sun, perhaps, or the window. I put the water down and opened the window to let the air in.

She beckoned me with her hand, and I came over to sit on the side of the bed. Her eyes were red and full. She said nothing, but she looked so sad, as if she'd witnessed a tragedy she didn't want to share. I looked for a way to comfort her. She shook her head very softly. That was her answer: *no, Günter. I am not. I won't. It won't.* Now I didn't want the truth. I wanted her to tell me a sweet lie. I wanted the truth to be different. She held up her thumb, forefinger and little finger. The little finger: *I.* The thumb and forefinger: *L.* The thumb and little finger: *Y.* She leant back against the pillow and put two hands over her chest. *Love.* Suffocation. I put my hand up to her mouth and nose. She had stopped breathing.

I pushed the emergency help button.

No one came in five seconds. Her hand was burning hot. I said, 'Excuse me,' to the corridor. No one came in ten. She looked like she was stuck halfway up a mountain. Someone ran in after fifteen seconds. She looked strangely at peace. A crowd had formed by thirty. They wheeled her away to a new room where I wasn't allowed. This wasn't something we could share. This wasn't somewhere I could follow.

And here, at the heart of the crisis, I was alone. Everyone else was busy. I was not. I was the only person here who knew my mother, but these things don't matter in the end.

My dad arrived soon after, having followed the ambulance, and Max followed straight from work. I sipped at the water and looked out the open window.

When I think of Mum in hospital, I picture the sparrow flying into our patio doors. It is that moment that my mind has replayed many hundreds of times, and the cat nudging it as it lay there, the little bird already unconscious, incapable of safeguarding its dignity. I suppose, if my father has always assured me that life isn't romantic, my mother inadvertently taught me that death is no better. It stops you in your tracks like an invisible wall. From a very acute angle, you can see it coming, but most people find it catches them full pelt.

4

The Plain Dealer

Avon College for Boys is one of those schools that no one wants to talk about after they've left. I suppose I'll have to. But no one really enjoys their schooldays, do they? If you were supposed to enjoy it, they wouldn't make the uniforms grey. It was a big school, which made it easy to blend in, or would have, if I hadn't had my early growth spurt. I'm 5'10" now, but I was already 5'8" by the time I was twelve, and the sixth-tallest in the year when we lined up for gym class. I'm sure I would have been the tallest except that I was born in August, so I was young for my year. They say that during puberty you grow up, then out; it was widely believed that I had already completed both stages of development, though as it would later prove I had yet to finish growing out.

You might think this ensured I was left well alone, but bullies do not, in my experience, pick on the smallest prey. They might reinforce the hierarchy every now and then, but there is no honour in felling a sapling. On the contrary, bullies most like to fight with someone impressive looking but ineffectual. One also has to bear in mind Tall Man Syndrome: having lower blood pressure, and not needing to vocally assert themselves, tall people are more laid back.[6]

---

6 DW: I never quite knew where he got this notion. As Günter's beloved Wikipedians might have put it, '[citation needed]'.

The fact of my height, coupled with my refusal to behave antisocially, combined to make me a conspicuous target amongst my peers. Although I had pointed out many times that my name was Günter, pronounced with the same phonetics as Oompa-Loompa, many insisted on calling me Gunter, to rhyme with Munter. I was sometimes alternatively addressed as Gunther, or Munter Arse, and over time my year group settled on the contraction Munt. Later, some of the worst boys substituted the first letter again, but I'd rather not dwell on that.

Karl Baggett was one particularly obnoxious classmate. He spent all his time with the football players and the rough kids but, lacking any particular skill which would have made him 'cool', chose to specialise in sadism.[7] He was in all my classes except English, Music and Science, and he would always sit directly behind me. I could go into some detail about the reasons I know he was disturbed, but to pick an example at random: he once stapled the webbing between his thumb and index finger during a maths exam, with the only apparent intention of putting off Tom, who was sat next to him, and who was scared of blood. In every lesson, he would prod me in the back, put things down the back of my shirt, flick ink on my shirt, and make it impossible for me to take in any of what was going on. The pleasure he took in sitting behind me would always outweigh the attraction of sitting with anyone he'd have wanted to call a friend, to the extent that against both of our wills, we became known as a sort of double act ('Where are Munt and Karl going to sit?').

---

7 DW: As you may know, sadism is when it gives you pleasure to cause other people pain. What I don't understand is that sadists often team up with masochists, who get pleasure from receiving pain. I hardly think sadists would enjoy knowing they are in fact causing masochists pleasure.

It is impossible to overstate the ability of idiots to think they have won an argument. Almost every day, we would run through a version of,

'Munt. Munt. Hey, Munt.' A prod in my back. 'Munt.'

'What? I'm trying to listen.'

'Teacher's pet.'

'What do you want?'

'Günter, pay attention please.' This from whoever happened to be standing, oblivious, by the whiteboard.

'Do you love your dad?'

'Of course I do.'

'GAY.'

'That's not what gay means.'

'Pretty sure it is.'

'Being gay is when two men want to have sex with each other.'

'Oh my god, you're like an *expert* on gays. Did you do a gay degree?'

Very occasionally – on a good day – I'd get a brief glimpse into the cankered swamp that bore him.

'Do you love your mum?' (Karl was not an innovator.)

'Yes, very much.'

'Motherf—'

'Don't you love yours?'

'No, she's a bitch.'

'Well, what about your dad?'

'He doesn't want to live with us when he gets out.'

And so I couldn't even hate my own torturer, but only feel a great sadness for the world that had made him this way.

Things got worse when Max joined Avon. Everyone except Karl was kind and inquisitive about Max's deafness, whereas Karl was just inquisitive, particularly when it came to Max's vocalisation. There followed some unpleasantness during which both Max's ego and Karl's testicles were bruised. As the older brother, I was apparently supposed to have leapt to Max's aid, but, as I tried to explain, he didn't need it. He told me it was a matter of principle, he felt betrayed, and there wasn't much I could say to that. The damage had been done. It was around that time that Max stopped speaking out loud in my presence.

My grades didn't improve, either. By the time of my mock GCSE exams, I was barely scraping by. In English, my marked paper had lots of question marks on it, with the comment, *try to be clear about what you're saying*. In Double Science, my papers were a mix of ticks and crosses. *Use the approved wording*, and, *it's not enough to know the answer: show your working*. Music was fine in theory, but there was no way to backdate keyboard practice, and my performances brought my average down. Karl put paid to my chances of success in other subjects.

Mum wanted me to get into college, and go to university. Dad thought it best that I 'start earning' since, by the time I had paid off university debt, I would be a 'middle-aged loner still living with his mum'. Max helpfully suggested that the latter would happen in either case. As it turned out, I got an A, two Bs, a C, five Ds and an F, meaning that I didn't qualify for college, so, if only by default, I took my dad's advice and joined the working world.

There was an advert in the *Salisbury Plain Dealer* for milkmen: 'cheerful, reliable, early to bed and early (3am) to rise'. Thankfully qualifications weren't mentioned at all in my interview with Mickey, the operations manager, who looked like an oversized, milk-fed baby. While I was too young to drive, I would work in the depot, stacking bottles on each of the floats to match the orders that had been requested on the system, and then after a year I could get my licence and drive my own float.[8]

I would come home from work about the same time the rest of my family got up. As I was to learn, I had entered a dying trade. You see, milk lasts much longer than it used to, so people can buy lots at the supermarket and keep it all week and half of the next. And then there's long-life – don't get me started on long-life.

But it was a good job while it lasted and did, at least, avoid the doldrums of a nine to five. I would get up while everyone was sleeping and walk to the depot, past drunks trading poorly aimed haymakers over their stilettoed princesses, the peal of war cries rising even as sirens burst through the stale air.[9] I would arrive at the depot crunching over broken glass, sober as a drudge and dressed in my white coat. I'd take my float and drive my figure of eight round the neighbourhood, picking up empties and delivering bottles of creamy white cow-juice, capped with red foil. The silence was impeccable at around six. The sun would rise pink or orange like a furnace. Sometimes there were squirrels, or foxes, or woodpeckers.

I felt a certain smugness that I had seen so much of a day before the other residents had even mastered consciousness. I'm not one of these people who snaps awake at six every morning,

8 DW: You would think Günter had to get a category B licence (car) so that he could obtain the category L licence (electrically propelled) in with the bargain. In fact all the floats were diesel, because only about one in eight people have their milk delivered in Salisbury. Günter passed his test third time, with thirteen minors (stalling x 2, signalling too early, signalling too late, approaching a junction too fast, passing too close to a parked car, stopping too close in traffic, failure to overtake a slow-moving vehicle x 2, lane discipline, ancillary control, undue hesitation x 2).

9 DW: Alcohol is one of God's stranger gifts. On the rare occasion that I am out walking late at night, I am reminded of Isaiah 19:14: 'The Lord hath mingled a perverse spirit in the midst thereof: and they have caused Egypt to err in every work thereof, as a drunken man staggereth in his vomit.'

while others dream of stretching out the morning as they fumble for the snooze. I am by nature a late riser, a lover of sleep. For me, the only thing worse than having to wake up would be not waking up. I have known what it is to doze like a cat through a summer's day and out the other side, woken only by my mother for the family dinner. And so, to wake so early, to have out-flanked even the early risers, was satisfaction enough. There were small pleasures, too, and each day I might find a little joy in the way an empty bottle trapped the first pink light of dawn, or the symphony of willows in wind.

I continued on in that job for some years, only realising I'd come out the other side of adolescence when I discovered, one evening, that I couldn't lie down properly in the bath. Suddenly, arbitrarily, it had been decided that I was now a Responsible Adult. At twenty-one, I couldn't just buy alcohol; I could sell it. I could adopt a child, and then drive it around in an HGV, such was the trust conferred on me by society.

As I towelled myself, dressed, went to the kitchen and hugged my mum, I saw that we were Russian dolls[10] that didn't fit any more. I was no longer a solid little offspring, but a big, hollow shell of my own.

The four of us sat at our kitchen table for dinner, munching while my mother soliloquised on her latest obsession (. . . Thomas Hardy, Norse mythology, Buddhism . . .), or tried to teach us new words. My parents had a tacit pact whereby Dad was allowed to stuff food into his mouth for precisely as long as her lesson lasted, at which point Mum would stand abruptly and sweep the plate out from under his fork. Over the years, this had turned Dad into an incredibly efficient eater.

---

10 DW: In Russia they obviously don't call them Russian dolls. They call them Matryoshka dolls, coming from the word for mother. So really the dolls are a metaphor for offspring, rather than the other way around.

As luck would have it, the subject of today's homily was Employment. We were having lasagne, Dad's favourite. He removed the top layer of pasta, scraped all the remaining béchamel away, grimaced, and shovelled a forkful of mince into his mouth. He really loved Mum's lasagne.

'Do you want a glass of wine?' asked Mum, hovering.

'God no,' said Dad, smothering his mince in Worcestershire sauce. 'Can't drink on a weekday. I'll never get up.'

'Oh, come on, live a little. You're retiring, you should enjoy yourself.'

'It's bloody boring. I want to be out there making a bit of money.'

There's more to life than making money, signed Mum to everyone as she sat down. *Why don't you sign up for a course?* she asked Dad. *Learn something? We should all keep learning, throughout life.*

People don't take courses any more, I signed. *If you need to know something, you can just google it.*

But learning opens doors, she signed back. *If you had more qualifications you might be able to get a different job.*

What's wrong with my job? I asked.

Nothing's wrong with it, she signed, *but it gives you options. Learning makes your world bigger. There are two ways to change the world. Go out there and make it better, or change the way you think about it. Knowledge gives you the option to do both.*

You can talk, I signed. *Even I've got more qualifications than you.*

Mum looked wounded. Max pushed mince around his plate, looking down, which was like putting his hands over his ears.

'We can all imagine a better life for ourselves,' Mum said judiciously, her voice wavering ever so slightly. 'And you're capable of so much more.'

I flushed with shame and pride. No one other than my mother

had ever really believed that I was capable of anything. I secretly nursed the idea that I might be an undiscovered genius, and sometimes googled 'Einstein's school report'[11] to cheer myself up, but I got on better with ideas than I did with people, and it is rarely left up to ideas to decide whether you're a serial underachiever.

'Don't go giving the boy ideas, Mathilda,' said Dad. 'He's hardly a bloody rocket scientist, is he?'

'Very supportive, Arthur, thank you.' She turned to me as Max looked up. 'Günter, you can do anything you set your mind to.'

Yeah, signed Max, *You're a regular superhero. Charmless, half-blind and fat.*

Clark Kent has glasses, I signed.

They're a cover. He can see through walls, you dick.

I walked into that one.

When someone you love dies, the first thing you have to think about is paperwork. You may have recently concluded that all human endeavour is no more than a way to keep our hands busy until we, too, die, our life destined to wink only briefly in a cold and unobservant universe. But the first thing you are asked to do is to ignore all that, and to help out with some good old-fashioned box ticking ('Mathilda. With an H. Glass. 2 February 1955. Salisbury. I'm her son. About ten days. Yes, I was there with her.')

Max's new employers said that, since he was new, he was only allowed to take a day off for the funeral as annual leave, so he couldn't help much with the arrangements. Everything happened in a kind of sleepwalk, fumbling along and saying the

11 DW: 'He will never amount to anything.' At twenty-six, became the most important physicist of all time, but hindsight, as we shall learn, needs no spectacles.

same things you would say if she was dead: yes, it's a terrible loss; hydrangeas were her favourite, but we might ask people to donate money to a charity. Dad sleepwalked more than me. Overnight, he became a wandering, forgetful shade. He didn't know when he had last eaten, or what day of the week it was.

During this time, others also referred casually to 'what she would have wanted', as if she had granted her approval over our every decision in advance. But Mum was full of surprises. I think she might have been amused by the idea that anyone in the family, least of all my father, had any inkling of her preferences. I suspect the whisky fire alarm was a typical misfire, and that Mum was so bewildered to receive it that Dad refused to own up to such an obviously poor pairing of wife and gift. I'm not saying we didn't love her and sometimes also pleasantly surprise her, but after witnessing Mum's brave face for twenty-two consecutive Christmases, all I know is she didn't like bath salts.

I wandered the streets around Salisbury a lot around this time.[12] I would often go and stare at the cathedral and think about how long it had been there. I would think about why people liked to see an old building, and whether all anyone really wanted was to weave themselves into the story of the world. Salisbury Cathedral:[13] now that was a big part of the story. People could

12 DW: It seems clear that during this time he was, if not depressed in the modern sense, at least melancholic. The Reverend Robert Burton defined melancholy as 'a kind of dotage without a fever, having for his ordinary companions fear and sadness, without any apparent occasion.' Rev. Burton wrote a 1,400 page book on the subject, *The Anatomy of Melancholy* (1621), during which he complained rather unselfconsciously that there was too much to read these days, and that 'our eyes ache with reading, our fingers with turning.' His remedy for melancholy can be summed up in the last six words of the book: 'Be not solitary, be not idle.'

13 DW: Or, to be accurate, The Cathedral Church of the Blessed Virgin Mary, in Salisbury.

try and be important for a day, like celebrities or politicians, or they could try and ingratiate themselves with the story by spending time with things that lasted, like vicars or academics. It was a question of how to find your place in the ecosystem.

One day, on my way back from the cathedral, I wandered past a primary school. I stopped by the tessellated diamonds of the fence to watch them play. The children were effortlessly happy, albeit in a volatile, slightly primal way. They were playing near a drain, which was overflowing with scummy water. To an adult, this was distasteful, but to a child it was Lucerne by moonlight, it was anything and everything. A boy ran up in his scuffed Velcro-fastened shoes and booted the water as if it were a football. It sprayed a nearby group of girls who squealed and shivered with mingled terror and delight, and the fattest girl – the enforcer – ran after the boy. Screams sailed into the air as they sprinted off towards the other end of the playground.

My thoughts were interrupted by a call from my boss, Mickey.

'Günter, you have to come back to the depot.'

'But I've delivered all the milk.'

'I know.'

'Have I left something behind?'

I heard the boss sigh.

'Let's say yeah. Would you be so good as to waddle down?'

'I'll be there in half an hour.'

I walked back to the depot, and found Mickey behind the same car-boot-sale desk he was always at. He leant back on two legs of the chair with his hands on his round, taut belly, the cold halogen strip lighting gleaming off his bald pate.

'So what did I leave behind, Mickey?'

He leant forwards and his chair hit the floor as he picked up a plain white envelope.

'This.'

It was a cheque.

'I'm sorry, Günter. You're a good lad but this is an old man's game. We're gonna have to let you go.'

'You're firing me?'

'Redundancy, yeah. People don't want their milk delivered in this day and age; they want to order it off their phones and have it delivered to their work address, they want long-life that lasts a year because they're never home—'

'Please, Mickey. You don't have to explain.' I shook my head bitterly. 'I've seen the rows of UHT in the supermarkets, they're taking over. I understand. But this is a very large cheque. Are you quite sure I qualify for this kind of severance pay?'

'Are you fucking crazy?' he asked me.

I thought for a moment.

'No.'

'Then keep the cheque. I'm not gonna tell anyone.'

'Does that mean I'm not supposed to have it?'

He rolled his eyes.

'Just do us a favour and leave, okay?'

On my way out, I took a bottle with me and peeled back the cap, sitting on a wall by the loading bay. I drank it dry and watched the sunlight play through the misty white glass. I wondered how the bottles looked when they were clean. Probably beautiful in the thankless way of everyday things.[14]

The next day I went to a recruitment centre in town. Everything was blue or grey, and after I filled out a clipboard's worth of information, they took me through to a little room with a sofa made out of two seating blocks pushed together, and a little plastic plant. I sat down with a recruitment lady and we talked over my skills – attention to detail, honesty and integrity, neatness, good with hands. She asked me if I'd ever considered a career in recruitment.

14 DW: For a long time, glass vessels or windows were the preserve of the rich. It is comparatively recently that they have swapped place with lobsters.

'No, I hadn't. Isn't that what you do?'

'Yes. A role has just come up. Not mine.' She tittered.

'So, if I did it, I would be recruiting people for jobs?'

'That's right.'

'And if I were in your shoes, would I be offering people jobs in recruitment?'

She looked less certain about this.

'I suppose I'm asking a two-part question,' I said. 'Is it a pyramid scheme, and if so, what will we do when everyone works in recruitment?'

'I can't really say. Shall I put you down as "quite interested" for that one?'

I said that that would be fine, and left.

5

Church Attendance

On the day of the funeral, Dad, Max, and I stood in the lounge not talking. I was so nervous I felt cold. Relatives and ex-colleagues started to trickle in, some wearing hats. When there were enough of us, we followed the funeral director, Ivan, who, despite his hunch, looked almost inhumanly tall in his hat, as various relatives put magnetic flags on the roofs of their cars. Dad, Max and I got in the hearse, which followed Ivan at walking pace to the end of the road, trailed by the other cars in a giant parti-coloured snake. Ivan got in and we proceeded through Salisbury, slowing traffic. White-van men let us out at roundabouts. Our line was broken once, by a BMW driver. I forced myself to assume that he hadn't realised what he was doing.

We arrived at the cathedral. When we had booked the venue, it had felt like a gesture of profound love for my mother, but now it suddenly seemed overblown and ridiculous. There were about forty of us, and the building could probably seat ten times that number. It was gargantuan. One of the life-sized statues built into the wall was holding his own model cathedral.[15] Each

15 This is Bishop Richard Poore, who is commemorated holding a scale model, in case visitors are somehow oblivious to the building on which the statue stands.

of the building's hundreds of arches were built into further, larger arches, spires multiplying on the spires, all pointing up. The huge central spire not only pointed up but seemed to be grasping at something beyond the sky. I thought I saw the very tip of it flash red.

People kept looking at us with dramatically turned-down mouths as the coffin was unloaded. Some of them came up to say they were sorry for my loss, as if it was really no loss to them, and they had only come out of politeness. I probably looked thoughtful, or mildly affronted, as I thanked them, but I was mourning too far below the surface to put up much of an appearance of mourning.

The nave was even larger than I had anticipated as we followed the coffin inside and our small band huddled up in the front rows, the majority behind them empty. A choir was singing a song I didn't know. We were asked to sing a hymn, and very few people sang along properly, perhaps not knowing the tune, perhaps feeling that this wasn't the occasion for an enthusiastic performance. We were asked to pray and I didn't say 'Amen', and I felt bad because almost no one did. A woman decked in long robes at the lectern, or whatever it was called, introduced herself as the Very Reverend Dean Angela Winterbottom.

'"So they poured out for the men to eat,"' she began. '"And it came to pass, as they were eating of the pottage, that they cried out, and said, O thou man of God, there is death in the pot. And they could not eat thereof."[16] Unfortunately, Mathilda's story is as old as stories themselves. So much has changed since the writing of the Bible, and yet, even in our technologically enhanced age, we still find ourselves afflicted in the most basic

16 2 Kings 4:40. DW: There's nothing like a cry of 'there is death in the pot' to put one off one's food.

ways, and the same things continue to matter to us: our search for family, for friends, for work and for meaning in God. We may have every right to feel that Mathilda was taken from us before she should have been, but seeing you all here today, it's clear that she made a lasting impact in this world.'

The Dean kept indicating the coffin as if my mother might somehow have a right of reply, or as if she was some bottled genie who might at any moment jump out to verify any grand claims made on her behalf.[17]

'And it may seem hard to tell whether the life she has lived was a good one,' the Dean continued. '"There is a way which seemeth right unto a man, but the end thereof are the ways of death. Even in laughter the heart is sorrowful; and the end of that mirth is heaviness."'[18]

Even as I listened to her vintage wisdom, I felt that my mother's funeral was being hijacked. I had to wonder if she'd have wanted to attend her own ceremony.

'Everybody will one day find that their time has come, and if one tries to bolt the door, one might just find that death is come up into their windows,[19] so to speak.'

I looked away from the Dean and the coffin. Light filtered in through stained glass, transforming it from white-grey to ruby, like water to wine.

'"For where a testament is, there must also of necessity be the death of the testator. For a testament is of force after men are dead: otherwise it is of no strength at all while the testator

---

17 DW: Günter related his experience of the funeral to me later. As far as I am aware, I did no such thing.

18 Proverbs 14:12. DW: People too often think of laughter and crying as opposites, when really they are at the same end of the spectrum. Their opposite is being underwhelmed.

19 Jeremiah 9:21. DW: If I'd known what was going to happen, I might have saved this one for the next funeral.

liveth."[20] And we can take comfort from that.'

I felt my shoulders sag. I glanced across at Max, who was biting a nail. Dad gave a defeated little huff, and stood, a handwritten page shaking in his hand as he made his way over to the lectern. He hated public speaking. He said hello to everyone, and glanced at Max, who gave him a tight nod.

All I can hear is echoes, said Max.

Can you lip-read? I signed.

Too far away, Max replied.

Okay, I'll sign: 'Mathilda was an amazing woman. I met her completely by chance when I was a door-to-door salesman. She answered the door and I started trying to sell her whatever I was flogging back then, but she'd just moved to England and barely spoke a word. Bloody hell, I thought—' (now he's apologising to the Dean for swearing) '—she's a corker. So rather than bother with my swatches or whatever, I told her I was an English tutor.' (Uncle Dave just did his dirty laugh.) 'She really went for it, though, so I started giving her these lessons, and before I knew it she could speak English better than me. I expect everyone here knows that won't have been because of my language skills. She was always looking things up in dictionaries, you know. She loved her weird words.' (A couple of people are chuckling.) 'She was clever and ambitious. But one thing or another clipped her wings. The move came at a bad time for her and she didn't get the right qualifications to go to a university here. She moved in with me, and I always think I didn't do enough to encourage her. Then we had the kids. When you're young, you always

---

20 Hebrews 9:16-17. DW: I am absolutely sure that life is one's only true message to the world, and to God. One's message can even be quite coherent if one dies young enough not to dribble a comeback album down one's cheek. For those who die young, their *oeuvre* is complete, their contribution known, evincing none of the compromise that comes with age. Can there be any word more antithetical to greatness than 'reunion'?

think you'll do everything, you'll beat life, and then you wake up one day and realise life's been beating you.' (He's stopped, he's crying.)

Max looked up. I had never seen Dad cry. It felt like stepping through my bedroom door as a child, and hearing it slam shut, and realising there was no handle on the other side.

'But she was a good person,' he said vehemently. 'She never did a bad deed in her life, and you all know it. She'd let you walk all over her, and she wouldn't bear a grudge. And she might have thought she had nothing to show for it at the end of the day, but God did it make you love her.'

Dad's eyes burned; Max shook my useless hand; I felt like I was falling.

And then that was that. My mother was buried. Everyone went back to their living. She had been; she was not. It had occurred to me before that my life somehow contained my death – that the story of my life had to end somewhere – but now I realised that the course of my life was determined all along the way by the deaths of others, her death contained in my life.

I could hardly find a job now. It seemed like an insult, the idea that I might turn away from thoughts of her and start squirreling away money. That I might just set her aside, like an unconvincing book, fending off guilt by telling myself that I would get around to preserving her memory one day. Before this, grief had been as inconceivable to me as a black winter coat in a summer heat wave. And yet here it was. I put it on and it fit. It formed a layer between the world and me. It was heavy and stifling; it tired me out, made me hungry. Without her and with Max now in a flat of his own, the routines of the house fell apart, and we rarely remembered to shop for food. One day, there was nothing left in the cupboard but the half-finished pack of Dutch waffles, which had gone stale. I ate each of them slowly at the kitchen table, willing them to offer some kind of bite, but they were soft and chewy. They were the last food she had bought. We had eaten every other trace. Time was undoing her effect on the world already. I went shopping at the big Tesco so that I could buy more Dutch waffles, seven or eight packs. It was good to have them there.

6

Back to School

Before I could think of finding a job, I decided to pay tribute to her, and to try to educate myself a little. I missed the way she would constantly feed me half-digested information like a bird to her chicks. It was only natural, then, that after her death I sought out a surrogate in the greatest pool of half-digested information in the world: Wikipedia. I did consider buying a selection of the popular *For Idiots* series when I found an offer on at W H Smith, but as I picked up *Self-Confidence for Idiots*, I wondered whether theirs was the right approach. And it wasn't as if the internet was still stuck in the era of my schooldays, when homework had involved triangulating a single line of information on the Encarta CD-ROM with the unlimited untruths of Altavista, Lycos, Yahoo! and Ask Jeeves. Now we had Wikipedia, and it was learning more and improving every day.

I started by learning about Wikipedia itself. The demographic for its top ten thousand editors was single males between eighteen and thirty with no partner, no children and a degree. Some people had made hundreds of thousands of edits, for no other reason than to contribute. It was a charity with 150 staff but four hundred million hits a month. *Nature* magazine said in a study that it was nearly as accurate as the *Encyclopaedia Britannica*. The *Encyclopaedia Britannica* only had about a hundred editors, but it did start in 1768. Some people had read the whole thing, all thirty-two thousand pages of it. I wondered if anyone would ever read all of the four million articles on the English language Wikipedia. I supposed it would be impossible now, that human knowledge had exceeded the capacity of any one human.

Now, I'd be the first, or the second, to admit that I don't know everything. But no one knows everything. By studying their behaviour, I had realised that many so-called clever people are really just people who know how to steer the conversation round to the things they know, and refuse to engage with topics that they don't know. So I decided there would be two phases to my education: the gathering of any old information I could find, and the proud disseminating of said information. My method was to start off on the day's 'featured article', and keep clicking through articles until I felt I had learnt everything I could take in that day. I became, to coin a word, a *Wikipedophile*. As I lay in bed each day surfing and eating my weight in Dutch waffles, I became fat (and as my vocabulary improved, corpulent).

Over those first months, my grief wore in and I felt a little give in the shoulders. If grief had an equivalent of the Schmidt sting pain index, it might have relaxed from a 4 down to a 2.[21] I felt guilty, in case it meant that I had begun to care less, but I was also seized regularly by a vague ennui. For all that Mum might have approved of my project, my life seemed to have lost its track. I decided that the thing to do was to retrace my steps. Whenever I used to lose something, my mother always told me to retrace my steps.

I went to the milk depot. They looked like they were doing a

---

21 DW: The scale only goes up to 4 ('Pure, intense, brilliant pain. Like fire-walking over flaming charcoal with a 3-inch rusty nail in your heel') though halfway up the scale, one is still in a great deal of pain ('Rich, hearty, slightly crunchy. Similar to getting your hand mashed in a revolving door').

roaring business. In fact, there was a brand new sign saying they had started offering long-life, the bastards.

I walked back past the school with its tessellated fence. There were no children playing today. It must be shut for the Easter holidays. A Rice Krispies Squares wrapper was caught in the fence, and a cherry tree had been snowing over in the corner near the vegetable patch. People ambled purposelessly by. I suppose most people don't have somewhere to be every minute of the day. At least, not in Salisbury, they don't.

I marched onwards until I reached the green by the cathedral and stopped to look up at the spire. I thought about my mother, the Russian doll, lying in two. My eyes watered a little – from the cold breeze. The clouds swam faster, and I began to feel a little nauseous as I stared at the tip of the spire. Again, I saw a red light flash on its tip. I wondered what it was for.

'For the aeroplanes,' said a voice. I looked to the source of the sound, which was a small lady with short curly white hair and hands clasped like a Grecian key.[22] I recognised her as Dean Winterbottom, who had given the service at the funeral.

'Do aeroplanes land near here?' I asked, a little dazed.

She smiled as if I had made a joke.

'Ugly little bugger, isn't it? Still, height regulations. The council insists.'

'It looks like an aerial for receiving God's thoughts.'

'I'd never thought of it like that,' she said. We stood in silence for a little while, looking up at the spire together. Then I felt her eyes on me. 'Would you like to come in for a cup of tea? It's rather cold, and you've been standing out here for a good hour now.'

'Have I? Well—' and here I looked back the way I had come

22 DW: My hands were cold.

to indicate the busy and fulfilled life that was waiting for me, 'I'm sure I could stop for a cuppa.'

We went inside the cathedral. I stared at the rich colours of the glass and imagined a great choir chanting. I wondered whether I was allowed to come and hear the choir if I wasn't a proper Christian.

'You see how it's thicker at the bottom?' Dean Winterbottom said, pointing to one of the larger panes. 'It has flowed like that over time.'

'That isn't really—'

'Not many people know, but glass is actually a very slow liquid.'

'No,' I said, knitting my brow, 'That isn't right, I'm afraid. Everyone says it's a liquid, but it's just the way they used to make the glass. Sorry.'

'Oh,' she said.

'Sorry,' I said. 'I wish it was true.'

For some reason I started crying. She looked at me kindly and held me by the shoulders.

'Come on,' she said. 'Let's get you that tea.'

Sitting in a little back office on a couple of worn and comfortable chairs, we talked a little about my mother. The Dean remembered the service, and my name. I really believed I was beginning to calm down. But when she started pouring out the tea in the little kitchenette, I sobbed with renewed vigour.

'Whatever's the matter?' she asked, standing holding the milk bottle.

'The milk,' I wailed.

'This?' she asked, sniffing at it.

I realised how absurd I must have looked, and immediately started laughing in the slightly manic way that follows a good cry.

'Please, pour the tea. I'm sorry,' I said, wiping my face on my sleeve. 'It's been a strange few months. I lost my job as a milkman. I don't know anything else. I'm trying to figure out what I'm doing with my life. I don't feel quite myself.'

'I can pour the tea without milk if you prefer?'

'No, milk is fine, thank you.'

She brought the mugs over.

'Well, you've come to the right place. As Jesus once said, "Trouble me not: the door is now shut, and my children are with me in bed."'[23]

'Did he?'

She sat down, leant forward and clasped her hands on the table. Her eyes were powder blue.

'So what is it you're searching for?'

'All I know is that I don't know,' I mumbled.

'Could it be God?'

'Maybe. I mean, I don't think so, but I'm not going to rule Him out. I suppose I just want something to do, like everyone else.'

'Mmmm,' she purred. 'Purpose.'

We thought about that word for a little while.

'And what are you good at?' she asked eventually.

'I pay close attention to detail. I'm honest, neat, good with my hands. I know a lot of trivia.'

'Are you good with heights?'

'I suppose so.'

'Mmm.' She pulled at a stray hair on her chin.[24] 'The Man Upstairs might have a job for you.' She must have seen me shrink back, because she smiled reassuringly. 'Nothing out of the ordinary, I promise you. At least, nothing that would

---

23 Luke 11:7.

24 DW: The rotter keeps coming back. It's on a mole and I could swear it grows faster than bamboo.

make it into a Dan Brown novel.'[25]

Nonetheless, I took a slurp of tea and checked my watch.

'Something else is troubling you.'

I squirmed.

'But you have the answers you need. You only need to strip away the impermanent. I'm not talking about the Bible now. God isn't bothered about eternity in the least, it is a very human concern. You need to find your little piece of eternity, wherever it is, and keep hold of it whenever you're unsure.'

She looked a little surprised at herself and when she unclasped her hands there were nail marks in her palms. We finished our drinks, she scribbled her phone number on the back of a Samaritans card, which I didn't think was much of a coincidence, and I gave her mine, pondering to myself that I rarely exchanged numbers with someone in good faith. Although, not to mislead you, I remained, at this point, very much a virgin.

I walked back out past streaks of stained light and into the whistling wind. I took the short route home. I supposed I was good with heights. But then, I supposed a lot of things.

25 DW: Everybody talks as if Dan Brown's success is an accident, when really it took a great deal of hard work, trial and error. First, as a musician, he made a cassette for children, then he tried releasing an adult album called *Angels and Demons*. When the music career didn't take off, he wrote humour books, then thrillers. So his success was assured eventually.

7

Then I'm Cleaning Windows

Dad was sat at the kitchen table wearing my mother's apron, his face wrinkled and red around the eyes where he'd been rubbing them. He had broken into the novelty gift on the wall to get to the minibar bottle of whisky. God only knew what the sell-by date had been. It was probably vintage by now. I sat down at the other end of the table.

'How are things?' I asked.

'Had a gap in the diary so I started early today.'

'Why are you wearing the apron? You didn't try to cook, did you?'

He scratched his cheek and I could hear the bristles. Back when he was working, he used to shave every morning and some evenings. He looked over at the oven, in case, at this late stage, it might reveal its mysteries to him.

'Why don't I make you a fish finger sandwich?' I suggested.

He closed his bloodshot eyes and nodded slowly. I made one for each of us while Dad dragged last week's newspaper over. He stared at the front page as if each line read 'you have cancer.'

After eating, I went to my bedroom and switched on the computer. I looked up aircraft-warning lights. Then I wondered if Salisbury Cathedral was one of the tallest buildings in England. Turned out it wasn't. The tallest building was a skyscraper called

The Shard that was just being completed in London.

On a whim, I googled 'glass'. It gave me some news results – one John Blades had been given an OBE for his services to the Queen, as her appointed window cleaner and sculptor of a life-sized glass statue of Churchill for the palace. He ran the country's largest window-cleaning business, as well as a thriving glassblowing and sculpting workshop.

I found an article which explained that the time it would take for glass to flow down a thick window would be many times longer than the existence of the universe. Flowing over thousands of billions of years like a tear down the face of God, dripping and splashing into the end of our world and through the beginning of the next. That was one of the reassuring things about glass, I supposed: its permanence.

I thought back to the glass museum, to the strange realities of bending light, the way that, when it was perfectly clean, it looked almost like a solid slice of air. It seemed odd, otherworldly, even noble, that there were people who spent whole careers making sure that glass was clean and clear. Their life's work was to preserve the ideal state of a unique material, a tribute to its timeless utility. Perhaps that's what I could do. There was nothing stopping me, I supposed. I didn't need GCSEs or work experience. If I bought the equipment, and cleaned people's windows, and said I was a window cleaner, then that's what I would be.

I quickly discovered that there are an unusually large variety of products in the window cleaning profession, including different kinds of holster. There were many ladders, belts, karabiners, suction cups, cloths, wipes, sprays, gels and squeegees – enough to satisfy even an obsessive compulsive.

There was only one person I knew who could wade through lists of consumer products with the galoshes of a practising Capitalist, and unfortunately it was my brother. Max brought meaning to his life through objects. They were his 'raisin of being', as the French might say.[26] If Capitalism was a fungus feeding off the Western world, Max was a truffle pig. I sent him a message asking for his thoughts, and within the hour he'd picked his definitive arsenal, with alternatives to each product rated one to ten.

A little of his excitement rubbed off on me, and in hindsight I ordered too much. I got a double-pouch holster and a 'sidekick' holster, which I decided to strap to my calf with a tiny squeegee, in case my primary squeegee somehow got disarmed. I ordered a scraper and various kinds of cleaning fluid. I resolved at some point to try them out on different panes round the house, and see which was the best. Because good wasn't good enough – for once in my life, I wanted to be flawless.

The ladder we had in the garage was not fit for purpose. It had three wooden steps, one of which was split, and a total height of about 1.2 metres. On Max's advice, I opted for an Extension Ladder with Integral Stabiliser, Overlapping Rubber Feet and Non-Slip Rungs. If I couldn't blame my tools, perhaps I wouldn't be a bad workman.

For two days I waited for my things to arrive. On the third day, nothing arrived either. I milled about, showed Dad how to peel potatoes, ended up doing them for him, and waited for the day to pass.

The next day, the doorbell rang. I opened the door to discover that a lorry had jammed its way onto our small residential road. A man lifted up the shutters, and pulled out a very long, very shiny ladder. Then he got a couple of boxes out and made me sign for it all. So this was it, I had my equipment and I was all set. All I needed to do now was learn how to clean windows. I picked up the ladder and turned towards the house. I

---

26 DW: The French don't say this, but Günter did, once or twice. Such are the perils of autodidactism.

heard a clang and stopped. I turned back round. As I turned the second time, I heard another small clang and watched the tip of my ladder bump into the helmet of one of my neighbours, who was sitting stationary on his moped, eyes screwed shut, helmet slightly scratched.

'Whoops,' I said.

'I didn't think people like you existed,' he replied quietly.

'I'm really sorry. You don't make that mistake twice, do you?'

'Apparently you do.'

'Well – sorry.' And as I turned round I lifted the ladder so it was more vertical, and he ducked just in case. At least I'd got that lesson out the way. Otherwise, it could have been very embarrassing.

I took everything out of the boxes and cellophane and laid it all out on the bed. Then I applied my belt, holstered the scrapers and put on my old walking boots. I looked in the mirror and saw something more than myself. At a glance I may have looked like a slightly overweight twenty-two-year-old with glasses. I may have borrowed my sense of personal armoury from a childhood love of spaghetti Westerns – and now that I looked at it, the leg holster might have to go – but for the first time since my mother died, I was a man with a purpose. I felt taller, my muscles taut, hand poised over the trigger of a cleaning-fluid bottle. I had a staring contest with my reflection. I squinted slightly, as if I was looking into the sun, and set my jaw like Clint Eastwood. Waiting, waiting. Who was going to make the first move? My left index finger twitched imperceptibly over the cleaning fluid.

Bam! I drew the bottle, sprayed my reflection, right-hand-pulled a squeegee and I was off at the top of the mirror, snaking left down right down left chasing the fluid as it trickled inexorably floorwards – but I got there first and overtook it. Now I had time to slow down, to take my time on the corners and holster the fluid, pull out a J-cloth, still crisply folded from the packet, and wipe the fluid from the frame. The outdoor windows wouldn't need such care, but this one wasn't just a quick cleaning job. This was me sticking my flag in my moon. I wasn't going to be a salesman or even a Silica-Based Window Panel Hygiene and Care Co-Ordinator. I was a window cleaner. I would make houses new again, let the sun flow freely into the corners of forgotten rooms. One day, I might even clean one of those giant glass erections[27] in the big city. I wiped the last smudge on the window and looked back at my shimmering face. Canary Wharf, or Manhattan. The Big Smoke and the Big Apple. I imagined people on their lunch breaks in America, biting into ripe, chunky apples, and then I thought of London – people huddled on doorsteps smoking. Perhaps London wasn't a city you lived in, so much as survived. But on the up side, it was only a couple of hours up the M3.

I decided to go round the neighbourhood and clean everyone's windows for free, and then drop my card through the letterbox. I didn't have any cards, and the printer was broken, so I got a notepad and wrote my name and number out hundreds of times, as if I was being punished for forgetting them. I folded them carefully and put them in a spare pouch. I walked round the side of the house and got the ladder from where I had left it. Then I started out on the figure of eight I used to do as a milkman.

At the first house I reached, the owners weren't in. I wasn't sure about letting myself in the side gate. I crept round to try and hear if anyone was out in the back garden. Something malevolent barked at me from behind the fence. I made an executive decision to skip this house, and to start ringing doorbells.

At the next house, a pleasant-looking man opened the door, and I recognised him as the owner of the shop at the end of the

---

27 DW: Günter seems to have used this word interchangeably with 'constructions'.

road. I asked him if he had a window cleaner already, as the last thing I wanted was a turf war.

'To be honest,' said the shop owner under his breath, 'we don't really like our window cleaner. He's foreign, you know.' I looked into the shop owner's big brown Indian eyes. 'One of those Poles. Coming over here, taking our jobs, the lazy bastards. Half of them are on benefits.'

'Hang on, do they have jobs or are they on benefits?'

'Whatever they can get their hands on. Both, probably. Worst ones are the asylum seekers. You'll never convince them to go back where they came from.'

'No, I suppose not. I tell you what, I've got all my stuff with me, so I'll give the house a once-over for free, and then just let me know if you want me to come back in a couple of weeks. This', I tore off a strip of paper, 'is my number.'

I cleaned the ground-floor windows, then got the ladder up and did the top ones. After that, I realised that the cleaning fluid had dripped down to the bottom ones, so I did all those again. Lesson two.

I worked my way round the neighbourhood until I'd run out of fluid, and then I walked home happy. I felt that I had accomplished something. My good work would be undone by the natural chaos of things, but I would be back again to sort it out. It would be a comfortable ebb and flow, a leisurely game of table tennis between the world and me.

As luck would have it, my home turf was unchallenged – the aforementioned Pole turned out to be an odd-jobs man who had been renovating their staircase – so I tended to pick up business just by walking around. People would stop me and I'd slow cautiously to a halt, making sure my ladder was parallel to the road. I'd take out a handwritten business card and offer it. Sometimes they'd laugh, often they'd look at me maternally as if I'd just done something incredibly sweet. Sometimes they'd survey my tool belt area with hungry eyes and tell me that I should come round for a cup of tea and talk things over. If they started staring at my lips I'd generally just keep walking. I think they wanted something I was loath to provide.[citation needed]

You really only clean a window for two purposes: to see out of, or to see into. 'Glasshouse' or 'fish tank', if you will. And the only way to tell whether you've done a good job on a window is to look through it. So I quickly discovered that, as a window cleaner, you tend to witness every joke in the human comedy. I very much enjoyed spotting a situation I hadn't seen before, although my soul withered a little every time I caught a teenage boy masturbating.

One of the women who stopped me in the street was called Paula Dorman, and by giving her my number, I instigated what would become known to me as The Dorman Affair. She had given me the normal spiel, about how her husband was always busy doing other things, and how she had too much to do with the washing and the shopping, and she didn't want to get up a ladder or the whole neighbourhood would see her big old backside (here she had paused, and I later realised that she had been waiting for me to contradict her). I had said I would gladly clean her windows for my standard ten pounds. She had written her address on my arm in lipstick.

I turned up at the appointed time, two days later, and Mrs Dorman invited me in.

'Please, call me Paula.' I had discovered by this point that I didn't enjoy doing the inside of houses. It made me feel like a burglar. She made me take my shoes off too; needless to say that I was truly uncomfortable. No one else was expected to get their work done without shoes on, with the exception of karate teachers.

I went through to her kitchen. There was a small TV on a

bracket in the top corner of the room, and a counter with stools. Not a comfortable chair in sight. We sat down on the stools and she poured us orange juice from concentrate. Her eyes were sunken and her peroxide-blonde hair only served as a contrast to the blotchy pink map of her face. She gnawed her lip as she poured the juice.

'So this is the kitchen,' she said.

'Yes,' I said. 'It is.'

'In a moment I'll show you everything else.'

I hoped her husband didn't teach karate.

'So what does your husband do?'

She waved her hand vaguely.

'He's some sort of consultant. He goes into businesses and tells them who they should fire.'

'He fires people for a living?'

'No. He just tells them who to fire. And then they give him a few grand. It's the perfect job if you're a coward as well as an arsehole.' I looked across at her patchwork face and, before I could wonder if she'd been crying, she knocked back the rest of her juice.

'Come on then, I'll show you the house.'

I stood up, knocked back my own and rested my other hand on my holster.

She showed me the lounge, replete with leopardskin cushions; the bathroom and its woollen toilet roll cover; the little utility room where she kept the shiatsu. It yapped at me and I wanted to growl back.

'Quiet, Napoleon.'

Small man syndrome, I thought.

She had left the bedroom until last. The tension was palpable. She walked up the narrow staircase ahead of me, bottom rustling gently in synthetic trousers. A long, manicured nail reached back to free some material which was trapped in her underwear.

At the top of the landing, she pushed open a door and waited for me to go in first. I tightened my grip on my squeegee. She followed me in and closed the door.

'This', came her ecstatic tremolo, 'is the master bedroom.' I surveyed the room: a bay window, double glazed, ten panes. East-facing, so the sun might slip in each morning across the heavily frilled king-size duvet. (You'd be surprised how few people close their curtains of an evening.) On the bed, there were more pillows and cushions than one could comfortably rest a head on, and a mirror was stuck to the ceiling. The politics of this marriage were, I ascertained, conducted in the bedroom.

'Very nice aspect,' I said, in what I hoped was a noncommittal tone. I tried to sense exactly how close she was behind me.

'Now make sure you give these windows an extra polish,' she breathed. 'I want them so clean you can't even tell they're there.' Something stirred in my Y-fronts. It was the perfect bay window, overlooking the lush garden and jacuzzi, and I would look forward to cleaning them thoroughly, but still I felt uneasy. I looked across at her and, just for a moment, I glimpsed something vulnerable in those squashed little eyes. Then her face hardened and she left the room. I was a little taken aback, but altogether pleased not to have been bundled onto the bed.

Downstairs, she asked me where I would start, and I explained that you have to do the top floor first, because the suds drip down to the lower windows. I would do the outside first, start round the back and work my way forward. I could do the inside if absolutely necessary. We agreed I'd start on the bay window. Then she asked me, very specifically, to come at twenty minutes past one the following Thursday. I happened to be available, but the specificity baffled me. She said that she wouldn't be around, but she'd leave my money and house key under the pot of sweet peas round the back of the house.

In the days leading up to Thursday, I did other houses, but something kept niggling at me about the Dorman job. I didn't know what it was, but our conversation had put me on edge. I had heard about exhibitionists before, and I was aware that there were any number of fantasies which might require the participation of a window cleaner. We are one of those few professions who, like doctors or teachers, must break social barriers as a matter of course in our daily work, and as such the humble window cleaner seems to occupy a disproportionately large space in the consciousness of the depraved.[28]

Thursday arrived on schedule, and the morning passed without event. At the appointed hour I unlatched the side gate and manœuvred my ladder across the side of the house. I thought I could hear noises within, but I couldn't be sure. I looked at my watch as nineteen flicked to twenty. Right on time.

I propped the ladder against the wall beneath the first floor bay window, steadying the bottom against the side of their jacuzzi. I took a deep breath, and steeled myself.

I had two options. I could treat the window as if it were opaque, setting my face and pretending that whatever was happening inside wasn't visible because of something unlikely such as glare. The second approach, and the one which I generally employed, was to smile, wave cheerfully, pretend to wobble on my ladder, and generally spread good cheer. The way I see it, there isn't really much choice but to admit that glass is designed to be transparent. To pretend otherwise is like being a mime: degrading to both viewer and participant.

But as I put my foot on the first rung of the ladder, I resolved

28 DW: Günter always professed ignorance of conjugal matters until his move to London, but the occasional slip seems to suggest that he may, under the privacy of his own duvet, have begun to educate himself. Admittedly, one doesn't necessarily tell the vicar about these things.

that, whatever I was going to witness through that bay window, I was going to marshal my admittedly undeveloped acting ability and pretend that I couldn't see it.

As I climbed the ladder, the noise became more defined and I began to make out individual words. There was a pounding beat like a kick drum, and a man's voice, shouting hoarsely, 'You're fired bitch! You're fucking fired!' over and over again. As I raised my eyes to the level of the window, I couldn't help but peer in to see the man I presumed to be Mr Dorman jackhammering away at a helpless woman who, for all her peroxide hair, was certainly not Mrs Dorman.[29] Maybe a small part of me was grateful to be learning first-hand about sexual technique, but I gathered myself and remembered that I was here to do a job, come rain or shine. So I grabbed my cleaning fluid and sprayed a liberal quantity on the top left window, before watching my squeegee zigzag down the pane. It squeaked a little, and I heard a scream. Everything went quiet, and I watched Mr Dorman dismount and cross the room, preternaturally quickly for such a large man, penis pointing up at me like the lance of a mounted knight. I heard a muffled shout of 'Pervert!' as he struggled to unlock the window, and then he opened it wide, and pushed me.

My ladder swung out into the air and for a moment I hung there, balanced between the house and the cool beyond. Then, as the angle of the ladder battled against the strength of Mr Dorman's push, and won, the ladder changed direction and came slamming back into the wall of the house. I lost my footing and fell twelve feet into the jacuzzi.

29 DW: It was ever thus. As an interesting historical aside, there was an unfortunate typographical error in the King James Bible of 1631, now referred to as 'The Wicked Bible', which caused Exodus 20:14 to be printed as, 'Thou shalt commit adultery.' King Charles I was not greatly amused and publicly ordered all copies to be destroyed, though if he had kept a private copy for his son, that would certainly explain a proliferation of Fitzes in the subsequent decades.

The next thing I knew, Paula was dabbing at my face with a cloth from my belt, her face a Pangaea of blotches.

'I'm so sorry Günter, I never meant for this to happen, I'm so so sorry.'

Back on my rounds a couple of weeks later, I mentioned the incident, if not the frightful specifics, to a neighbour. The neighbour revealed that, since Mr Dorman managed the finances for the both of them, Paula couldn't have hired a private investigator without arousing suspicion. But she had known that something was going on, since she always came back from her Pilates class on Thursdays to a badly made bed, and she might be a lot of things, but she wasn't a slattern. So when she had seen me walking along with my ladder, it had seemed the perfect opportunity to 'smoke the rabbit out of the hole', as the neighbour put it.

The Dorman Affair was perhaps my first inkling that I'd make a good private detective, although if anyone ever wanted to compile a comprehensive survey of the masturbation habits of teenage boys, I'm sorry to say I could do that too.

Around the time I was called as a witness for the Dorman divorce hearing, I got a phone call from an unknown number.

'Glass Cleaning, how can I help?'

'Günter?'

'Yes?'

'Oh good. Dean Winterbottom here. I was wondering if you might like to come over for a cup of tea? We have some wonderful loose-leaf Darjeeling in at the moment. Best served without milk.'

'I'm all booked up this week,' I said, looking at my diary.

'I quite understand. However, it is rather pressing. I don't mean to put pressure on you, but we don't want to have to close the cathedral.'

I thought about telling her I'd already found a job, but a part of me was still intrigued.

'Are you free this evening?' I asked.

'Always free, my dear, always free. God is a freelance.'

'Okay, I'll pop over around six.'

I went downstairs to make an early dinner for Dad, and found him sitting at the kitchen table with a bottle of whisky.

'Fish fingers again, I'm afraid,' I said, opening the freezer.

'I can't eat now.'

'You've got to eat something.'

'Sit down and have a whisky.'

I went and sat with him. He filled up his glass and nodded to himself.

'You're a real man now, with your job. You're independent. You must be making some proper money now, eh? You'll probably move out soon. No use in worrying.'

'Look, Dad, if it's about my cooking, I can learn. We both can.'

He drew his hand down over his face, like he was wiping an Etch-a-sketch.

'Look, if you want to stay here, I might have to start charging rent. I can't keep supporting you. All I've got's my pension, and it's smaller than the mortgage. So the longer I live, the more I owe.'

'That's okay, I can help to clear it,' I said. 'The window cleaning is going well, and I have a couple of hundred pounds left from my redundancy.'

'We're talking about thousands of pounds of debt, Günter. The bank won't give me any more money.'

'Oh. What about Max?'

'Tight as a bunny's arse.'

I looked up at the wall clock. It was quarter to six.

'I've got to run, but we'll talk about this later. Eat something.'

'Thanks for your concern,' he said, eyeing the whisky bottle, 'but I'll start what I've finished.'

8

Miracle Worker

I arrived at the cathedral a little late. The sun was hitting one side of the building, casting a long shadow which pointed out east like a giant sundial. I walked in through the main entrance, where tourists were milling around, some of them dragging children or dogs.

I went through to the back where the little office was, and knocked on the door. There was no answer, so I opened the door to find a young reverend goggling at a computer screen. Statistically, it was likely to be either a video of a cute animal or pornography.

'Evensong was at half five,' he said without looking up.

'I'm looking for Dean Winterbottom,' I said.

'Who are you?' he asked.

'Günter Glass.'

'Anne!' he shouted, still staring at the screen. I very much wanted to see what was on the screen.

Dean Winterbottom came through from the kitchenette, looking quite radiant.

'Sorry I didn't hear you come in, my dear, I was just feeding Moses.' I must have looked bemused, because she explained, 'Our cat. I found him a few months back wandering around outside. He looked lost, and the vet said he needed lots of tablets, so I called him Moses. We are stewards of all God's creatures, are we not?'

She directed this last question at the young reverend, who carried on staring. The cat strutted through and rubbed itself along his leg. He gave it a little kick and it decided to lick itself instead. It probably wasn't a cat video.

'Come on, let's take a walk outside. The quality of light this time of year is quite spectacular.'

Outside, the sun had gilded the tops of the trees.

'Just look at it,' she said, squinting up at the cathedral. 'Still beautiful, no matter how many times you see it. You always notice something different.'

'Why has the light stopped flashing?' I asked.

She beamed at me and clasped her hands.

'You did say you paid close attention to detail, didn't you? And you're good with heights. It's all worked out splendidly.'

There was an ominous rumbling in my bowels.

'This job that you mentioned—' I began.

'We had a very good chap who used to replace the light. It normally lasts a year or two. He'd come every May. But he is almost as old as me now, and he had a little scare last time. It does get windy up there, but karabiners so rarely fail . . .' She trailed off.

'I see.'

'It's not exactly a common job, so I've been having a little trouble knowing where to find a replacement. But when I saw you standing there looking up at the spire for so long, I thought I might lean tentatively on God's Providence. Of course, one mustn't test the Lord, but I thought I might see whether or not you were one of his little jokes. So I invited you in for tea.'

'I thought you were just being nice.'

'No, no,' she said, waving at an invisible fly. 'It wasn't anything so trivial as niceness. I had a purpose to deliver, and you were searching for one. "That which hath been is now; and that which is to be hath already been; and God requireth that which is past.'"[30]

'I'm not sure I follow.'

'There is a right time for everything, Günter, and I believe that you came here for a reason. Whatever you were looking for, I believe you'll find it up there.' I looked back up. It really was very high. Four hundred feet, Wikipedia said.

'I suppose I wouldn't mind doing it, but all I have is a fifteen-foot ladder.'

'Oh, I'm sure we can sort all that out. And you'll be remunerated, of course. We used to pay Mr Giddings a hundred and fifty pounds, I hope that sounds reasonable.'

I thought of Dad.

'I'll do it.'

'Sterling,' she said. 'Let's go and get the harness.'

She set off towards the cathedral, taking me by the arm. We walked through the back office and into a sort of broom cupboard, where she bent from the hips and started rummaging around in an old Asda carrier bag on a low shelf.

'Now what you must do, when you get outside – I was sure I had left it here – there should be two ropes, you see, one for – oh no, here it is, I could have sworn I'd put it – it's crucially important to make sure that you – and here's the other.' Flushed and triumphant, she handed me two sets of ropes and a harness. Her part of the task was over. I wasn't sure I had understood

---

30 DW: Ecclesiastes 3 suggests that 'to every thing there is a season, and a time to every purpose under the heaven.' There's even apparently a time to gather stones, presumably not regularly. But since God is omnipresent through time, from his perspective it's all happening at once. Though our meeting seemed a coincidence from our perspective, I tried to imagine how it might have appeared to God: two sharp lines on an infinite sheet of white paper, angled infinitesimally towards one another, seeming to run parallel but eventually converging at a point predicted exactly by their vectors.

her instructions, or even whether she had given any.[31] We went to the bottom of the spire, and walked upstairs in a spiral so uniform that it made me wonder whether I was travelling at all, or whether I was stuck in a nightmare by Escher.

After some time, we reached the bell tower.

'The world's oldest working clock,' she said. 'The day this bell stops chiming I'll be listening for the sound of sixteen hooves.'[32]

There was another staircase leading off from this main platform, with a black metal chain on which hung the sign, DANGER OF DEATH: DO NOT CROSS. Dean Winterbottom cheerfully unclipped it and waved me through.

'Good luck my dear, and remember what I said about the ropes. Oh – and do come down if it's too windy, won't you.' She handed me a screwdriver and a red bulb that she'd been carrying, almost like a bicycle light, but much larger. On the back it said AIRCRAFT WARNING LIGHT. I stepped into the harness, tied the bulb to my belt and pulled as hard as I could on anything that looked like it might break or come loose. Matters had progressed more rapidly than I had anticipated. My palms began to sweat. I wiped them on the thighs of my jeans, walking up the remaining stairs, which creaked and grumbled, until I came to a little door, about the right size for a hobbit. I opened it onto the cool evening air. All of Salisbury was laid out before me. Shaftesbury, too. Hardy country, I'm told. Stonehenge and rape fields. It was too high for mosquitoes. If I fell, I would have time to worry on the way down.

Except that I wasn't worried. As if for the first time, I felt alive. Of course, you always know you're alive – rationally you

31 DW: I thought I'd been quite clear, but the subsequent news article in the *Salisbury Plain Dealer* seems to contradict this.

32 DW: It dates from 1386. Don't listen to the Bishop of Beauvais if he tries to tell you otherwise: ours is the oldest. Beauvais couldn't even finish building their cathedral.

know, you can feel your pulse and think and move and all that –
but now, up here, I really *felt* alive. I could feel my skin buzzing
and the sharp geometries of my surroundings hung in the air
before me like they were the only real things I had ever seen.

I looked down at the green, where tourists were swirling like
dust. A sharp gust tore at my hair as I located a little metal loop,
onto which I clipped my first safety rope. I put my hands on the
frame of the door, then got a foot up, turning myself around to
face the spire. I looked up at the climb, and tested my weight
on the black metal structural ladder. I felt I knew how to do
this instinctively, almost as if it was coded in ancestral genes.
Another gust wrapped itself around me, and I shifted the second
rope on my shoulder. I went one rung at a time, slow and steady,
methodically, tantalising myself with furtive thoughts of the
drop below. I got to the top of the ladder and took a breather.
My fingers were tingling. I wondered how long it had been since
I had last eaten, and wiped my palms again, one by one, on my
jeans. Here was the spire. I gulped down air. I was at the highest
point between the horizons. Beside me in all directions was sky,
and beyond that, space.

The wind changed direction twice in short succession. I held
the spire itself and stood upright on the topmost rung of the
ladder, trying to get myself steady. I couldn't see anywhere to
clip my second rope – the spire and the rungs were too wide.
I unscrewed the first of four attachments on the warning light
and caught the screw in the same hand as it fell – a moment
of unwonted grace. I did the second and third without trouble,
stowing the screws in one of my marsupia, but as I started to
unscrew the fourth, with the plastic casing now hanging off, a
new gust caught me front on and I lost my footing. I grabbed
the spire as the wind took me and, for one fraction of a second,
hung in perfect balance, supported almost horizontally by the
wind. Then the air under me went still, and I fell through it.

I caught a rung on my second attempt, hitting the ladder with various extremities as I jerked myself short of oblivion. I didn't trust that rope to hold a normal adult, let alone someone of my dimensions, so it was a relief to find myself clinging hard to the ladder, held fast, breathing heavily, alive. I had nearly conquered the spire. I would conquer it.

I climbed the ladder again, removed the shell, replaced the light and, triumphant, took the old spent bulb in my hand. I heard a cheer as from a far-off stadium, and looked down at the tourists, who had converged in the middle of the green. Little pinpricks of xenon flashed out in the murky light, and I lifted the old lamp to show them. If I could do this, I could do anything. I could clean skyscrapers. I was breathing hard. Here a man could really breathe.

I was in the local paper the next morning.[33] There was a photo of me outstretched in the air, one hand gripping the spire, the other wielding the screwdriver as if I were a British Superman, flying in to attack the warning light at speed. Say what you like about Japanese tourists, they know how to take a good picture. I even had a suspicion that my safety rope had been photoshopped out.

The article itself seemed to suggest that I could be likened to Jesus, because we both had facial hair. This didn't seem like a fair comparison, although I can't pretend I wasn't flattered. And when they had phoned me up about it, I had asked them to mention my window cleaning, so the phone had been ringing all morning. I ended up enlisting Dad as my secretary, because otherwise I wouldn't have had time to attend any of my appointments.

When I came home after a long day of cleaning, I was tired. My knees and elbows hurt from the fall, and I'd hurt one of my

33 'Miracle Worker', *Salisbury Plain Dealer*, 15 May 2012.

fingers catching the ladder. To Dad's dismay, I cancelled every-thing for the next day and went straight up to bed, taking a mug of herbal tea and a long list of missed calls with me.

A lot of the people who had phoned were too far away for me to reach by foot, so I had to reject them out of hand. But I did fill up my potted schedule for the week ahead, and confirmed what I already knew: this neighbourhood was mine. If I carried on like this for a few months, I might start making enough to pay the mortgage, and if he found some work too, we could start eating into the debt.

This had all of the characteristics of a good, solid plan, the kind of plan that a man could live by. Prudent. Except that I didn't want to be prudent. I wanted to be way up there in the sky, close to the sun.

As I scanned down the list, one name stuck out from the rest (possibly because my father had written it in capital letters and underlined it urgently. JOHN BLADES. I felt a searing heat run through me. John Blades had called me. John Blades OBE, the man who cleaned half the skyscrapers in London, had called me, Günter Glass, of Glass Cleaning, Salisbury. I should have whooped or punched the air, but as it was, I tiptoed across the hall and went to the bathroom. Those herbal teas go right through me.

9

The Spinnaker Project

The next morning, I ate some Dutch waffles and had a pot of coffee. Then I put on a pot of camomile to calm myself down. I cleared my throat and tested out various professional phrases before my dad could wake up and start goading me. Then, just as I picked up my phone to call Blades, it rang.

I picked up. A silky voice said, 'Open your curtains.' Stunned, I walked across to the kitchen window and pulled a curtain aside. The window was blacked out as if the house were buried under earth. I walked through to the lounge and opened the patio curtains. The patio window was caked with thick mud. Someone had tried to seal the whole house from sunlight.

'You have eight minutes,' said the voice, 'to clean those windows. If you can do it, you've got the job.'

'What job? Who are you?'

'You know who I am, Günter. Your time starts now.'

The line went dead, and my heart sprang to life. I hurdled the stairs three at a time and grabbed my belt from the back of my door, fairly jumped back down the whole flight and ran out to the garage, where I picked up a spray I hadn't used before. The label was filled with orange and black warnings, skulls and crosses, and a tag line ('wipe filth away for good'). The front said simply, GOMORRAH. I holstered it and ran out to the ladder, which I mounted faster than I've ever mounted anything. I took a scraper and chipped at the mud on my bedroom window, which wasn't yet dry enough to crumble off, flicking it into the flowerbed below. Then I pulled out the GOMORRAH and sprayed it onto the mud in the top left corner. My eyes streamed at the acidity as I worked the panel snaking left down right down left. The mud was dispersing under the assault of the spray and I cleared the window in just over a minute. I almost slid back down the ladder and did the bottom window nearby to save running time, all the while making a mental calculation and deciding that I would have to work quicker. I ran round the bottom windows spraying GOMORRAH, hoping it would start to break up the dirt while I worked the top windows. I checked my watch and it had been four minutes. I was working quickly but it felt like my face was being stung by hornets – it didn't matter, though, I'd finished the top floor. With one minute to go I raced round the bottom windows scraping with my right hand while I squeegeed with the left. I got to the last window with twenty seconds to spare and finished it just in time to answer my ringing phone.

'How did you do?'

'I finished.' I looked up at the crystalline glint of the young sun in the windows and wiped my brow with my sleeve.

'You finished?'

'Yep.' I looked at my ghostly reflection in the pane in front of me, savoured the feeling of steam rising from my cheeks as my glasses misted up.

'Oh.' There was a short pause. 'Hang on, I'll come round.'

A minute or so later, I heard someone unlatching the side gate. A man appeared wearing tight trousers, a blue silk shirt and a watch that looked as tacky as a market-stall counterfeit. Both his eyebrows and his designer stubble had very defined edges. In fact, they were almost exactly the same length, as if he had trimmed them to match. He gazed at me appreciatively.

'You know Günter, I set you an impossible task to see how

you'd work under pressure. No one ever finishes the job. I just wanted to see how you'd cope – whether you'd argue or get on with it.' He looked around my feet. 'Where's your bucket?'

'I don't really use one. I use an array of fluids.'

He laughed good-naturedly. He had long canines.

'A revolutionary. Well, you won't be allowed a bucket with what I've got planned.'

'Do you like camomile? I've just put a pot on. It'll be getting on the strong side, by now. It's been brewing for a little over eight minutes.'

He set his face and handed me an envelope, then half-nodded, half-bowed, making prayer hands, and disappeared round the side of the house. I ran after him.

'Wait,' I said.

He stopped on the driveway. A heavyset man was getting out of a black car.

'People don't normally follow me,' he said irritably.

'What is this?' I asked.

'It's an envelope,' he said simply. 'I've got another one of these to do this morning, so I'm in a bit of a hurry, okay? See you there.' He got in the car, which sped off with a brief shriek of burnt rubber.

I turned the envelope over in my hands. Dad came out holding his dressing gown closed, badly.

'What in God's name are you doing? It's eleven in the morning! How am I supposed to sleep with you banging around the house?'

'You should be up by now anyway.'

'What's the point? I'm old and I'm tired. What have I got to get up for? And who was that man? What are you holding?'

Dad was always confused when he first woke up. Explaining would only confuse him further. I opened the envelope. I was being invited, in copperplate,

To undertake the proud task of cleaning
The Spinnaker Tower
on behalf of the City of Portsmouth
this May 29th, 12 midday
RSVP spinnaker@johnblades.co.uk

There were no further details, but I knew I would do it. This delicate gilt lettering was the sign of my ascendancy.

I went in and drank the camomile, thinking about Blades and listening to my dad's constant questions about the job, the money involved, whether there was more work coming, and what was for breakfast. When he drew breath I escaped to my room and discovered eleven new emails from Max, who seemed to have been compiling revenue-projection graphs and finding new equipment all night. One of them was a list of his top ten grappling hooks. When on earth would I ever need a grappling hook? The last email read, 'Just say no. Between emails I've been cleaning the house and I've rubbed away all the skin on my hands. Coming down now. Typing hurts.' I knew there had to be a reason why he was being helpful. I wondered briefly about staging one of those quaint American 'interventions', but on reflection I decided not to validate him. It was probably just a cry for attention.

The rest of the morning passed slowly. When I had been unemployed, days had drifted past like clouds or mobility scooters, but now that I was in the habit of being useful, doing nothing was just annoying.

I went downstairs to get my dad but I couldn't find him anywhere. I retraced my steps, like Mum would have told me to. I'd put him down in the kitchen in front of some pancakes, but he wasn't there now. What did I normally do with him?

I found him curled up back in bed.

'Get up.'

'No!' he moaned.

'You can't waste a whole day in bed. What do you normally do?'

'Sleep and watch telly.'

'Well today we're going outside. Come on, it'll do you good.'

'Don't want to.'

'If you get dressed I'll buy you a pint.'

'Fine,' he scowled, jumping up.

'I'll be waiting downstairs.'

When we got to the pub, we sat for a while in the manner of locals, silent with our thoughts, occasionally scraping the head off our top lips with our bottom lips, or saying, 'Mm.' Eventually, Dad rested his palms on his thighs, elbows out. His 'man to man' pose.

'Günter, we still need to talk about our home.'

'What's there to talk about?' I asked.

'I'm getting red letters. Unless we come up with eight grand in the next few weeks, we're going to be spending our evenings fighting over Special Brew.'

'Come on, Dad, don't be so melodramatic. It can't be that bad.'

'It is that bad.'

'But Mum had savings. She wouldn't just let us—'

'No, Günter. She had a few hundred pounds.'

It shocked me that she had not left us provided for. The day I had lost my job to that cruel slump in dairy, she had stopped me at the bottom of the stairs, and stroked me pacifically on my upper arm.

'You will always have a home here,' she had said. 'No matter what happens.'

But here we were. How could I blame her, if she had no way

of knowing that she was lying?

Dad slammed his fist down on the table.

'She didn't deserve it.'

'Who?'

'Your mother. She didn't deserve to go like that.'

'I know.'

'She didn't deserve to . . . we could have—'

'It was no one's fault,' I said soothingly.

'But what if—'

'No.' I put down my pint. 'Just try not to think about it.'

He threw back his beer, staring into the bottom with desolate eyes.

The remainder of my day of rest was spent buying us more beer and playing Scrabble until our stomachs were full and my father finally accepted that *gumshoe* wasn't a word. I know he was depressed, but I wasn't about to give him a triple-word score.

Over breakfast the next day, I pondered the unique ability of Dutch waffles to get a heart racing so soon after sleep. They were so heavy and sugary that, in all likelihood, my heart was pumping harder just to get the syrupy blood around my body. But just as exercise made me feel unwell, doing things which surely brought me closer to death made me feel truly alive. Perhaps that was why I was genuinely beginning to like the idea of dangling up high.

I checked and cleaned my gear, hitched it all onto my person, and set out for the train station before dawn. Heading out for work like this reminded me of my days as a milkman, and I felt a warm nostalgia for the job. The depot's fleet of diesel and electric floats had been a useful and environmentally sound mode of transport, and one I wouldn't easily replace. It was so hard to act in the world without indirectly harming someone else, or contributing to the net misery brought about wherever human-ity flourished. One couldn't buy from fast-food shops, because they were cruel to their chickens, exploited their workers and deforested the Amazon to farm cows, which in turn contrib-uted to global warming with their imperfect digestion. One couldn't buy cheap clothes because they would have been made in a sweatshop, but expensive clothes played into the hands of the fashion world, which peddled insecurity as their stock in trade. Besides, cotton was too often grown and wasted on T-shirts that were never bought, and fair trade only served to elevate a few lucky landowners. And if you were rich enough to be buying everything fair trade, you probably had one of those jobs that creates inequality in the first place. Thinking my way through the world's complex web of injustices as I trudged along Fisherton Street, I realised that the best I could hope for would be to break even on the moral scales. If it was true that people were reincarnated according to their karma, most people must end up as ants. That would at least explain why there were so many ants everywhere.

I passed a man who was asleep in the front seat of his car, the bonnet propped up to reveal the innards. I had a quick look at it, topped the radiator up from my water bottle and checked the oil. All seemed fine to me, so I knocked on the window. He woke up a little startled as I had expected, and thrust the door open hard into my kneecap.

'Ow! Why did you do that?' I asked.

'Get the fuck away from me! I haven't got any money. Get away from me now or I'll kill you, I swear!' He brandished a car jack at me.

'What are you going to do with that? Give me a quote on my undercarriage?'

'I told you to step away.'

'I'm only trying to help. What's the matter?'

He studied my boiler suit. 'Are you AA?'

'No, I'm . . . helpful. What's the matter?'

'I ran out of petrol.'

'Oh.' I rubbed my knee. 'There's a petrol station just up by Waitrose, you know.'

'Is there? Nothing came up on my satnav.'

'I'm going that way. I can show you.'

'No that's okay. I need to, ah . . .' he cast around.

I smiled to prove I wasn't a murderer. 'Well, have a nice day,' I added as an afterthought. I limped off. One good deed in the bank and the day had barely begun.

I reached the station, found a bench and watched the sun climb steadily. The sun must have made a good god. It had a constancy not often achieved in the average deity, and one experienced its benefit and absence daily. The odd eclipse probably provided a decent unknown variable to ensure worship.

By the time I arrived at Gunwharf Quays, the day was bright and I was hungry. I had the second half of my breakfast in a mock-French café (a buttery, stale croissant), and caught up on some news from an old newspaper. Nick Griffin had been invited to the royal palace as a Member of the European Parliament, and apparently the billionairess owner of L'Oréal, whose father had been a right-wing extremist, had illegally funded Sarkozy's campaign trail. I abandoned the paper on the grounds that it was depressing.

There was patriotic bunting strewn everywhere in preparation for the Jubilee. It looked a bit much to me. I'd always thought one of the nicest things about being English was how quietly we held our pride, as if flag-waving and shouting the anthem were faintly embarrassing and, old and wise as our country was, we'd got that kind of adolescent demonstration out of our system two hundred years ago.

I watched the people of Portsmouth go by. They were a good-looking bunch. I have often thought that people are more attractive outside of one's home town – it's like you're on holiday, and you get that spontaneous, carefree sense that you might never meet again. Either that or I come from an ugly town.

After a time the heavyset man appeared and motioned silently toward the others. We walked the few hundred metres down the quay, with seagulls hurling abuse above our heads and a ferry honking out to sea. The Spinnaker Tower loomed up ahead of us, a giant white spear dominating the quay, twisting up like DNA into the sky. It looked like a lighthouse from the future.

I had thought that there would be a whole team of us, but as it turned out, we were just three including Blades. Dressed in a yellow hard-hat and a boiler suit done up to the waist, he had the spry build of a rock climber, and I felt not a little ashamed at the hairy gut peeking out between my buttons.

The other man introduced himself as Pete, an Australian Greek with a harsh accent and the casual manner of an unrepentant alpha male. He wore his boiler suit done up to the collar and lit a new cigarette off the stub of his last.

'Now,' said Blades. 'You may be wondering why I've brought the three of us together for this job. We don't necessarily have a great deal in common. You've both got your own freelance work and I'm sure you don't need my patronage. But the thing is this: I'm trying to get us some good PR, in advance of a major contract that's come up. I need this contract. Failure is not an option. And both of you have something that I have, something you can't buy. It's something unique, something that other people want. I can't explain it except to say that you are the kind of guys that make headlines. And the thing is – I'm sharing a secret with you now – window cleaning doesn't make many headlines. It's something to be proud of, guys. It's what made my company stand out from the crowd in the first place.'

'Oh yeah,' said Pete, looking at me askance. 'You're that fuck'n . . . superman guy.'

'I should say that it wasn't as windy as it looked from the photo. It was a rogue gust. What did you do?'

'Peter wrote an advertisement with a well-placed typo,' Blades cut in. 'Certainly caught people's eye.'

'It said, "I do widows. First time free."'

'It went viral,' said Blades excitedly.

'That's quite a commitment. Did you actually have to "do" any widows?' I asked. Pete pushed his bottom lip up into his top lip and tilted his head back. Lucky widows.

'Gentlemen,' cut in Blades. 'Back to business.'

Blades explained the layout of the tower, the all-important anchor points, and last of all the dreaded glass floor. Blades would go first, to clip on our safety ropes, and then we'd work from the top down, using equipment that he had provided. The heavyset man took all my own equipment back to his car and I felt a little naked. Then we walked round to the service stairs, strapped and buckled everything we could and ascended. Another spiral staircase, this time aluminium with little embossed shapes like blown up rice. The tips of my fingers itched; my head went hot.

We did the inside first, which gave Blades a chance to flash a few smiles and introduce himself to the visitors. The female contingent all promised to video the event on their phones and upload it to YouTube when they got home. All except one tall, broad woman who stood in the corner, looking out to sea, if anything actively avoiding Blades. I walked up to the window next to her to try and see what she was staring at so intently. I couldn't see anything, but my eyesight was imperfect, so I opened my mouth to ask.

'Wh—'

'Nothing in particular. I just love the sea.'

'And do—'

'Just visiting. I'm a medium, amongst other things.'

'I'm a large,' I said. I always think a bad joke is better than no joke at all.

'Leave.'

'I'm sorry?'

She turned to me and held out her hand. I shook it, befuddled.

'Günter. Pleased to meet you.'

'Enchanted. Leave-ah.' She touched her significant bosoms with her free hand.

'Okay. Well, I suppose I'd better be getting off anyway.'

'Oh.' She looked vaguely put out. What on earth was this woman up to? I went to rejoin the other two, and she watched me go. I felt her eyes boring into me. Was this what women felt like when they walked past builders?

I helped Pete clean the glass panel on the floor of the observation deck, glancing occasionally down at the ground below. It was a cloud's-eye view of the world, suspended high above the human scale, looking down at the nothing between our feet. It made me delirious – happy, possibly.

We went back out to the service stairs, and then up and out. Blades chalked his hands and disappeared. Pete and I looked at each other. Then his smiling head appeared in the doorway, and he gave us the thumbs up. We pulled our ropes taut, and then we were out in the thin air. The noises of the city filtered up to us like heat waves, and the sun washed down as we hung like urban commandos. The trick was to take quick, light swipes at the window. If you pressed with any force, you'd start to swing, and then you had to wait while you regained equilibrium. The alternative was to use the suction cups we'd been provided, but if you leant on one and it came loose, it set you swinging, sometimes into the window you'd just washed, and you'd have to do it all over again. It was an amazing design, though. You can't make curved float-glass, so they had attached several panels at slightly different angles to give the impression of a curve. Marvellous in the truest sense. I worked with care, paying service to the slightest blemish while Pete cracked jokes about the chicks in Adelaide. He seemed unaffected to say the least. From his posture, one would have thought that we were sunning ourselves in deck chairs, or abseiling. I looked over at him and then, with a horrible lurch, I realised I couldn't see Blades. I couldn't see him anywhere.

'Where's Blades gone?' I asked.

'He'll show up,' said Pete.

He mightn't just 'show up'. It wasn't as if we had split up to save time in a supermarket; we were hanging from a modern sculpture five hundred feet in the air. I looked down and couldn't see any sign that he'd headed in that direction. No police tape or screaming, which had to be a good sign. I saw how small people looked. I heard my breath in my ears.

I pulled a bit too hard on the release and dropped a couple of metres down my rope, leaving me hanging from the building in mid-air. My stomach lurched again and my heart beat hard as my sidekick squeegee fell from its holster and spun into the distance below. I heard a sharp crack and shouts. I looked down. No one was injured.

The only way to get back up would be to hoist myself up sharply while I released the catch, but when I released it I had to make sure I was gripping hard enough, or I would fall further, run out of rope, and then there really would be police tape below us. This was one of those odd situations that was not serious until it was fatal. I began to get the feeling of dread that I always got at the possibility of dying ignominiously, a feeling I had first discovered when I was eight and I realised, swimming in the sea, that my feet weren't touching the bottom, and the tide was strong. My mum had waved to me happily from the shore. The tide wasn't vicious, but there had been a small chance that I would start losing ground with each backwash and that, despite swimming as hard as I could, I might not make any progress towards the shore. I was struck with horror that I might never reach the sand, which was so close and yet just out of reach. If I were pulled out to sea by the tides, I would be fighting a lost cause before anyone had even noticed I was in danger. I would never see my family again.

And now there was a small chance that I would fall to my death.

I was far down enough to see Blades on all fours, upside down with his suction cups, scrubbing at the glass. He glanced across at me and winked. Can't anyone ever tell when I'm in trouble? Knowing my luck, some tourist would probably snap my last moments in some stupid pose.

'Just checking on you,' I shouted to Blades cheerily.

'I'm fine,' he smiled. 'You?'

'Yep. Yep.'

My rope uncoiled slightly and I span to face the sky. There was nothing out ahead of me until the nearest star many light years away. There was nothing below me to put my feet on, nothing solid to grab onto. I was falling, but for three inches of rope. If I pulled the catch on my karabiner now, I would head backwards, picking up pace, approaching terminal velocity, before smashing into the cold hard fact of the concrete below me. It was almost tempting. And it might make a nice follow-up piece for the local paper. I could just pull a little on my karabiner, and never think again.

Still, nothing makes less sense than committing suicide without thinking it through, and I had a job to finish. The task of pulling yourself back up is not difficult, I told myself. The thing to remember is that you only get one chance. You either get it right, or get it wrong. If there has ever been a time to fully concentrate in your whole life, it is now. Okay, stop thinking about thinking about it. Just look at the rope. Firm grip. There's the release. Release and heave. Just do it a bit at a time. First try – agh! Okay. Good. Now one more. I really need to eat less. Stupid . . . gravity. Nearly. There. Good.

I was nearly back at eye level. Pete had finished his window.

'Do ye want me to finish yours, mate?' He indicated the window, in case I needed help identifying it.

'I can finish it myself,' I snapped.

And I did, under the gaze of the rogue medium. She stood at the window keeping a watchful eye on me until I was back on solid steel. Something about her unbroken attention was discomfiting, and yet I felt safer, up there, with her watching me.

When we were back inside I went into the viewing room to find her. I didn't know exactly why I was going to find her, as she had been so rude to me before, but it turned out not to matter since she was no longer there.

I went back down and took off my gear. The heavyset man appeared swinging car keys round his index finger, holding a little book in the other hand.

We three squinted up at the tower, which gleamed like a kiss in a toothpaste advert.

'I guess we done all right,' said Pete.

Blades handed us each an envelope.

'I'll be in touch boys.'

Pete tore his open immediately. I opened mine too, using my little finger as a letter-opener, and found a cheque for £500. Crikey. Perhaps it was danger money.

I started off the way I had come, back down the quay, past the *faux* French café, and I spotted the strange woman, sitting at a table by the window. I thanked the driver and waved Blades off. I didn't know what I'd do if she asked me to leave again. The car hummed off down the road, blaring classical music. A seagull strolled past between us. I hadn't realised seagulls were quite so big. Up close, it looked like it'd put a decent dent in my leg with that beak.

'Would you like to sit down?' the strange woman asked, staring at me under a poster for Chat Noir.

'Thank you, I will.' I tried, unsuccessfully, to catch the waitress's eye. 'So your job, is it based at the tower?'

'Of course not. I was in the area visiting a client, and I thought I would look at the view before I left. It's not often I get out of London.'

She opened a large purple purse filled with bank cards, loyalty cards and what looked a lot like a deck of cards. From their midst, she pulled out a business card and handed it to me. *Lieve Toureaux.*

'Your *name* is Lieve!'

'Yes. Yours is Günter. You have a bad memory, Günter. You must be thirsty after your work. Let me get you a glass of water.' She summoned the waitress instantly and asked politely for water.

'This card says you're a psychic and a medium.'

'I'm not exactly psychic. It's hard to explain. The best way to put it would be to say that I can see into the immediate future. Say, half a second. I asked my GP to help me prove it to the scientific community, and he told me that, in his opinion, I was deranged.'

'Are doctors allowed to use the word deranged?'

'I don't know. I assume it was his professional, and not his personal opinion.'

'Are the two any different?' I asked.

'It's important to keep work and private life separate,' she told the sea. I was too busy thinking about her ability to see into the future, albeit the immediate future.

'So can you—'

'Yes, but people find it annoying when I interrupt them, so I try not to.'

I sipped at my water. The waitress had put a slice of cucumber in it. It tasted pure and clear. I wondered why I never used to drink water on its own. I rather liked it. Lieve saw me eyeing the glass.

'The cucumber is supposed to help cleanse your palate.'

'But I haven't eaten anything.'

'Perhaps your breath smells. Breathe on me.' I leant up close to her and whispered *haaaaa* as I stared into the clear grey-blue pools of her eyes. She looked directly back at me and smiled. 'No, you're fine. You smell quite nice actually. Is that your natural odour?'

'I suppose it must be. I'm not wearing aftershave.'

'It's a good sign. It means we're sexually compatible.' She looked at her watch. 'I should catch my train. It was a pleasure to meet you, and I don't say that to everyone I meet.' She got up, grabbing a gargantuan handbag, which sagged with its unknown contents. I knew that this was the moment to ask for her number, but I was unable.

'My number's on my card,' she said. 'I already gave it to you. Take care.'

After she left, I sat on the cheap wicker chair, my fingers edging around her business card in my pocket, looking out at the sea. The seagulls fought a vicious air battle over a couple of scraps of bread, and I saw that I never would have survived in nature.

10

My Lady of the Slabs

When I got home I noted Max's four-by-four in the drive. There was no sound in the house. I walked through to the kitchen, where the two of them were sitting. Dad looked up at me as I came in and Max turned round to see me.

We were just talking about you, Max smirked.

Dad assumed the serious face that he had always used when Mum laid down the law. *You know you can talk to me about anything,* he signed.

I nodded. Dad opened his mouth a little while before speaking.

'It's just Max has been looking out for you, and he's noticed that you haven't had a girlfriend since – well – ever. He's been explaining to me that it's actually quite normal to be gay now and a lot of people don't think it's disgusting at all.'

'Thanks Dad, but I'm not gay. Max is winding you up.'

I'm not! Look at his vest top.

This is a T-shirt! I signed angrily.

It's a cutaway at best. And you've got the church trying to convert you before it's too late. When have you ever shown an interest in women? You didn't even watch that porn I sent you.

I very much had watched the pornography,[34] and felt a flush

34 DW: Following a slightly terse exchange about the relevance of this research detail, Max explained that he had received a 'download confirmation' email minutes after sending it – so Max was simply goading Günter here.

of righteous indignation.

As a matter of fact I met a woman today. Her name is L-I-E-V-E. I made a sign close to 'beautiful' to stand for Lieve's name.[35]

Max snorted.

I'll believe it when I see it.

Dad looked a bit confused at this new development. Presumably it had taken some persuasion to convince him that I was gay, and now I was clambering back into the wardrobe of heterosexuality before his very eyes.

'Well, you know that I'm here for you if you are gay, and we're not going to judge your choices,' said Dad. 'But if you're not gay, that would be ideal.'

'I'm not sure people choose to be gay, Dad.'

'They bloody do. Some of them have kids, so it's not as if they can't get it up.'

'Dad, please.'

You're making him uncomfortable talking about his people like that.

'They're not my people! I mean, they aren't *not* my people, but I'm just not – look, the point is I'm not gay. I like women.'

Give him time. Anyway, I should go. Hey Günter, look at my new Mido. Swiss-made. It s a work of art. He proffered his watch. I have to say, it did look very nice. But if he could afford Swiss watches, why was he letting his own father drown in red letters? I shrugged at Max and he sloped off down the hall, slamming the front door loudly on his way out.

I wonder when I stopped liking my brother. Perhaps I never liked him. I just never really understood why he had to talk about how much money he was making all the time.

'I made five hundred pounds today,' I announced to Dad,

---

35 DW: One typically assigns a gesture to a new name, so that you don't have to spell it out each time.

showing him the cheque. His eyes filled like fish bowls, and he hugged me.

'Good lad, good lad,' he cried, and I felt how fragile he was in my arms. He was getting older now. I would look after him. I patted him on the back, unexpectedly disturbed that there was no one left who could look after me, no safe place, no more summer holidays, no one to pat my back. I didn't really want to have to provide for myself. Perhaps I should give God a try. I didn't much like the idea of giving up my weekend lie-in, but I supposed it was all *quid pro quo.*

When Sunday came round, I found myself awake at dawn. I looked across at the clock. 07.04? I didn't know times like that existed on a Sunday. I could even *get up.*

I sat in the kitchen for a while eating my waffles. Sunday morning. What a surreal thought. I could go to church. I could just get dressed and go to church. I'd woken up; anything was possible.

I didn't want to wear my black funeral suit ever again, if I could avoid it, so I went into my dad's room, where he was snoring face down into a pillow, picked an inoffensive-looking work suit and squeezed myself into it. He was not quite so broad as me, so I developed a cunning way of pulling back my shoulders so as not to rip the material. I reasoned that, as it looked like a warm day, I could probably take off the jacket once I was safely installed in a pew.

It was a pleasant walk to the cathedral, and for the first time in days no one bothered me for my autograph, or snapped me on their phone. I simply walked, shoulders back, head held high, past the school, over the green, and joined the patient worshippers queuing for entrance. It was cool when I got inside, and no one took off their jackets. I would just have to keep mine on. The young man who had been staring at the screen before now stood near the lectern, dressed in gold and red and white, staring at the people passing like an angry customs official. I hoped he didn't expose me as a charlatan. I felt he would be the kind to cast people into the flames.[36]

Everyone was filing in with quiet, almost-fearful reverence. The bishop stood taciturn in an imposing golden gown with a white hood draped back over his shoulder blades. Lit candles illuminated pools of light around the young choir, who wore white gowns over green with little ruffs. The powers that be seemed to have chosen a particular moment in history to stop moving with the times. They must have felt that their age captured the very essence of religion. I wondered if God would wear a ruff and light his way round houses with candles. If so, what did he do before ruffs? Was he just waiting until they were invented? And if so, why wasn't Jesus born then?

Oceanic blue light poured from the windows at the end of the hall, magnifying the artificial feeling of twilight, and everything, everything pointed upwards. I must have looked out of place, because a nice old lady took my arm and led me on to a pew. Her face looked like a parched desert, the skin cracked into slabs, and her lips seemed to have imploded in on her mouth, but she led me with silent understanding and I was grateful. We were seated while the bishop spoke and I had a good deal of time to look around me. I noticed a little crystal prism inside a cabinet to the side of the hall and wondered what it was doing there. A memorial, probably.

I was just beginning to get used to the gloom and the strange uniformity of the participants when the congregation stood. Everyone's expressions were caught between the purposeful and the downright miserable, and so I set my face in the same way. But then the choir started and I couldn't help but perk up. Their

36 DW: He really would.

young voices sailed up in such beautiful harmony, echoing round our heads with an intertwining sound that seemed to lift itself out of all worldly ceremony and gloom. I was so transported by this glimpse of purity that I forgot who I was, what I had grieved for and what I meant to achieve. So lost was I in the holy rapture that my Lady of the Slabs had to prod me rather viciously in the ribs before I would open my eyes and acknowledge the bishop. He glared contemptuously, rubbed his thumb in a bowl of the Godly era and then made a wet cross on my forehead, saying, 'Remember that you are dust and to dust you will return.' The mark itched immediately. I was irritated that the bishop had interrupted the music. Frankly, it was too dark in here and everyone was behaving strangely; on top of which my shoulders were starting to cramp up. But I realised, caught in these tight pews with only one, very public, escape route, they had made leaving impossible.[37]

This was a bad idea. These people repelled outsiders. They lived off rites and customs and reverence and deference and acted as one; I was in a cult. A cult with beautiful music, but a cult nonetheless. This was what cults did, wasn't it? They trapped you and then they brainwashed you with their weird repetitive rituals and then you gave them all your money. I saw a collection plate being passed around. I tried to breathe carefully through my nose and mouth and focus on the music but now the deep bass of the organ was filling the air and people were taking wine and bread with one hand cupped under the other and I didn't want to be a part of their mind games, their chanting, their low words. I looked across at my Lady of the Slabs, and she was crying, wiping tears from the wrinkly channels in her cheeks. For all I knew those channels were cut by

---

37 DW: I still don't know exactly why Günter reacted quite so strongly against the service. Most people profess to enjoy the Choral Eucharist.

tears over many debilitating years of worship. I couldn't hear anything over the deafening crescendo of the choir but I could see that, two rows away, a baby was crying. It wasn't natural to want this.

My eyes darted around for exits and there were none. Doors had been closed, a service was in progress. The collection plate edged closer. The bass of the organ enveloped me. I stood wedged in the middle of a line of ten and prayed – to whom, I don't know – that I would not be sacrificed as an unbeliever. Everyone around me turned to prayer books and recited together while I tried to peek at the page number over the shoulder of my Lady of the Slabs. The same words, repeated in endless permutations by endless voices. This was entrapment.

I moved my Lady of the Slabs aside and said, 'Excuse me,' at the other worshippers on the pew until they let me past. People had started turning around to look at the troublemaker. The bishop and his retinue were patrolling the main aisle so I turned back the other way, nudging people aside, and bolted along the side of the building, ripping the shoulders of the jacket, tearing out of a small door and into the cool, fresh air as cries of consternation rose up behind me. I supposed I must have violated some holy sanctum on my way out, but it was too late now: I was off across the open field and free. I looked back and saw the aircraft light flashing, turning the cathedral into a beacon and dragging it into a century it had never wanted to be a part of. That building stood as a monument to the unbounded ambition of humanity. Its stonework, the stained glass and the wrought perfection of the choristers were eyewatering, but it had all been achieved for one purpose. I supposed that I had been drawn to the cathedral because it was a place where a certain kind of art had been perfected, without realising that its art was persuasion. They were a tribe, united by the unbelievers circling them around. I was looking for something else, something high up in the rafters. I supposed that I wouldn't come back, and that I would miss it, in a way. But then, I supposed a lot of things.

I had to get away. Not just from the cathedral – from Salisbury, from my life here. Since my mother had died, I had begun to see what a life might look like if I were to choose it for myself, no longer relying on the world I had inherited. I might live where skyscrapers defied the downward pull of time, standing out against the chaotic jumble of mere buildings. I might find someone to love and to make memories with, so that there might be some brief record of my existence. High up, away from the earth, I had had some glimpse at my purpose, my permanence, and I had to chase it, because it wouldn't be there forever.

11

Calling

I waited for the call from Blades, but it didn't come. I kept getting calls from people who lived miles away, who had heard how well I had treated poor Mrs Dorman, or had seen me in the paper and were pleased to see a good Christian at work in the neighbourhood. Those were the worst calls, the ones that implied that it wouldn't do to have one's windows washed by the ritually unclean.

And so, with nothing to get up for, I slept. We all sleep, but like my father, I do not believe in half-measures. Sometimes I would wake at 10 a.m. to find that my father and I had fallen asleep together in our dinner fifteen hours before. At least he could plead senility – I had no excuse. I would only wake up because my phone was ringing through to my dream. Another unknown number, another suburban semi-detached. To get a cold call was annoying enough, but to interrupt the unburnished beauty of a good dream was unforgivable.

I did try to call Blades. His phone rang, rang and rang. I wanted to leave a voicemail but it just kept ringing. I hung up.

About half an hour later, I got a text from him, just saying:

I'm busy don't ring again I'll call you

I went downstairs, disheartened, to heat dinner.[38]

38 DW: Günter could not cook, according to Arthur. Shortly after Max moved out, Günter found a website that sold out-of-date airline food, which he bought in bulk and microwaved for the two of them.

Hours later, at the kitchen table, Dad prodded me awake and, wiping 'chilli con carne' from his cheek, asked me:

'Why aren't you out there working? You're not just going to give up again like last time are you? Sit around here all day playing on your computer?'

'Calm down, Dad,' I said. 'You're confused because you just woke up.'

'You calm down! You ingrate!'

'Dad—'

'Don't "Dad" me!'

'You've got a kidney bean in your nose.'

'Don't change the subject. I want you out of the house and working tomorrow.'

I looked at the pink rashers of dawn streaked against the sky. I took up our plates.

'Go to bed, Dad. Let's speak when we wake up.'

'I mean it, Günter. I want you out there in the morning—' he looked out the window '—tomorrow morning. And pulling in a wage.' As if to emphasise his point, he put an index finger over one nostril and ejected the kidney bean.

I went upstairs and took a shower, watching the white fat of the chilli mince melt from my eyelashes and blur into the stream by my feet. I vowed never to tell anyone how many times I had slept face down in food. I wondered if it was possible to drown in chilli con carne. I thought about the way my mother had gone.

When I woke up later that morning, I decided I was ready to check my phone. I had many missed calls from many unknown numbers. Three were missed calls from Blades. *First new message. Received today at 9.30 a.m.* 'Günter, hi, it's John here, John Blades. I'm going to send Frank over to get you, I've got a great job coming up in London, I've pinged the details across by email so you'll have it all there but we should meet mano-a–mano. I know you check your mail regularly so I'll send Frank now and you'll have a couple of hours to pack.' I looked out of my window. The heavyset man was standing outside my front door, reading a little book which he held open with one meaty hand. He was about halfway through the book.

I felt a familiar rush of excitement as I grabbed all my gear and stuffed a few bits and bobs into an overnight bag. I scribbled a note to my dad saying that I'd gone to London to work (here, perhaps spitefully, I underlined the word) and didn't know when I'd be back. I walked my bike round the side of the house and saw the heavyset man. He looked up from his book and bobbed his head appreciatively.

'Frank?' I asked. He looked at me, neither confirming nor denying, and put his book in a large jacket pocket. Then he reached out and grabbed my bag with one hand and the bike with the other. I had decided to cycle everywhere from now on. London wasn't that big, really, and I could use the exercise. 'Oh! One last thing.' I ran back inside and grabbed my new grappling hook, still in its box, and brought it out to the car. As I sank into the soft leather, I felt my nervousness sink into obscurity. *There is no need to worry now*, the seat seemed to say as it massaged me with the rhythms of the journey. *You are in safe hands.*

Frank was humming along to an epic, swooping piece of classical music. I stared into the tinted glass. It could almost have been a sulphur-based smoked glass, but something told me it was photochromic, and reacted to how bright the day was. Very tasty. I chuckled to myself and saw Frank glance at me in the rear-view mirror. I decided that I would make him talk to me. Unless he spoke sign, in which case I wanted him to keep hold of the steering wheel. I looked at his eyes in the mirror. They were sunken and the surrounding veins had risen to the surface like dead fish.

'What were you reading, Frank?'

'A book.' He spoke softly from the throat, as if unwilling to make use of his huge lungs in a confined place.

'What's the book about?'

He didn't reply, so I watched the countryside. It was all much of a muchness, fields of green and beige. We continued winding down a quite lovely stretch of the M3, which had been dug through a hillside where rare butterflies were once found. England held a very broad definition of progress.

'My nan used to live in Salisbury,' Frank offered.

'Oh yes?'

'Yeah. She's dead now.'

'Oh,' I said. 'I'm sorry to hear that.'

'Doesn't bother her, does it?' said Frank. 'So you German or something?'

'My mum was German, but I don't really know anything about it. The country, I mean, or the language.'

'So you're not German?'

'Well, I'm half German. Half Welsh, actually.'

'Blades likes Germans. Probably why he hired you. In his book, Germans are the next best thing to a born and bred Englishman.'

'Right.'

We watched more scenery pass. I declined to stop at the service station. I found them odd and disturbing places. I preferred not to think about who had developed them, or where their employees came from.

'So where are we going?' I asked.

'London,' he said.

'Where in London?'

'London Bridge.'

He swerved out of the way of a car in the fast lane, undertaking it at pace. I noticed that Frank had a habit of almost doubling the prevailing speed limit. The car was so silent inside that it was hard to believe the speedometer, although the blur of traffic outside suggested that it was accurate.

That, and the fact we arrived in London almost before we left Salisbury. I was glad, because the conversation wasn't exactly flowing. Just as I spotted the great spike of the Shard up ahead, we veered off the main road and down an alley, stopping in a concealed car park from which I could see the Thames and a warship that seemed to be lodged between two bridges. Frank got out and opened my door wordlessly, as he was wont, and led me out through a small path to the main promenade and then into a neat little bar which was sandwiched between two restaurant chains. Blades sat alone at a table by the window, enjoying an ale, watching the football. I suppose I had thought that, because we both cleaned windows, we must be similar people. But I am no lover of football. I was once shouted out of a pub during an international match because I asked what colour kit we were wearing.

Nevertheless, in the important spirit of camaraderie, I sat down and turned my head to the screen. After a few minutes someone kicked the ball at the wrong colour player and Blades slammed his fist on the table.

'That's right, just hand it to him on a plate you silly black bastard.'

'He is a silly . . . bastard, isn't he?' I said, shaking my head. 'I was thinking that last game.' Was this too far? I hoped the bad player had been on the pitch last game.

'Palace fan, are you?'

'Well . . . I suppose I'll be watching the jubilee. Quite fond of them, really. Though I'd hardly call myself a Loyalist.'

'How can you be when they play like such – THROUGH BALL, YOU – OUT LEFT – I SAID LEFT—' Blades threw his hands up in dismay. 'Well they've given them the game. They don't know their arse from their elbow. Half of them don't even speak the same language. How are they supposed to work as a team if they don't speak any bloody English?' He turned away from the TV set as the waiter approached. 'What can I get you? Scotch? You a Scotch man?'

I thought about Dad drinking whisky at the kitchen table and gradually shrivelling like a prune.

'Just a water please.'

'Sparkling,' said Blades.

'I don't really drink sparkling water,' I said.

'Really? It's a great palate cleanser. I always have a glass after sex. Keeps you fresh,' Blades said, checking a BlackBerry.

I considered this hypothetically, not knowing what anything was like after sex. I wondered if the world seemed different. The waiter brought a bottle. It hissed open and he poured about a quarter of a glass' worth, as if demonstrating a new kind of vessel to the uninitiated. I poured the rest of the water into the glass, as if I too was trying out this new vessel.

'I'm going to cut to the chase, Günter. I want you to work for me.'

'Okay.'

'I saw you slip up back at the Spinnaker Tower, but you kept a level head, and that's the important thing. Don't let it scare you off the idea of skyscrapers.'

'I'd love to work on skyscrapers.'

'The money's good.'

'I said I'd be happy to.'

'I wasn't listening. So what IRATA level do you have?'

'I'm sorry?'

'You know, rope access qualification. Level 3?'

'Oh, I don't have one.'

'What?' He bared his canines in surprise. 'Then why in God's name did you dangle off the Spinnaker Tower?'

I faltered.

'I don't know. I suppose I wanted to see it clean. I like being out there, up high, the idea of . . . uh. Purity. I suppose.'

He smiled, his canines protruding further, and held my gaze.

'Purity?'

'Well. Yes.'

He made an amused noise at the back of his throat and seemed to relax.

'Me too. So: we'd better get you enrolled on a course. You'll start Monday. We have three weeks left and then, I think, things will get interesting.'

His eyes drifted back to the game. Frank came tactfully to my side. No one else, including Blades, seemed to have noticed Frank's arrival. He was a subtle creature, for one so heavyset.

'Where now?' he asked me as we got in the car.

'I don't know. Can you recommend somewhere to stay?'

'Do I look like a phone?'

I was struck by that British paralysis that occurs just after being the victim of rudeness. Presently, I decided to get out of the car.

'I'm sure this area will do nicely,' I said, opening the door. 'I'll pick up the rest of my things later.'

'All right, all right,' he replied. 'Look, the hairy Aussie is staying down here on the left. Hostel California. Just keep your head screwed on. They'll see you coming.'

A few minutes later, I found myself staring at a peeling door tagged with artless graffiti. The buildings next to it were all single-storey, but this one teetered at three floors. Next to the front door stood two skips full of fermenting rubbish. I supposed it would probably be nicer once you got inside.

I opted for the cheap twelve-bed dorm, since the same musty smell permeated the whole building, and took my belongings up the rotting wooden stairs. At the top, the landing was painted a sort of livid puce, and one door stood ajar, apparently no longer able to shut itself in the event of a fire. I pushed it open and made a beeline for a free bed. It was unmade, but then, all the beds were unmade.

I looked around the bare room and saw a pile of duvets bundled up on one of the mattresses. I went over to pick one up and realised that it was rising and falling with the breathing of whoever was sleeping underneath it all. There was a shuffling, and Pete the Aussie Greek slid out from the bottom of the pile.

'Give us a minute, mate? I'm cracking one out.'

'Oh. Gosh, yes, of course.'

I went and sat on my bed and started to unpack my things. A toothbrush, a glasses case, a few changes of clothes, my gear. I didn't want to wait for Pete on my bed, so I decided to head back out. It was raining heavily now, but I had my cagoule on so I didn't really mind. I went and bought a copy of *Loot* to look at the accommodation on offer. Anything would be better than the hostel. Much as I admired the internet, one could find a better quality of advertisement in a proper physical paper. It took a great deal more effort and expense to take an ad out, whereas on the internet you could just throw it up for free in two minutes.

I circled the only likely-looking place - a bachelor in a two-bed Hackney flat. The oddity of the advert caught my eye, requesting that applicants appear in person on a Friday. The man was looking for a live-in cleaner, rent free, male only. I would have to brace myself in case it was a den of iniquity. The problem was, I started the course on Monday. Two days did not seem like a very long time to find somewhere to stay, let alone live. I felt like a hermit crab between shells, and if the bailiffs came for Dad it would feel very much like they were stomping my safety shell underfoot.

As I walked back to the hostel, my hand came upon the business card in my pocket. Lieve had told me she lived in London. *Psychic and Medium.* I decided that I would try to convince her, against her better judgment, to go on a date with me. It was easy, I told myself. I dialled the number before I could think too hard about what I was doing.

'Lieve Toureaux.'

'Hello! It's Günter. I met you in Portsmouth. The window cleaner?'

'Hi, Günter.'

'I'm in London.'

'Okay.'

The line fuzzed.

'I was just wondering if you were free, by any chance?' I asked, wincing slightly.

'When?'

'Oh yes, of course, sorry . . . Tonight?'

'No.'

'Oh. Well that's . . . Another time, perhaps.'

'Meet me on Saturday at 8 p.m. My address is on the back of the card you're probably holding. Bring wine.'

'Brill. See you then.'

I put the phone down in dismay. When had I last used the word *brill*? No one ever used that word. *Brill*?

In the dorm, Pete was sitting up against his pillow texting, and we had been joined by one of the other occupants, a man with a threadbare suit and mild pneumonia who, it became obvious, was a permanent fixture. He had an office job near London Bridge but couldn't afford a rental deposit. A Swiss backpacking couple joined us soon after that, apparently upset to have to be around the three of us, and then a young, silent man who spent his whole time doing press-ups. We made a motley company, to say the least, so I was glad when Pete suggested that we go out for a drink. On the way over there, he explained that there was an Irish-themed pub he liked visiting because it was where all the tourist girls drank.

'I just tell 'em I'm Irish and halfa them don't know any better. Bit of local chahm.'

Pete came to life at the prospect of meeting ladies. His method was to walk up to them and say, 'Hi, I'm Pete.' It sounds simple now, but he did it with such confidence, as if they must have been dying to ask his name, and he was only doing them a common courtesy by introducing himself. Before I knew what was happening, we had installed ourselves with two backpackers called Brigitte and Kali, and Pete was buying us drinks. I asked Pete for a fruit cocktail with no alcohol, as it was a bit early for me, and the barman shouted 'Virgin!' in confirmation just as I went to sit down next to Kali. 'One of these a virgin?' he shouted again.

'Yes!' I hissed.

Kali smiled at me.

I couldn't talk to women.

I could when they were being people. But when they were being women, wearing sexy clothes and looking at me in the eye, I tended to seize up. Kali had already stopped paying me attention and had joined the conversation with the other two. I could practise speaking to women another time. When the opportunity arose. When I was settled. But ideally before my date on Saturday.

After a little while, Brigitte and Kali decided to go to the toilet together – a phenomenon which I am yet to fully understand – and it was just me and Pete.

'What happened to divide and rule, you dumb fuck?' asked Pete.

'Sorry.'

'You're killing me out here.'

I shrugged. 'Sorry.'

We sat without speaking for a little while, Pete bobbing his head to the disco song in the background, I trying to clear a clog in my straw, presumably caused by some chunk of fruit. I gave up after a little while and put down my glass.

'So are you excited about working with Blades?' I asked.

Pete snorted derisively. 'Wouldn't trust that prick as far as I could shit him.'

'Oh.'

He leant forward. 'Now, back in Oz, a guy might call me a wog, and I know he doesn't mean any harm. But that fuck'n . . . Nazi.' He shook his head. 'He's got a screw loose or summ'n. Right now I need the money, and when we're done I'm goin' home.'

He couldn't be that bad, I thought.

Once Pete had gone to stay with both Brigitte and Kali, and I was lying in my mattress, which felt a little like a hammock made of springs, I thought about Blades. There was something disconcerting about him. But then, being disconcerting didn't make you bad. I would take him as I found him. It was probably just a misunderstanding.

Max texted me: *you dead yet? where you staying?*

I replied: *five star, can you believe it! I have my own jacuzzi!*

I hoped that rats liked eating cockroaches.

Before I knew I'd fallen asleep it was the middle of the night and the businessman was coughing in the bunk above. I was still wearing my clothes and glasses. I undressed clumsily and put my glasses on the floor by my bed. I don't remember what I dreamed, but I awoke with a sense of melancholy. There was something beautiful buried deep in my imagination that I had lost when I opened my eyes. I wondered whether Dad would be asleep by now, or whether he'd be drinking at the kitchen table, trying to make himself as tired as possible so he could sleep through the next day. Though I tried to pretend it was a symptom of laziness, I knew he slept out of the exhaustion of grief, and also to escape himself, because in his eyes, life had amounted to less than a good dream.

12

Wolf and Cork

It was one of those cold, damp mornings that follows heavy rain, and I pulled my windproof cagoule about me as I exited London Fields station and started in the direction of the flat. People were pushing prams; groups of hooded men hunched in doorways. A lot of people seemed to be cycling here, perhaps because the tube didn't service the area. Despite the name of the rail station, it seemed completely different to the London I knew. People were dressed as if for an Edwardian carnival, with bright lipstick, furs, strongmen moustaches and horizontally striped vests abounding. I tried to check my map, but I had no data, so my blue dot had turned grey and was still hovering around the station. I flagged down a passer-by whose woolly hat, sleeves and trousers were all rolled up. His T-shirt sported a printed simulacrum of a double-breasted cardigan, and he was wearing a four-finger ring or knuckle-duster on his right hand which said TAWT.

'What's up, feller?' he asked, sniffing sharply.

'I'm just trying to find this block of flats.' I showed him the red drawing pin on my phone map.

'Oh, easy squeezy, feller.' He pointed behind him. 'You wanna go down Mare Street and pop a right on Paragon.'

'That's very helpful, thank you.'

'No worries, feller. Love that working-class hero thing you've got going on by the way. Très prole.'

He ran off for a few paces before splaying his legs and lifting his toes, rolling away on his wheeled trainers.

I was beginning to worry that I might not fit in here as I ascended the stairs. But the flat was seven floors up, which I took as a good omen. When I got to the plain white door, there was no letterbox, no knocker and no doorbell. There was only an old hole for a deadlock and a thin metal rod propped up against a plain brown doormat. Several months' worth of unopened letters sat outside in a scattered pile. I knocked on the door, which gave a muffled thud, but to no avail. I cast around. I needed to find a new home and I was buggered if I was going to turn away now.

After about half an hour of knocking and looking for alternative entrances, a neighbour came out of her house with a big hemp bag full of laundry. When she saw me, she gave a nod of recognition and came over. She picked up the white rod, threaded it through the deadlock, and stuck her tongue out as she jiggled the rod around. I heard an old-fashioned doorbell sound from within. She replaced the rod and chuckled.

'You'll have to indulge him. He's a bit—' she tapped herself on the temple. 'Nice though,' she said, as if I might take offence. Before anyone could answer the doorbell, she scuttled off with her laundry bag.

The door swung violently open, and I was confronted by a haggard and hairy face, with eyes protruding so far that I thought they might escape their host. He stared at me for a second. Then he receded into the flat, past a second front door, which had a doorbell with scratch marks around it. The whole of this ante-chamber was upholstered with cork board, including the doors. I felt like I might be entering a wine bottle.

Past the second door, I entered into a relatively normal kitchen cum living room. There were no windows, but there was a bright lamp in the corner which shone light on an ivy plant that was growing up one side of the fridge. On the fridge were hundreds of tourist magnets, decrying *CYPRUS: the birthplace of Aphrodite* or *mi otra isla es IBIZA*. I couldn't imagine the man who had opened the door ever going anywhere that he might tan, and strongly suspected that the magnets had originated with the previous owner of the fridge, but they did add a nice homely touch. Some of the furniture was paint-stained, there were empty bottles everywhere and the regular routes of the room's occupant were mapped out in geometries of dust. On one side of the room was a vast bookshelf filled with hardbound volumes in various languages. A flotilla of Post-it notes bobbed between pages, under the breeze of a wall-mounted fan.

'To keep the books from dust,' said the haggard man. His voice was gravelly, with a hint of an accent that I couldn't place. 'You are here about the room?'

'Yes, that's right. Günter. Pleased to meet you.'

He bared his yellow teeth. It was a smile which I felt was designed to affront, and yet I found myself reassured. There was an honesty there which was missing in the more charming smile of, say, Blades. It was a smile that said, 'I am forcing you to take me as I am.' And I was inexplicably touched that he had invited me in before he knew who I was.

'This is my contact room. As you can see, there are all of the things which you would expect in a house: a fridge, a sofa, a toilet.' There was indeed a urinal hanging casually from the wall, which had been graffitied with the name R Mutt 1917. 'My retirement fund,' he said mercurially.

He led me through to a second room, which was also lined floor to ceiling with cork board. There was no light but for a small gas lamp. Pillows were plumped up in the bed, which was moulded into the negative of a sitting man, and leaves of paper were strewn about the room. The air was thick and cloying. I suspected that the room had not been cleaned for a long time.

'This is where I write for six days a week. Fridays are my days of contact. I come out for other things, such as placing orders for books or washing myself.' There were a number of fish skeletons on plates around the room, which must have been contributing to the unusual pungency. 'You will not come in here, except perhaps on Fridays.'

We went back to the first room.

'What are you writing?' I asked.

'For many years I have been writing a guide to living. An essential guide. Nothing extraneous. But it is difficult,' he said sadly. 'Life obscures my effort.' He stroked the cork board on the wall fondly, as one might a beloved pet. 'I must have silence for my writing. I must not have any sign of our frivolous modernity in my room – it would be too distracting. I must not hear planes or traffic. Above all, there must be darkness. Darkness is the friend of thought. We are no more than animals, you see. We must be in darkness to awake our animal instincts for danger and preservation, to awaken our desire to see and not be seen.'

'I see.'

'Do you?' he asked, searching my watering eyes. At such proximity, his halitosis was like a punch in the nose.

'You don't like being distracted,' I summarised.

'It is very pleasant to be distracted, but one cannot capture life while living it. It is like trying to understand the oceans while you are drowning.'

I'd have thought drowning would be the most efficient way to become better acquainted with the sea, but I let it go. He moved off to another room and I followed.

In the third room, there was a large window. There were no furnishings except for a plain white futon. The window was open and the sun glided in like a paper aeroplane to rest on the plain wooden floor. The lamp shade was a paper globe, similar to traditional Japanese lights.

'I have fitted this room in the manner of a normal capitalist IKEA customer,' he said proudly. 'Do you like it?'

'It's very nice.'

'Good. Then you must move in today. Otherwise next Friday.' He handed me two keys. 'This one is for the front door, and this is for the front door.' He smiled at me again.

'I didn't catch your name,' I said.

'I didn't give it,' he said. 'Every person calls me the Steppenwolf. It is a little joke we have. You do not know to what I refer?'

'Is it because you look a bit like a wolf?'

'Do you not read the great German novelists? Or our philosophers? Schopenhauer, perhaps? Kant?'

'No, I don't really read many books, I'm afraid.'

'You are German, though? Verstehen sie deutsch?'

'Um,' I said.

He laughed.

'Go and get your things. If you must contact me, I have a telephone, although I have disabled the bell, so I must guess if it is ringing.'

He ushered me out the door, and I found myself back out on the street without his number, his real name, or any details of the tenancy. I knew I didn't want to spend another night in the hostel, so I supposed I would just have to check out and hope for the best.

Not wanting to get straight back on the train, I decided to have a quick coffee in the Ride-Thru Pop-Up Cycle Café near the station. Inside, there was a man sitting behind the counter, and a couple of customers sitting around in Lycra. The man behind the counter wore a very low-cut vest, and across his bare chest I could see a tattoo of two swallows fighting over an anchor. Though at first he appeared to be talking to himself, I could see an earphone cord trailing down under his long, thick beard.

'And I was like, Well, I'm going to Alibi, and he was like Agh, FOMO, and I was like, YOLO, mofo. And he was all like

FML bro. Anyway, gotta go, I have a customer.' He pressed his headset button. 'How can I help you princess?'

'Just a coffee please.'

'To park or to ride away?'

'Take away, please.'

He sized me up.

'We only do flat whites, is that okay?'

'I'm sure it's fine.'

'We just free-pour the stretched milk. You can't customise it at all.'

I smiled at him. Eventually, he smoothed down his moustache, before printing out a receipt which included a service charge, and sliding it to me on a porcelain plate not unlike our nice set at home.

Another customer rode in, carefully dismounting his penny farthing and parking it in a spare bay.

'Cycling is very popular here,' I said as he made the coffee.

'It's the only way to travel,' he replied. 'Go fast, get fit, no carbon footprint.'

'Apart from the carbon you eat.'

'It's basically about saving the planet. By the time our kids grow up, they'll be like, what's a bike yo? They'll be travelling by pedalo. You ride?'

'I, um. I do occasionally. When I can find the time. You know. When it's nice weather.'

'I'm sorry, but that's not good enough. You have to minimise your impact.'

'But you sell your coffee in disposable cups,' I said.

'The customer experience is very important to us,' he said coldly, handing me my coffee.

Back at the hostel, I gathered my clothes and gear. The Steppenwolf's flat remained detached in my mind from what I thought of as 'proper' London, and I wondered how I might connect the two – the problem with the tube and the train was that they bypassed the normal human routes through the city, passing over, under and behind the streets and buildings. It felt like I just went in one station and popped out somewhere else. After a bit of googling, I discovered that there was a bus, which started in London Bridge and cut through the eastern part of the city, winding all the way up to London Fields, which might help me get my bearings, so I hoisted my things on my back and found my stop under the shadow of the Shard.

When the bus came, I sat at the front of the top deck and (in the privacy of my own head) pretended that I was the driver. We soon crossed the river, and I could see the great glass buildings of the City rising up ahead like an icy forest, each fighting its way ever upward to the light at the top of the canopy. The gherkin loomed up on our right – though I can tell you, a gherkin wasn't the first thing that came to mind. The top of its bulging erection even had a sort of glans.

As we passed into Shoreditch, the glass offices gave way to brown stone buildings, railway bridges and big clusters of council blocks. We passed over a parochial little bridge where I could see canal boats and the bright little sprays of balcony gardens, and I saw that all the pedestrians had knapsacks, none of them socks. Yes, this was the place. I got off, retraced my steps to the flat, and was soon threading the white rod through the keyhole again.

The Steppenwolf answered the door apparently surprised that I had returned.

'Could I see a copy of the contract?' I asked, as I put my gear down.

He smiled yellow, his eyes almost vaulting the thicket of his beard.

'We are not lawyers, Günter. Give me a deposit of £500. You

will get it back, I think. You need not pay me anything further, but I am not very . . .'

'Clean?' I suggested.

'Organised. If you simply do these things like washing dishes, and on Fridays take my fish from my room . . .'

'You do love your fish, I've noticed.'

'I hate fish. I eat them only for the important oils. The oil is very important to life,' he said. 'I explain in my book.'

'How long until you finish it?' I asked.

'I am beginning to believe that it will be finished on the day I die,' he said. 'The book started off very large, about one and a half million words, and for the last fifteen years I have been stripping away the unnecessary. It must be an essential guide to life. Everything necessary, but nothing extraneous.'

'Has anyone read it?'

'No. On my days of contact, I may read brief excerpts to you to check the validity of my suppositions about the outside world. Tell me, do people still watch television?'

'They do.'

'Good, good.' He stared at an empty wine bottle with unfocussed eyes. I backed away slowly, lest I scare away the idea that he was coaxing out of the dark tangle of his mind.

So, no rent but some cleaning. It sounded like a perfectly good plan to me. I took my wallet and phone and went to my nearest bank branch, where I deposited my £500 cheque, and then I went to buy a bigger T-shirt. I was conscious that my belly was beginning to protrude from almost every top that I wore, and that I should probably stop eating waffles for breakfast.

Since I was out already, I decided to go to Oxford Street to look for furnishings. My room was very bare, and if I was to live there I wanted it to feel like home. I made for the biggest department store I could find, strolling past electronics and kitchenware, sofas, beds, fireplaces and garden furniture. I mentally calculated the money in my bank account. I had earned five hundred pounds, but I'd spent a little on living costs, and the deposit was five hundred pounds, so I must have a little less than nothing.

I continued to wander idly through the various sections of the store. Max would have been in heaven. He lived for these rows of tat; his favourite tactic was to buy a budget-range item only to ditch it for a mid-range item and then later, if the object was to become an obsession, a premium-range item: overpriced and barely perceptibly better than the one he owned. If these objects really did bring meaning to his life, he wouldn't keep replacing them so often. When I did finally have the money to spend on these things, I would simply buy one of each thing and make it last. If I wanted a telephone, I would save up for the sturdiest, most timeless telephone that money could buy. I would sit on the floor until I could buy my life's armchair; the armchair that I would be sitting in when, pale and liver-spotted, my years out-stripping my energy, I finally joined the rest of infinity. I'd rather have one perfect chesterfield than a whole room full of badly made MDF. For now, I couldn't afford anything, so I bought nothing.

When I got back, the Steppenwolf was drinking red wine and kept playing and replaying the same thirteen seconds of a Gregorian chant. He was playing it on a turntable, and instead of moving the needle back to the start of the section, he would push the record anti-clockwise, playing the chant backwards. The effect was disturbing. It reminded me of Satanism,[39] but I'm not sure what use Satan would have found for that particular exercise.

---

39 DW: Satanism is the only truly contrarian belief system. Either Satan doesn't exist, or he does and he is out to destroy you and everyone you love. There's no use in trying to get on the good side of the embodiment of evil.

I picked up a call from Dad.

'So. You lef' me.'

'I didn't want to wake you. I'm going to be in London for a little while, but if you need—'

'You di'n'even say g'bye.'

'Dad, you're drunk.'

'No I'mno'.'

'In fact, you're not just everyday-drunk, you're smashed.'

'Wha'makesyu think tha'?'

'For a start, you can't even pronounce words like "you".'

'WHERE'S MY MONEY‽'[40] he yelled. I removed the phone to a short distance from my ear.

'I needed the money as a deposit. But now that—'

'Y'ra fucking liar! LIAR!' he shouted.

I'd never been called a liar by my father before. I was so hurt I couldn't begin to formulate a reply. I looked at the screen and hung up with a firm press of my thumb. Frustratingly, there is no efficient way to slam a mobile.

A quick google revealed that Lieve lived in Baron's Court, which was on the District Line (the Green One). Luckily I had left an hour's leeway because, as I learned the hard way, there is more than one Green One – which, to my mind, slightly defeats the point of colour-coding them. I stood outside her house, just three minutes early, trying to think of any last-minute preparations before I rang the bell. I had eaten a mint. I had combed my hair. I felt like a schoolboy in my white shirt and black trousers. My shirt was still creased in squares where it had been folded in its packet. I tried to smooth it down. I looked at the label of the bottle I'd brought – it looked like decent plonk to me. My

40 DW: The interrobang (‽) is a tremendous typographical invention, used where a question is too loud or emphatic to expect that the speaker will listen to the answer.

heart picked up pace. I rang the bell. I was excited. Or scared. Yes, scared.

Lieve let me in quickly, her fingers brushing my neck as she took my coat. She went to open the wine at the kitchen bar. I looked around. The walls and ceiling were decked with rugs and there were several mirrors decorated with sequins and semi-precious stones. Thick smoke trailed from an incense stick which was burning in the corner. The table, which was about knee height, rose up out of a pile of cushions, which had been herded into one half of the room in lieu of furniture. She came back with two massive glasses, each of which looked like it could hold a good litre of wine, and I sat cross-legged on one of the sturdier cushions, which may in fact have been a pouffe. She looked into my eyes. Her lips were very dark.

'So what brought you to London, Günter?'

'Don't you already know?'

'Why would I know?'

'I thought you could see into the immediate future.'

'Yes, but I'm asking about the immediate past.'

'Oh I see.' I didn't. 'I've moved here for a new job.'

'Staying on friends' floors?'

'As a matter of fact I've just found a sort of . . . bachelor pad. There's only two of us, it's going to be quite . . .' I couldn't think of a good adjective for what I thought it was going to be like to live with the Steppenwolf.

'Well you're always welcome to stay here. I have a spare room.' It did seem like a big house for one person.

She fixed a piercing look on me. 'My husband left me two years ago. So, tell me about your eyes. Do you have to wear the glasses all the time?'

'Yes. I mean, I thought about wearing contact lenses but the idea makes me a little squeamish.'

'How bad are they?'

'I suppose I'm about a minus 3.'

'That's not unmanageable. Any male-pattern baldness in your family?'

'Um – not that I can think of.'

'Any hereditary illnesses? Diabetes? Any early deaths?'

'Well there was my mother. But she died when – well . . .' I tapered off.

'I'm sorry.' She didn't look sorry. In fact she looked slightly pleased with herself. This wasn't turning out at all as I had expected. Was this really what people talked about on dates?

She took up our glasses to refill them in the kitchen and I tried to guess how old she was. It was hard to tell. She had a very inexpressive face. It was hard to focus on the details. All I got was a strong impression of stern, raw sexuality.

I let out an involuntary moan of pleasure when I took my first bite of the starter. The flavours were familiar, like the best home cooking, but combined in such a way as to feel both comforting and new. The salad was like any Mediterranean salad, dressed in olive oil and vinegar, but she had added thorny caper leaves which prickled in the mouth before yielding to my frenzied mastication. The main course, lamb, had a sweet dressing which I hadn't expected, sticky with the sort of plummy richness you'd expect with duck. The lamb itself had been slow-cooked and practically dissolved in my mouth, the flavour spreading like a warm bath all the way to the extremities of my tongue.

The presence of a starter had led me to believe that this was to be a three-course dinner, but before I could be offered any pudding, Lieve went and got her purse. She looked like she might be about to offer me money, and I began to worry that she might have invited me over to clean her windows. She took out a deck of cards.

'Ooh, good idea! I was starting to worry that the conversation might dry up after dinner. Do you know how to play Steeplechase?'

Lieve laughed as if I had said something funny and took out the deck. It was printed with unrecognisable symbols and suits. She started sorting the picture cards from the numbers, and then she shuffled the picture cards and held them out to me.

'Tarot de Marseille,' she said. 'What everyone wants to know more than anything is what the future holds. So hold it.'

I looked into her face to see if she was serious. I thought it was probably very stupid, but I didn't want to offend her.

I turned over the first card. *Le Bateleur*. It looked like the joker with a big table of games in front of him. He looked like a bit of an idiot.

'That's you,' she said.

'Are you sure?'

'It must be. Turn over another.'

Bloody insult, that's what it was. I grabbed the pack from her hands and chose one from the middle, just in case the future was thinking about dealing me a mixed hand. *La Maison Dieu*. It looked like a big tower being ripped open by a sunbeam with two men falling to the earth.

I looked up at Lieve. She said nothing, but searched my eyes. I took two more from the middle. *Le Soleil* and *Lemonde*. I wished I had paid more attention to French at school. Lemonade, perhaps? The pictures didn't give much of a clue, but there were two people with their arms round each other in the one with the Sun, so that was something.

'Let me do it,' she said. She pushed all the cards out the way except *Le Bateleur* and turned the next cards over from the top of the deck, which she put back in the centre of the table. *L'Amoureux*. Cupid shooting a man point blank. No prizes there. Next *L'Imperatrice*. It showed a woman on a throne, holding a shield. I had no idea what that might mean.

'These are the cards of persuasion, love, and fertility,' she said.

'Fertility?'

'I mean lovemaking.'

She stared at me in a manner I can only describe as forthright. To relieve my embarrassment, I turned over the next two cards to see what they were. *Le Pendu* was a man who was hanging upside down by his foot, and the next one, though there wasn't a name on it, showed a grim skeletal figure doing some reaping.

'You can't just choose cards at random,' she snapped, picking up the cards and shuffling them all back together.

'Now look what you've made me do,' she said. Then she tried to shuffle the deck quickly, somehow causing cards to fly in all directions. I went to pick them up but she stopped me.

'It isn't important. They have told their tale. You are the magician,' she said, regaining her composure. I looked at her black lipstick. I heard the candle flicker. She advanced towards me holding out her hand and I fell backwards over my pouffe, landing on the soft cushions behind me. She unbuttoned her shirt and straddled me.

'Shh,' she said. I had the urge to speak. I didn't know whether I wanted to speak because she'd hushed me or whether it was the other way round. My head was sluggish. I'd drunk a lot of wine. And it was so dark in here. She pressed her great bosom against my face and my vision was eclipsed. All I felt was tugging and a great release of pressure as the button of my black trousers flew off. Was this romance? It seemed gentler in films. But even in the face of the evidence, it was hard to believe that I would finally be rid of that cruel nun Virginity.

She sat on me, knees pressed against my lowest ribs, her dark fine hair hanging down over my shoulders. I was pinioned by the soft, smooth flesh of her thighs, bare under her skirt. I could just reach out and touch one. As we kissed, I raised my right hand and placed it gently on the outside of her leg, just above the knee. She didn't stop me! I moved it up a little, towards her hip. If anything, she seemed to actively enjoy it. This was a surprise. Just as I began to contemplate the furtive, almost unbearable possibility of moving my hand over the top of her leg, and towards her inner thigh, she raised herself on her knees, tore my trousers and pants down, and began to touch me on . . . well, to touch me. I didn't know what to think. I was still wearing my socks. Not that I wasn't enjoying myself, but this was a first date, after all.

As she took my hand and guided it up her skirt, I felt my interior monologue begin to slow and fade, and even, for whole seconds at a time, to disappear.[41]

. . .

. . .

'Stop,' I whispered.

'What's wrong?' she asked.

'No, nothing – it's just that I'm sort of . . . I don't want to jump the gun. Do you see? I don't want a false start, or I'll be . . . disqualified. For the, ah, tournament.'

'Shhh.'

She kissed me and positioned herself above me before, finally, inevitably, we came together. I don't mean to say that we both had an orgasm, as I'm quite sure only one of us crossed the finishing line. But we became together; we were intimate, together.

Somewhere, in a part of my mind removed from our grasping, heaving bodies, I wondered whether there was a word for a pleasure that was forced upon me. I wouldn't have done it if I hadn't been forced, but I was glad that I was doing it. There should be a word for this, I thought, for the moment a reluctant parachutist is thrown out into the glorious skies by his commanding officer.

41 DW: The Dalai Lama says that we are only one and indivisible with the universe at the moment of orgasm, and the moment of death. I know he's on the wrong team, but he's a lovely chap.

Perhaps there was a word for it in some other language. It was probably a German word, like *Schadenfreude*. Perhaps I could ask the Steppenwolf.

Her face had grown softer now. It was over. She stroked my cheek.

'I'm going to get you dessert.'

She strode off to the kitchen, and came back through with a glass of tap water and a whole chocolate tart. We ate from the same plate. I'd never felt this sort of intimacy before. She had saved me from a life alone. It was as if I had gone back to visit the house that I grew up in, and discovered a whole new room that I had never been in before. It wasn't just unlikely, it was a travesty. No wonder people went so far out of their way for sex, got themselves in tangles with their secretaries and launched fleets of ships.

Lieve looked down at me on the cushions.

'You look smug,' she said.

'Do I? I suppose I am, a bit.'

'We can do it again if you like.'

'I think it's stopped working.'

'Wash it with cold water. It'll help.'

Was there anything she didn't know? But her knowledge was hidden by the smoke of the incense, the low lights, the locked secrets of Tarot. Lieve didn't want to brush the dirt off of her life, so much as bury it in the garden for safekeeping. But she stroked my hair and we muttered things that didn't make sense to each other, and we laughed. I couldn't remember the last time I had laughed since I'd outgrown the bath. I told her so. She laughed. And then, under the fug of the incense, a heavy sleep seeped in.

I woke naked and clammy. My throat burned like I had drunk a litre of GOMORRAH. The glass next to us was empty. I looked over at Lieve, who was peacefully asleep next to me. She had opened my eyes to the surreal pleasures of rubbing and licking. I was reminded of lonelier times, when I had been so happily affected by the casual intimacy of having my hair washed at the barber's. The women had run their hands through my hair, massaged the shampoo into my head with their fingertips. But this was twenty times as pleasurable, a hundred times as intimate.

I detached my tongue from the roof of my mouth and stood up. My bladder was the priority here.

There were five doors leading off the landing. I had no idea which might be the loo. I opened the first and found lots of towels, socks, a selection of the large, dark lace undergarments to which I had been so recently introduced, and a dream-catcher. I closed the airing cupboard and moved onto the next. One of them had to be the bathroom.

I opened another door to what looked like a study room. There was a desk with a big black leather office chair. A big whiteboard was leaning against a wall next to several cardboard boxes marked JOHN, which had been taped up. The white-board had been wiped clean, but traces of a complicated web remained. I could read the words 'Fasci', 'Falange', 'Cagoule'. This certainly wasn't the toilet.

The next door opened into a large, dark room. I switched on the light. The blue pastel walls and wall-hanging mirror spoke bathroom, but the mobile and empty cot did not. Nor did the pile of shop-tagged toys in a cardboard box in the corner of the room. I listened for any sounds of movement downstairs, but there was nothing. I closed that door gently, and found the bathroom.

I pondered that last room as I relieved myself. I gently hummed the tune to 'There's a Hole in My Bucket'. I don't know much about the subconscious, but I secretly suspect it to be a rather savage and ironic part of the brain.[42]

I went back downstairs and drank straight from the tap. This had to be the longest that I'd been naked (outside the shower) in my entire adult life. The cool water ran down the side of my cheek and I hung free. Then I walked back through to the lounge, where Lieve stirred. I felt like a man. A man standing in front of a woman. Fully naked. With my willy out. No one could cast aspersions on my sexuality. Not now.

I lay down beside her, put her arm over my torso like a seat-belt, and fell asleep. I woke again in what seemed like no time at all. The sunlight was cut into neat slices by the venetian blinds in the kitchen and stacked up like a plate of waffles on the opposite wall. Lieve stirred and kissed the side of my throat. I felt her lips there for some time afterwards, even as she moved her hand across my body.

We spent the best part of Sunday lying there, occasionally taking breaks to eat bacon or make cups of tea. She drank a rancid concoction involving stinging nettles, which she seemed certain was good for the health, though I didn't see how it could be. People often mistake uncommon foods for good foods, just as people mistake quiet people for nice people. But I drank my normal tea and she drank her nettle tea, and just as the sunlight had brought the day, so it left with its train of warmth, and we showered and dressed once more, I in my white shirt and black trousers, which seemed unnecessarily formal now, and she in her silk dressing gown, which couldn't have provided much insulation.

We parted with a kiss, and I weaved back through London's

---

42 DW: On a personal note, I'm not sure how seriously one should take Freud. He was a cocaine addict who wrote papers with titles like 'Character and Anal Erotism' or 'Dreams and Telepathy', and only became a doctor so he could get married. He was, however, correct that 'time spent with cats is never wasted'.

streets. I saw a great billboard which boasted a company that delivered 'milk and more'. Let them deliver their milk, I thought. I'd jumped that ship. I walked past several churches: some bustling with dark-skinned ladies wearing their colourful Sunday best; some Orthodox, their worshippers dressed only in black; some Anglican, and empty. I walked past a Scientology shop offering free 'stress' tests to pick at the spiritual realm's low-hanging fruit. I wondered who, if anyone, spent their Sundays not engaged in some kind of mob activity. Even the atheists were communing in cafés, sharing stories of the night before with their ritual roasts and fry-ups, or watching football in vast crowds.

When I got back to the flat, the neighbour was just returning with her hemp bag full of shopping.

'Hello!' I said.

'Oh, hello again. Did you manage to get in in the end?' she asked.

'I did. I'm living in the spare room now, in fact.'

'I didn't know he had one.'

'I think he keeps his cards quite close to his chest.'

She smiled at me and then there was a pause.

'Well,' she said, hefting the hemp bag, 'I'd better get this in.'

I unlocked my front doors and went in. The flat stared blankly back at me. There seemed so little point in sitting on my own on the sofa, or reading a magazine, when I could be with Lieve, filling in her uncharted past, finding out where on earth she was in all that time I was somewhere else. Why was I somewhere else now that we had finally met? It seemed pointless to be eating toast on my own, like telling a joke to an empty room.

Mum would never get to meet Lieve. I'd never find out what she thought of her. I found it hard to imagine what they would even have said to each other. They were so different. Mum would have fussed around in her bag for something or other so that she didn't have to make eye contact; I imagined Lieve watching her steadily, reaching over to take my hand. *Mum*, I'd say. *I'm so glad – this is – I'd like you to meet – she's my* . . . Well. Mum would probably have pretended to like her no matter what. *I'm happy that you're happy*, she might have said. *You are happy, aren't you?*

I unlocked my phone and stared at the screen. No missed calls. I flicked through my contacts, found Mum, and deleted the number.

13

Chapter 133

When I opened the second front door, I saw a pair of bare feet sticking out of the doorway to the Steppenwolf's bedroom. They weren't moving. I approached slowly, my hand automatically feeling for my most dangerous impromptu weapon, which was my keys. I put the heaviest key between my index and middle finger, for all the good it might do. I crept up on the doorway, in case the killer was still in the apartment. Many months of post-redundancy internet surfing had equipped me with my fair share of amateur detective knowledge,[43] and the Dorman affair had confirmed my instinct for suspicious activity. I crept up as quietly as my haunches could manage, and then spun into the doorway to confront the Steppenwolf, supine, naked, holding a paintbrush, the remnants of a fish hanging from his mouth, very much alive.

'You should be careful with fish bones,' I said.

He squealed, leapt up and slammed the door in my face. On the outside of the door, in fresh paint, there was a notice saying I AM ALWAYS PLEASED TO BE OF SERVICE UNLESS IT IS NOT FRIDAY. And by my feet was a sheet of paper, which was presumably meant to have been trapped inside the room. I picked it up and read it.

43 DW: Allan Pinkerton was a particular favourite: the detective who codified the first surveillance and undercover strategies, founded the US Secret Service and supposedly died of gangrene of the tongue.

Chapter 133: From womb to tomb

We are completely secure in the womb, where we are fed without eating, warmed by our environment, protected by a second skin. But we find ourselves born into a cold and brittle world. Human life mirrors these patterns of security and uncertainty, and we take control of these patterns ourselves in an unconscious attempt to master them. We tear ourselves from our warm bed to confront the cold air, we have a 40°C morning shower to prove to ourselves that we can relive the liquid embrace of the womb. And at the end of the day we turn off lights, close curtains, bury ourselves in beds. It is a nightly dress rehearsal for the unthinkable; a semi-colon to put off the full stop. This is the approaching oblivion that the insomniac dare not articulate. Is it any wonder, then, that children don't want to get out of bed for school, or that they are afraid of the darkness at night? We are those children, if we only knew it.

As with so many of the things that came out of his mouth, I understood what he was saying, but not what he meant. It was as if he had created a parallel universe out of the language everyone else used, the regular train of thought parked in the sidings. He was on his own runaway train, within sight of the main track, the iron sleepers of his words guiding it away by inches. There was no phrase I could search to help me understand, no fact or article that might shed light. Nothing agreed upon. The Steppenwolf seemed to be trying to write a kind of anti-Wikipedia, a new world made of old words. As I slipped the fragment under his door, I heard a scream of rage from inside.

I lay down on my futon and flicked through *Professional Window Cleaner Magazine*. It all seemed to skirt around the topic of glass, to beat around the bush without ever actually hitting the bush itself. It was easy to find articles about cleaning glass, glassmaking practices, the chemical processes, the cultures that developed it, but it seemed almost impossible to find anything describing the thing itself, as if its transparency extended to its very definition. You could almost believe that glass was a liquid, that it might escape like sand through your fingers, if you waited patiently.

The phone rang.

'Hi, Dad.'

'Hi, Günter.' He sounded sober in every respect. 'I was just calling to apologise for the other day and to say thank you.'

'That's okay. What are you thanking me for?'

'The money.'

'What money?'

'The Dean just called round with the money for your work on the cathedral spire.'

'Oh, that money. Which of course I promised to you in a sort of hypothetical way.'

'I also can't accept it.'

'Really?'

'Günter, I'm in more debt than you realise. They'll take my possessions, the house, even Mum's things.' He breathed deeply. 'I'm beyond help now. My only real hope is to declare myself bankrupt, or throw myself off something.'

'Okay, well you can just post me a cheque, and you know, once I start earning properly—'

'Günter, when you get to my age you realise that you're supposed to have been spending the first three quarters of your life piling up possessions, friends, memories, money. And then for the last quarter you just have to hope that you have enough of everything to lose some, because every year that passes, you lose a few memories, break a couple of keepsakes while you're drunk. You want to be able to look back and say, "That's what I was doing." All I'm thinking is, "What the hell *was* I doing?" I took your mother for granted, I wasted myself in a job I hated—'

'You didn't hate your job.'

'I bloody did. I just never told you I did. Just like I never liked your mum's lasagne.'

'But lasagne was your favourite!'

'No. At no point in my whole life have I ever said that anything good can come of sandwiching mince between two slices of pasta. I'd rather have a sandwich. At least you can hold onto the thing without the filling coming out the side or getting béchamel all over your fingers.'

'But you can use a knife and fork.'

'The point is, Günter, that I'm too far gone now. I haven't got much left for me here, and soon I won't have anything at all. I want to join your mother.'

'Well, tough. You're not allowed.'

I ended the call. I knew he had lost someone he'd shared his life with for decades, but so had I. Weren't Max and I a reason to stick around? Why did he have to be so self-centred about it? What about me?

By the time I had finished making my packed lunch I had worked myself up into a fury. I lay back down on my futon and could read no more. As I looked at my last email from Blades, I realised that I was also nervous about my first day of work, and that I might not be able to eat the next morning, so I decided to make myself some food to eat in bed. I heated a tin of beans in a pan and, in the absence of a toaster, put some bread on to grill in the Steppenwolf's old metal oven, scoffing it vengefully before settling down to catch up with my old friend, slumber.

I awoke before the day had drawn its shadows. It was early, but I felt good. I had now recovered from the various injuries

I had sustained, on church spires and from angry motorists, although I did have some elbow burns. I wondered whether this was a standard casualty of the sexual fray, or whether perhaps I was doing it wrong. I tried to put thoughts of protective elbow pads from my mind, as I was quite sure these were intended for rollerskating.

I grabbed my liver sausage sandwiches and went downstairs to find Frank and the waiting car. He was stood by the entrance to the flats, reading from his book, which he stuffed into an inner jacket pocket.

'Good morning, Frank. I was going to cycle today.'

'Sure you were,' he said in his quiet, throaty voice, opening the door for me.

'Can I sit up front with you?'

He closed the back door and opened the front passenger door. I sunk down into it, stowing my Tupperware by my feet, and listened to the quiet wailing of an opera. He seemed to listen to a lot of opera.

'What are you listening to?'

'Ring cycle.'

'Right, right. And who wrote that?'

'Wagner. It's fifteen hours long. Good for driving.'

'I imagine so. Do you have any idea what they're singing about?'

'Dead Vikings.'

He nodded appreciatively. I thought of my mum, her Viking myths, her wordsearches. I had almost never asked her anything about herself, and now I couldn't. So much treasure must have sunk in the shipwreck of her mind. All I held now were little fragments, and they didn't make sense on their own.

We glided through London's backstreets, turning down alleys, creeping the wrong way up one-way streets and shortcutting through car parks. I should have insisted on cycling to work, but this was such a comfortable way to travel. I would start cycling next week, once I was settled.

The training course turned out to be as boring as anything I have ever done, and I say that as someone who used to collect Roman coins.[44] I spent the majority of the next five days plagued by the supervision of pedants. The first thing they did was weigh me to check I was under the safe limit of 100kg, an indignity which I suffered in mute consternation. (I passed, incidentally, weighing a mere 96.6kg. I may have had one foot a tiny bit on the floor.) Next they took us through the appropriate clothing to be worn; proper equipment; equipment care; pre-use equipment checks; risk assessment; controlled descent; safe rigging (the point on which I had failed at the Spinnaker Tower, which is to say, I got the knot wrong); rescue; short ascent . . . The list goes on, and gets more boring. We were given reading materials at the end of each day, which all had names like *Industrial Rope Access: Investigation into Items of Personal Protective Equipment*, or *Five Steps to Risk Assessment*.

You could divide the class into two kinds of people, the Alternatives and the Blokes. The Alternatives were getting into rope work as a lucrative way to fund their extreme-sports habits – they would work on an oil rig or a skyscraper as a freelance for just long enough to earn the money for their next venture, and they spent the breaks excitedly swapping tips about wing-suits and mountain ridges. The Blokes were window cleaners who wanted to make more money, and were generally hard-working men whose few words were reserved for football or women. In the absence of a fitting phrase, I would call them 'raging straight'.

---

44 DW: One of Günter's shorter-lived obsessions, his collection ran to just a few dirty bronze coins, which he kept in a shoebox with some old (valueless) stamps and a surprisingly large number of novelty keyrings.

By the penultimate day I felt lobotomised with knowledge. I could have divided the course materials into eighty pages of *Things That Are Essentially an Extension of Common Sense, Such As Make Sure You Attach Your Rope to Something that Isn't You*, and then about three pages of *Actual Facts Which You Wouldn't Know Unless Someone Told You*. My salvation came in the form of a text from Lieve, saying that she was free on Friday night. The lecturer had just finished expounding on the virtues of kernmantel semi-static rope over dynamic mountaineering rope, and I gave a little yelp of glee, which elicited derisive laughter from both the Alternatives and the Blokes.

That night, instead of reading a leaflet on *What You Need to Know About the Control of Substances Hazardous to Health Regulations 2002*, I watched pornography. Not, you must understand, out of some kind of base carnal urge, but so that I might educate myself on the finer points of the sex act. After some frustrating googling, I determined that the language of pornography was a law unto itself, and that in order to get anywhere at all, I had to search for phrases such as 'XXX hot college teens'.[45] I didn't know what the Xs stood for, but I assumed it was a question of strength, like the anonymous gin bottles in old Western films.

After I had found what I was looking for, I ascertained that I was actually very staid. I didn't want extraneous body parts involved, nor did I need helping along with prosthetics, medieval weapons, extra people or multiple sexual organs. I wanted heterosexual sex between me and a solitary, human, fully female woman of roughly my own age. But even this simple dish could be served in a dizzying variety of ways, with a leg over a shoulder or a knee on a tumble-dryer. I personally couldn't think of

45 DW: As we have discovered, he sometimes knew more than he let on.

anything less sexy than foreplay in a utility room, but it seemed to feature as one of the more likely scenarios.

Eventually I abandoned the research as confusing and unhelpful. The problem with crowd-sourcing information was that, once mob rule was established, people were unlikely to speak out against it. I didn't recognise any of the men's actions in myself. They seemed to favour violent oral sex. I am too optimistic a person to believe that they represented the general approach.

I finished the rope course on the Friday and opted out of going to the pub with the others afterwards. I went home instead and was surprised to find the Steppenwolf emptying a box of cornflakes into his mouth and generally over the floor around him.

'I am lacking fibre,' he munched. 'Very hard to defecate.' He picked up a bottle of prune juice from the coffee table and started chugging like Thor. In the short time he had spent out of his room, he had made an almighty mess. I supposed I would have to clean it up.

'I, uh, read that chapter of your book,' I said, sinking into the old sofa.

'Which chapter?' he asked.

'133.'

'Ah no, it is at the heart of what is wrong with the book. I have burned it.'

'Burned it? Couldn't you just throw it away?' I asked.

'No!' he laughed. 'Then I might become contrite, like the lover who has spurned, and return to those parts of it that charmed me. I must not allow my future self to become lazy. So I have gone back to the beginning once more, recognising that my tenth draft was unsatisfactory. I have written a new introduction. May I read it to you?'

'I don't think . . .'

The Steppenwolf looked steadfastly at his little leaf of paper, his moustache drooping, his eyes filled with longing.

'I understand,' he said.

'It's not that I don't think you're very good,' I said. 'I just don't know how useful I would be.'

'But it is written precisely for the common man.'

'I, um. Sorry.' I pulled down my T-shirt, which relaxed back to its position above my waistline. 'I'm just going to . . .' I put my hands on my knees and rocked forwards out of the depths of the sofa.

'Where are you going?' he asked anxiously.

'I have a date tonight.'

'Ah, the courtship process,' he said wistfully.

'Yes. Complicated business, all this,' I said.

'I couldn't agree more,' he said, as if I had just made a very profound and life-changing statement.

'Any tips?' I prompted.

'I can only tell you of the fallacies of this concept, love,' he said. 'I have fallen into its pit before. 1958 was the year. But that was in another country, and besides, she is most likely dead now. Of course, to love is to give oneself up to the act of loving. One must love when one is compelled to love. It does not respond to reason. We are drawn to the qualities of the present hedonist, the spontaneous, the impulsive, the rash and the irresponsible. But the qualities we need are precisely the opposite: the Lutheran, the future planning, the impulse control, the responsible, the caring and nurturing. So it is that many cultures divided the role of wife and mistress, and is it fair to expect such disparate qualities in a single social role? Are we not so often unhappy because we define the cause of happiness as a thing beyond our grasping? A friend, a lover, a mother for my children? No, it is fallacious to presume such a hybrid exists. If I ever thought I had met her, I was wrong. Man's tragedy is to think that he has, in the face of all human history – the rational, happily arranged marriages, the miserable, impulsive elopements – become the first to utter the word love in reference to a woman who will be careful with his heart. For . . .'

The momentum of his speech dropped, like a sailboat suddenly becalmed. He looked lost, for the moment, in another country and another time.

'All good points,' I said slowly. 'Fingers crossed for this date tonight, though, eh?'

'Yes,' he murmured. 'We must continue to act as if these grand narratives have not collapsed.'

'So I thought I might take a shower.'

'Of course. You must.'

I wondered if that was a veiled insult. Under the circumstances, I let it slide.

I had recently discovered that a turtle called Archimedes lived in the bath, so I had to watch my ankles. I considered getting down into the tub, as I prefer baths, but I thought that it might nip at my exposed parts, and the water was cold regardless.

On the way to Lieve's, I stopped off at a little wine shop. A little man with a devil goatee stood filing his nails at the rough wooden counter.

'Good evening,' he said over his glasses.

'Hi. Can you recommend a good bottle of wine?' I asked.

'I wouldn't be much good at my job if I couldn't. Red or white?'

'You choose.'

'We have a wonderful Echézeaux. A very solid, fruity red, deriving from the excellent Domaine Romanée-Conti.'

He showed me the bottle. It wasn't far off £100.

'Have you got anything around the eight- or nine-pound mark?'

There was a pause. One eyebrow floated up towards his hairline. 'Cooking wine, sir?'

'No, I'm going to attempt to drink it.'

'Of course you are.'

'And could you put it in one of those nice boxes behind the counter. It's a gift.'

He broke into a smile. 'She's a lucky lady, whoever she is.'

'Have you ever heard of Tycho Brahe?' Lieve asked me over a lovely bit of venison.

'I can't say that I have.'

'Why is that?' she asked.

'Because I haven't.'

She put down her fork. 'He was an astronomer, the best of his generation,' she said proudly. 'Recently I've been dogged by the six of cups in my Tarot and I've been trying out past life regression to see how it all fits. And I had a breakthrough just before your message on Thursday: I *was* Tycho Brahe. In a past life.'

This was something of a dilemma. Delusional people made me nervous. But, in my limited experience – and by experience, I mean watching MTV – there was a remarkable overlap between women I found sexy and women I found crazy. Though the two traits have apparently very little in common, perhaps some small part of me believes that a woman would have to have poor judgment in order to justify having sex with me. It makes the whole fantasy more plausible.

I looked up the Wikipedia entry. 'Tycho kept an elk with him that got drunk at a party and fell down the stairs and died,' I read from my phone. 'He also enlisted the services of a clairvoyant dwarf called Jepp.'

She leant back in her chair as if to say, 'Case closed.' It did amaze me how independent her beliefs were from their natural parents, evidence.

We had finished our meal. I smiled at her. She was really, properly weird. What if I was too, and that was why she liked me? She bit off a tiny bit of skin on her lip and ran a finger down the hairline on her neck. Slowly, I reached across and took her hand, which seemed like the thing to do. She leant across the table towards me, and I leant out to meet her, but the table was too wide, and we couldn't reach. Her eyes were laughing, now, as I pushed my pouffe out behind me and it fell over and I walked on my knees round the table and she knelt to receive me. I pecked her softly on the lips. She put her hands on my ribs. She kissed me on the lips, harder, and pressed her bosom into my chest.

She took me by the hand and led me up the stairs to her bedroom, where we lay down side by side on the covers and I let my hand stray down towards her hip. She had her hand under my T-shirt, now, and held me close, her head resting on my other arm. We were still kissing, our eyes closed, but all I could feel was her hand trailing down my side, my stomach, my navel, to the top of my jeans.

'Shouldn't we get a—' I began breathlessly.

'It's fine.'

'But what if—'

'I said it's fine. I'm on the pill.'

She unhooked my button with élan and I was in an ecstasy, our tops went over our heads, we were skin upon skin, kissing and stroking, and it was forgotten.

I tried to get her to try some different positions, but she remained stubbornly on her back with a cushion underneath her pelvis.[46] I didn't give it much thought. Not to be too crude about it, my mind was on other things.

Afterwards I traced my fingers along her side, languid, looking at the shape of the eyeliner she'd painted on, which was

---

46 DW: The popular 'missionary' version of this position tends not to require a cushion, since missionaries are expected to travel light.

very slightly different on each eye. She kissed me on the nose.

'I'm going to fetch a glass of water. Do you want anything?' she asked, getting up.

'Um . . . Do you have any sparkling?'

'You sound like my ex-husband.'

'Come again?'

She came back through with a glass of tap water. 'I said, you sound like my ex-husband.'

'Your ex-husband..?'

'John. Blades.'

'No. Really?'

'Yes, really.'

'John Blades who I work for?'

'Yes,' she said.

'Oh dear. That's not good.' She shook her head, sitting back down next to me in silence. 'Dare I ask what happened?' I asked eventually.

'Well, what do you want to know?'

I thought about that.

'I suppose I want to know the reason why you loved him, and the reason you stopped loving him, if that's not too much to ask.'

'God, well. I'll try. I don't know if the reasons will make sense to anyone else.'

I made a gesture for her to go on.

'He was very . . . Traditional. He would open doors for me. He insisted on paying for everything. He punched men who looked at me a certain way. I told him off for that but it made me feel . . . Everything he ever did came easily, but it didn't make him lazy. He had worked his way up from nothing and I loved him for that.

'We wanted a family. We both did. But we found it hard to conceive. He wouldn't go to a doctor to see what we could do.

He was too proud to have his sperm checked. And so it took us years of trying, but it happened, I got pregnant, and we were so happy for that. It was perhaps the first time the world hadn't relented to the force of his will, and somehow that made it so much more beautiful when it finally did happen. He bought us this house, and I sat on a chair holding my belly and watching as he lifted everything in himself. He was so stubborn, he couldn't just watch while the removal men did their job, he always had to be involved, always had a better way to do things.

'Then at six months I had a miscarriage. I remember feeling heavy, thinking my waters must have broken because the baby had grown so big inside me. But I looked down and there was only blood.

'When they took me to hospital, I already knew the baby was dead. I could feel it sinking in me like a lead weight. The doctors told me I had to give birth to it anyway, that they would induce me and I would give birth to this dead thing, this object. So that's what I did, and I went through the senseless pain, and felt the loss of it, which was worse. The little body was taken away like refuse.

'The doctors explained that it was just a terrible accident. There was nothing to prevent me from conceiving again. But John . . . The moment he walked into the room and looked at me, I could see that he hated me. He thought I had killed it.

'We never really recovered from that. We couldn't touch each other. He claimed that he understood and that he didn't blame me, but I truly felt that he would rather I had died, and the baby lived.

'I looked for reasons elsewhere. I discovered there was a whole world, the spiritual world, and it could explain everything. There is a reason for everything, you just have to know how to read the signs. It wasn't my fault. Do you see? The stars, they . . .'

She broke off, wincing to trap the tears in.

'It's okay,' I said. 'It's okay.'

I took her hand.

'So he left,' she said. 'He didn't even pick up half his stuff, it's all in boxes upstairs. He didn't return my calls. We never saw eye to eye on everything, but to pretend I didn't exist, it was just too much. So I decided to confront him. It took me all of five minutes to find out where he was making his next press call. I thought Portsmouth would draw a nice big crowd, so I could tell the world what he was really like, humiliate him on his own PR campaign. I stood waiting on the viewing platform, and he appeared, and I couldn't. Seeing him again, the prospect of causing a scene seemed so undignified. I didn't want anyone to remember me that way. And he sees everything in black and white, once he turns on a person . . . He just makes these snap judgments of people, all the time. I know it will sound rueful, however I say it, but I'm glad it's over. Now that I've given up trying to make it work, I have finally let myself see how vile he can be.'

She smiled at me and squeezed my hand.

'Well, if we were married, I would certainly treat you better than that,' I said.

'But we're not married, Günter.'

'No, we're not. Quite right. But if we were —'

'Do you have intentions to marry me, Günter? Is that what you're saying?'

'No! I don't . . . I mean, that's not what I was —'

'Why not?'

'Look,' I said, holding my palms out in a gesture of futility, as one might during a bear attack,[47] 'I have to admit that I'm not

---

47 DW: Actually – if you're interested – the best thing to do if one encounters a bear is to back slowly away, keeping one's posture erect, preferably carrying pepper spray. Though I'm not sure this approach would have worked analogously with Lieve.

very good at talking to women. I sort of just say things to fill the gaps and often I don't know what—'

'Günter,' she said, with a finger to her lips. 'It was a joke. I was joking.'

'Right, okay. I mean, I know. Obviously that last part was a joke. But generally.'

I had made a tiny tear into our vacuum of intimacy, and now the silence was rushing in to fill it. She got up.

'Look, I'm sorry but I should probably get an early night. I have a client coming round early in the morning.'

'A client?' I asked.

'Were you listening when I told you what I did?'

'Oh – Oh! Yes. Sorry. Of course. Tarot, and uh . . .'

We were already in the corridor. I left quietly, walking out through the sodium-lit streets, the air muggy enough to carry smells of cooking and popcorn far from people's houses. So I was having sex with Blades' ex-wife. It would be best he didn't know about that. Ideally, I wouldn't know about that. So those were his boxes up in the study. And that was his whiteboard with the web of strange words on it. I tried to remember what had been written on it. It had looked like something out of *A Beautiful Mind*, but written by someone more paranoid and less clever. Now I'd have to go back to work with him, and pretend that everything was normal. I hated keeping secrets, particularly because I was so bad at it.

Back in my bedroom, I flicked through my emails. I had one from Max asking when I was coming back to Salisbury. That was one thing that I didn't understand about Max: when I spoke to him, he scowled back at me as if he resented my very presence. And yet, far from being glad to see the back of me, he seemed to want to stay in contact now more than ever. I'd had a couple of texts from him during my course, which I'd ignored. I would to go back to Salisbury soon anyway.

I emailed Max back: *I'm trying to make some money to help Dad pay his mortgage. I'll be home soon to check he hasn't died in your care.* I knew full well that he wouldn't be giving Dad any money or helping out around the house. Sometimes I wondered whether he was even self-aware enough to see the meaning in my reproaches.

I came out of my room to find the Steppenwolf rolling sushi on a space he'd cleared on the tabletop.

'It is nearly Saturday,' he growled amicably. 'I am preparing for my exile.'

I watched him for a while, first laying down the seaweed on his bamboo mat, then adding splodges of rice, patting them down, adding lengthwise cucumber and tuna, then rolling it carefully, like a giant cigar.

'I wonder what will happen first,' he said, baring his teeth in an honest smile. 'My mercury poisoning, or the extinction of fish?'

'It is hard to be good,' I said, half to myself. Then, 'You know how you're writing a guide to life?'

'I do know.'

'Is there anything in there about hate? Why people hate other people? That sort of thing?'

He huffed nostalgically. 'Oh yes. A great deal. Hate is a tremen-dously complex emotion. I explore hate in three sections of the Work. First, "Pulling Up The Ladder and the Perception of Finite Resource". Second, "The Loneliness of Misunderstanding". Third, "Spiting the Better Self: William Wilson, *The Double* and the Salieri of *Amadeus*". I will show you these chapters.'

'Could you just summarise them?'

He picked the knife up and began to approach me.

'Are you making a joke with me?' he asked, brandishing the knife.

'No!'

'You think it is easy to take all the tinnitus of existence and make a nice little phrase?'

'I, no, I'm just – I don't even know anything.'

He turned, walked back to the chopping board and started attacking the California roll. 'A sculpture is hewn, not built.'

'That's a nice little phrase right there,' I muttered under my breath. He swivelled round, baring his teeth.

'Good. You are learning. Very good.'

14

Bundles

The morning I was due to help Blades clean the IMAX in Waterloo began badly: I had run out of Dutch waffles. For the first time since Mum had died, I had to eat something else for breakfast, and what's more, the only thing in the house was sushi. Deciding it would be an insult to mother's memory, I went hungry, and going hungry is something that I am very loath to do.

I had told myself that I was definitely going to cycle, but, with the morning I was having, I decided to let Frank drive me today. I would cycle next time. Also, I had a bit of a fight with Blades over using my own equipment.

'Why do you need your own pouches?' he asked. 'Why can't you just wear what everyone else wears?'

'You hired me because I do things my own way, so let me do things my own way.'

'But it doesn't make any sense. What do you need different sprays for?'

'This is regular cleaning fluid, this one's distilled water in case of any problems with the solvents, and this is something called GOMORRAH. It "wipes filth away for good".'

'I thought that stuff was banned in Europe?' he said.

'Well . . . It gets the job done.'

'What is it about the regular equipment that offends you? I've been using it for years. You're good, but you're not better than me. Until you are, it's my way or the highway.'

'I just don't understand why you have to be such a damned fascist about it! I get the job done, don't I?'

'I'm telling you, Günter, don't bring it again.'

We continued cleaning in silence. I spent a long time on my own, up a rope, thinking about how, on my first proper day of work, I had called my new boss a fascist. It had just slipped out. To calm myself down, I tried to think up various scenarios in which the conversation could have gone better, most of them involving not calling him a fascist, and, in a broader context, not sleeping with his ex-wife. Was it better or worse that I'd done it twice?

We had split off in different directions around the circular building, and so, inevitably, we met on the opposite side of the building. He grabbed me by the safety rope, ensuring that I couldn't escape.

'You know, Günter, the word fascist is very misunderstood.'

I couldn't think of anything to say except, 'Oh?'

'You young people have been fed all this liberal trash by the media, and you don't realise that there are different sides to every story. I won't even ask what they taught you about World War Two.'

I glanced out at the cars on the roundabout, looked down at the drop, and tried to carry on window washing.

'Fasci were just like-minded political groups,' he continued. 'It means bundles. People naturally bunch together, don't they? You wouldn't mix a bundle of hay with . . . Well, anything else. Fascism was about strength through unity. People don't realise nowadays that by tolerating all these different religions and what have you, they're diluting the country, destroying its purity. You see this building we're hanging from?' he asked.

I nodded meekly, running my squeegee down a window.

'Well, a few years back it had glass cancer. When you introduce an impurity into the glassmaking process, it's as if the glass knows; it can feel a traitor in its midst. The impurity may be opaque, or have a different melting point; it might have a hundred other properties. In some ways it doesn't matter what the impurity is; the important thing is that it is not glass. The glass around it will fracture. Sometimes whole panels have been known to shatter spontaneously, seemingly without provocation. But there was provocation in the very making.

'And no one can tell when the trouble will start. It might look fine now. But it's a time bomb without a timer. In the IMAX, it happened a year after the building was opened. There were a few pedestrians walking under it at the time and a pane shattered above them suddenly, raining splinters.'[48]

I tried to imagine a rain of glass and thought it must be like a hailstorm. The drops would hit me on the head with sharp little digs, then nestle into my hair and my clothes. But rather than getting wet as they melted away, I would be dry, and covered in sparkling prisms of light, flashing agelessly like stars.

'I'm not saying foreigners can't be good people,' he said. 'I'm just saying they don't belong here. If you're from Poland, you belong in Poland.'

'What if your own government wants to kill you? What if you had to leave your home because you were being persecuted there?'

Blades shook his head gravely.

'Don't even get me started on all these illegal asylum seekers.'

48 DW: If we're being a stickler for the facts, the 'pedestrians' were some young boys with a slingshot ('BFI Smashes "Glass Cancer" Riddle at Avery's £20m IMAX,' *Architects' Journal*, 7 September 2000).

'You can't have an illegal asylum seeker. The only way to seek asylum is legally.'[49]

'I'm not interested in the fine print. The point is they shouldn't be here if they don't want to work.'

'Asylum seekers aren't allowed to work.'

'Well then they should force them into work. Get all the asylum seekers and all the convicts and make them work in a call centre or something.'

Maybe I was hallucinating. Maybe I hadn't woken up for work yet, and it was still the early hours of Monday morning, and this was all a dream. I gently knocked my head with the titanium end of my scraper to check. It hurt.

We unlatched ourselves and started packing our equipment away. Neither of us spoke for a good ten minutes. Eventually, Blades reached out to take back my rope, and said, 'I know it isn't popular to say you're a fascist now, but back in the day lots of ordinary people were proud of it. We have a lot in common with Fascists.'

We started heading down the stairs, back towards the solid earth.

'Let's agree to disagree.'

'No,' he said. 'This is important.'

'I just don't think I have anything in common with Fascists,' I said.

'But what evidence are you basing that on?' he cried passionately. 'They wanted the whole country to be a single, secular community, to keep the economy strong and foster consumer demand, same as us. They wanted a single leader of the country – sure, he had to pretend to be appointed by a king or voted in to satisfy the little people, but everyone knew it was just a

---

49 DW: It's one of those oxymoronic phrases that has somehow made it into usage against all sense, like 'devout atheist' and 'good grief'.

ceremony. Same as us. They wanted a strong national identity, and that meant pulling people together. Easiest way to get your people to pull together is to start a war or two. Same as us. And they didn't think women were much good at anything except cooking and fucking. If you dispute that, you should meet my ex-wife.'

My heart beat so hard that my vision shook. I would confront him, but not now. Not yet. First, I wanted to find out more about him, to figure him out. Maybe I could record our conversations and have him dragged through an employment tribunal. Something like that. But first, I had to let out enough rope and see if he hanged himself, or dropped off the end.

The main advantage I had, being me, was that no one expected me to know anything about anything. I could wear my clumsiness like a camouflage net. No one ever suspects the tubby window cleaner.

Max texted me to say that he was going to be in London the next day for a foreclosure auction, and asked if I wanted to meet for lunch. Naturally, I was suspicious, so I asked him why, and he explained that Dad had been behaving strangely. I said I couldn't get away from work for long, but he said he could meet me anywhere, so I didn't have much choice.

Max picked me up in the four-by-four. Naturally, I didn't agree with him using it, although it was actually quite fun to be so high up, bearing down on the other cars. It made me feel authoritative and powerful. It was a shame that so many of the things which made a person feel manly were bad for the environment. Apparently you shouldn't eat meat, either.

As we drove, I watched the little monitor that he kept on his dashboard, which gauged the volume of ambient noise. Someone slammed their hand on a car horn as Max changed lanes, and the gauge jumped from green to amber and nearly into the red.

Max didn't seem alarmed. To him, it didn't ultimately refer to anything. He might be able to hear a little, with his hearing aids, but it wasn't how he processed the world.

Max talked a little bit about his job. He was the guy at the bank who financed big 'consumer purchases' like cars and yachts and diamond watches. It was perfect for him because it required only deftness with arithmetic. He was simply employed to calculate whether the applicant could pay back the loan or not. He had always seemed to be more keen on the language of arithmetic than the written word. It was complete, precise, self-referring, where words were vague and pointed out at the world of experience, the world hearing people lived in. Despite having had his new job for less than a year, Max had thrown himself into it, and intended to become a true connoisseur of the talismans that people exchanged for money. He had even started going to foreclosure auctions to capitalise on others' misfortunes (hence the new watch).

After we'd ordered, he told me his department had just funded a car dealership which had got hold of a Koenigsegg CCX, one of the rarest cars in the world. It was shipped from Sweden to the USA, where the dealership was planning on trying an experimental biofuel upgrade which would put its horsepower at over 1000. It was bought before they could start to modify it – before it was even listed. As one of only twenty-five in existence, its movements were being tracked by some very wealthy people. The head of the dealership wasn't too happy about having to part with a flagship car so soon, and since he might never see one again, decided to take it out for a little spin before he handed it over. Rumour had it that he had been challenged to a race by a rival car dealer, but whatever he was doing, it took the whole front off the car. Today, Max had received an email from the guy who'd crashed it asking for finance to buy one of the twenty-four remaining Koenigseggs, because his customer had read about the crash in the paper and was getting worried.

Max laughed heartily at this, a stuttering, nasal laugh that turned a couple of heads. Oblivious, he speared a bit of ravioli on his fork and went serious.

It's a shame though. The CCX is like an endangered species. It's like shooting a panda in the face.

It's not like that, I signed.

How is it different? he asked.

Pandas have feelings. They're part of what makes this planet amazing.

Well, the guys at Koenigsegg have feelings too. You wouldn't understand. Those guys, they're trying to make something perfect. He picked his fork up again.

I decided to let it go. Max wouldn't know perfection if it killed him.

So what is going on with Dad?

Max shrugged.

He's just not doing very well.

How do you mean? I asked.

Now that there's no one around, he replied. *He's drinking too much. He's stopped opening the mail. Poor bastard can't even make a Cup-a-Soup without fucking it up.*

Why don't you go round? I asked.

Max glared at me.

The thought had occurred, he replied jerkily.

I imagined the spent case of the emergency whisky still hanging from the wall in the kitchen, the fake glass broken, the emergency ongoing.

So why are you telling me? I asked. *To shift the blame?*

He looked down. No one knew we were arguing. The beauty of sign.

How are you helping Dad? I signed in front of his face. *What are you actually doing?*

He looked angry. Good. He tapped his fork on the table a few times, the way people bite their lip to make sure they don't say the first thing that comes to mind.

Well, what are you doing? he signed. *Why don't you get down off your fucking high horse and do something yourself?* He hastily finished up his plate. Clearly we were enjoying each other's company as much as ever. Max wiped a hand on a napkin, and we sat looking at each other without speaking. I couldn't think of anything to say.

Well, this has been a real treat, he signed.

He tapped his watch face at me as he got up, both to indicate that he needed to leave and, I'm sure, to point out the watch again. He left me seated, thinking about his watch, black and chrome, or silver or platinum. The neutral blackness of it seemed to mirror and accentuate the qualities of the things around it. Elegant, raunchy, morbid, comforting, mysterious, empty. Black was nothing but what was made of it. The new black.

I looked around me at the other diners. They appeared to know we had been arguing. The waiting staff weaved around my table in such a way as to make me aware I wasn't wanted any more. Max hadn't put any money down.

I just didn't know how we always ended up arguing like this. We had to try so hard to get on, even for a minute. Weren't siblings supposed to be close? Weren't we supposed to feel automatic affection for one another? He'd grown up beside me for twenty-one years, and he still felt like an acquaintance – the kind that you try to avoid making eye contact with in the street.

Over the next week, I didn't text Max and he didn't text me. If I contacted him first it would be an admission that I was in the wrong, which I definitely wasn't. And if I was in the wrong, which I wasn't, I didn't want to look like I was.

It's not as if we would remember this argument in ten years' time, or twenty. Well, perhaps we would remember the fact that we had argued, or the fact that we always argued. But in the grand scheme of things what did it matter if we never got on? He would die eventually and so would I, and then it wouldn't matter to either of us. Everyone I knew would die some day, a thought which, if not exactly reassuring, at least put things in perspective. Everyone always lived as if the people around them were permanent fixtures, but it was the biggest, fattest lie of them all.

The whole week passed in solitude. The Steppenwolf had locked himself in his room and Blades left me off the timesheet. I texted Lieve to see if she was free at all, but she didn't reply so I just sat in the flat. www.what-do-turtles-eat.info said that turtles eat all kinds of food depending on their age. It said that eggs were a safe bet, so I boiled two for myself and one for Archimedes. After unpeeling and throwing it in the bath with a satisfying plop, I stood at the Steppenwolf's door listening for signs of activity, but I heard nothing.

I unwrapped a new packet of Dutch waffles and took one out while I pulled up a new tab. I do love waffles. They're so sturdy. There is a reassuring weight to them, a corrugated, cast iron promise of their syrupy yield, like a honeycomb flattened. I spent a couple of hours looking up the tallest buildings in the world, most of which were in Russia, America and Dubai, and then there was the Shard, which was just being completed at London Bridge. At a thousand feet high, it was one great spire starting from the floor and converging somewhere under the clouds, scratching at the intense blue of the sky, a great temple to human endeavour. It would tower over St Paul's, the once vast cathedral glowering over on the north bank like a one-time school bully who'd stopped growing at fourteen. Imagine scaling the outside. It made me short of breath just thinking of it. A thousand feet wasn't height; it was elevation, it was altitude.

Blades had texted me to ask whether I wanted to come and

watch the Palace game with some of the guys at his house. I had to accept the proffered olive branch – but if I was going to work with Blades, even in the short term, I had to know what I was getting myself into. I looked up the words I could remember from his whiteboard. 'Falange' were the Spanish version of Fascists. But 'cagoule'? At the end of the day, a cagoule was basically just a bin bag with sleeves. Rainproof: yes. Intriguing? No.

I texted back to say that I'd be there, and would bring 'beers'.[50] It is very important to conform in these situations, especially if you don't know anything about the sport in question, and perhaps more especially if you suspect your boss hates you.

I left the flat just as the sky's colours thinned and the shadows started melting into pools, stopping at the off-licence. There were youths hanging around outside the shop and one of them approached me. He looked at me like he wanted to kill me.

'Buy us some tinnies will ya? Guy in there's a right—'

'No,' I interrupted. 'I don't know you, but if, as I strongly suspect, you are under age, what makes you think that you and only you should ignore the law? If we all ignored the law we'd all be dead by now. So if you're old enough, you can bloody well buy it yourself.'

He went back to his mates and told them I was a bender. I went into the shop, grabbed two four-packs (buy one, get one free – I'm not an animal) and took them over to the counter.

'Can I see some ID?' said the man at the counter.

'I'm twenty-two.'

He didn't say anything about this, so I showed him my licence.

'I can't serve you if you're going to give it to minors.'

'I'm not. I'm going to watch the game.' I hoped there wasn't more than one game going on. That would cause confusion.

'I just saw you talking to that kid.'

50 DW: Football fans pluralise.

'I told him to go away.'

'Sorry. They'll take my licence away.' He didn't look sorry. He looked gormless.

I found another place to buy beer, but I was very nearly late for kick-off by now. It was a posh French off-licence that mostly sold wine, and the only beer was imported and expensive. Mayfair was so pristine that I hadn't seen someone with bad skin for four streets. This was someone's version of purity, with litter and the homeless swept away, pressure-hosed masonry and tailoring from first principles. For my part, I had never felt more like a manual labourer.

When I rang on the doorbell it was 19.43. A severe-looking man with a shock of blond hair answered the door. For some reason I had been expecting Frank. I followed him through an atrium with a great marble fireplace and down a corridor, lined with arty photographs of the World Trade Center[51] and other famous skyscrapers, then through a door to a massive lounge. A home projector had been set up against one wall, and six Blokes were sitting on couches which had been pushed back to the wall opposite. Blades sat in a lazy chair in the corner of the room, and I saw Pete the Australian Greek squashed shoulder to shoulder on one of the couches. I sat on the arm and realised I didn't know where the bottle opener was – but too late, for the whistle blew and the game kicked off.

The match started hurriedly, with all the players keen to get an early goal and demoralise their opponents. This went on for fourteen minutes, during which time people were talking excitedly. There was a transition period of about four minutes during which people made the odd comment, and by the time we were twenty minutes in, the blond man was getting up to get another beer.

51 DW: *Sic.*

'Could I grab the bottle opener?' I asked in what I hoped approximated football man talk.

He made a sound that was almost a 'yeah' and left the room.

About thirty minutes in, there was a decent shot on goal, but it was saved easily. Not having much else to comment on, the TV commentators went over the shot, and then some statistics about the striker in question. The fans at home and in the stadium grew restless.

'D'you remember when Jimmy Cannon used to play?' someone asked the room to murmurs of assent.

'They're too young to remember, Albie,' said Blades.

'No I'm not,' one of them said.

'When were you born then?' asked Blades.

'Seventy-eight.'

'Ha!'

The blond man came back with the bottle opener and his beer.

'If you were my age,' said Blades, 'you'd remember Jimmy Cannon properly. He was a hero. You still see him sometimes up in the boxes. Player of the Century for Palace.'

There was a pause, before the 34-year-old said, 'No he wasn't.'

'What?'

'Player of the Century was Ian Wright.'

'Don't be stupid. You think they'd pass up Cannon for some gold-toothed nigger?' Blades laughed and so did the blond man. Pete kept his eyes on the game. The guy next to me took a swig of his beer. There was no one black in the room. I didn't know whether this made it better or worse. 'Look at you, flinching at the word nigger,' Blades went on. 'If I see a spade, I call him a spade.'

'Wright was the best forward we ever had, before he went to Highbury,' said the 34-year-old, trying to bring the conversation back to safe ground.

'Yeah, he was good,' I said. He must have been, if I'd heard of him.

'Don't be fooled, Günter, he's the same as the rest of them. When it suits them they play off this image that blacks are really cool, they can all dance and they've got big dicks. And then when they want something, they play the minority card, they're all, "It's very hard growing up in Bongo Bongo land," and they end up getting the job over a decent, hardworking Englishman.'

'He's all right,' said the 34-year-old, aggrieved.

'He's a foreigner.'

'He grew up in Brockley.'

We sat in silence until the second minute of injury time, when a couple of guys stood up to go to the bathroom. The 34-year-old was one of them, and he didn't come back.

'Good riddance,' said Blades. He turned to the blond man. 'Impossible to find a red-blooded workforce these days. He'll have to go, too.' The blond man nodded. 'It's a wonder we get anything done. Still, we've got to stick together.' Blades caught my eye and gave me a little nod. I didn't nod back, but it felt too awkward to contradict him.

After the game recommenced, people started to expound their various perspectives on the players, and made predictions about the final score. Sixty-seven minutes in, everyone seemed to have sunk into boredom, and when the opposition side scored in the seventy-first minute, boredom was replaced by a kind of fatalistic anger.

'Well, that's it, isn't it?' said Blades, swigging violently.

I left as soon as the game was over. I didn't want to hear the post-match debrief, and I'd taken a dislike to the blond man. I hated football anyway. It was just a kind of tribalism, none of them understanding that the team they had pinned all their hopes on and built up in their mind was no different to any of the other teams; none of them were innately better or worse, none of them destined for greatness or relegation. It was just the amount of money they had, and the way they had been divided up. They could have been divided any number of ways, but it happened to be the town they came from, and nowadays the town you came from didn't make much difference to the place you ended up. It was an almost random process of constant buying and selling, each team held together by nothing more than physical continuity. How could you believe in a club when you knew each of its component parts had been replaced? What was left of the original, other than the story of its existence, reprised for the benefit of its young? At its heart was tribalism,[52] nothing more and nothing less.

I reached the main door of my building at the same time as the lady with the hemp bag. She wasn't carrying her hemp bag. She was wearing a sparkly dress and faded lipstick. I held the door open for her. I couldn't quite put my finger on how she looked – worried, perhaps.

'Hello,' I said.

She smiled as if she might run away, but she got in the lift with me.

'So, how is it? Living with the German man?'

'Well . . . quiet, really. I don't see him except on Fridays, and I'm out at work most Fridays anyway.' I assumed this would become true over time.

'I always thought he was a bit of a funny one.'

'It's just his mannerisms. I think deep down he's the same as everyone. He just wants to be liked, wants to make something that outlives him.'

---

52 DW: There is a story in the Bible (Judges 12:6) in which two tribes are at war. In one tribe, people pronounce a word 'shibboleth'; in the other, 'sibboleth'. They use this to identify the enemy, and to kill them, little realising the real tragedy that this is the sum total of their difference.

The woman started to cry.

'Oh dear, was it something I said? Why are you crying?'

'I'm not crying!' she said, tears streaming down her cheeks.

'But your face . . .' I began.

'Well *now* I'm crying!' she cried. A hand rooted around in her bag. The lift pinged. I held it open while she found herself a tissue.

'Would you like to talk about it?' I asked. She nodded sheepishly and rooted around in her bag again for keys.

Inside her flat, we sat at the kitchen table. She offered me tea but I only wanted water. Pure, clear, cold water. She sat down, her black eye make-up smudged rather prettily, like a sad panda.

'May I ask, is it trouble with a man that you're having?' (I could ask these sorts of questions now, as something of a relationship veteran.)

'Yes – well – man, men. I went on this date, he seemed nice online but he turned out to be an utter – anyway they all are. I mean no offence, you seem lovely, but they are, aren't they? And I only really need to find one nice man to settle down with and have kids but I'm a bloody lawyer so the only men I meet are lawyers and who wants to marry a *lawyer*?' She reminisced into her tea. 'When I was a little girl, I wanted to have eight babies. Eight! Imagine. But at least I'd have had a full house. Right now I just feel so empty. I know it's just the hormones, everyone gets broody, don't they? but it feels like I have another stomach inside me and there are no pipes attached so it just sits there empty and hungry all day, every day. I have all this love and nowhere to put it. I make cakes with love, I love characters I see in films, I imagine that they've got lost out in the cold on London Fields and I bring them in and give them blankets and make them soup.'

'Perhaps you should try to weave your way into something bigger than yourself. A cause, something more permanent.

Something pure, something that doesn't just blow away in the wind.'

She looked at me as if I hadn't listened to a word she'd said. 'Like what.'

'Well . . . Take this glass of water. It's probably as old as the earth itself. I drink it and it merges with my body, becomes a part of me. It's pure, unchanging, simple, clear. It doesn't matter what happens to me, I will always . . .' I could tell I was losing her. 'Look, what do you most want? What one great thing do you want to be able to hold up and say, "I was a part of this"?'

'I don't know. Love,' she said sadly.

I did something quite uncharacteristic, then, by standing up, going over to the woman and giving her a hug. I didn't normally hug people. She cried a bit and I did too, in sympathy, I suppose. It seems very hard to bear, the idea that all life is flashing by without ever returning: events, people, buildings, everything, blinking in and out of existence quicker than anyone could track them.[53]

I lay in bed that night awake for a long time, listening to the darkness. Just beyond my thin wall, there was a woman who was very uncertain about the world. It was comforting to know that she was there. After a while I heard her close her bedroom door. She unplugged something from the wall and then plugged in something else. A phone charger, I guessed. Then I heard nothing for a little while, until there was a light brushing, like someone stroking the wall. I stroked it back. I didn't know if it made a sound on her side. But I was here and I was human. It was something.

I woke up with sunlight warming my nose. A cold Friday, but a sunlit one. The Steppenwolf finished grilling his mackerel and

---

53 DW: Perhaps not in the East, where they rush to embrace impermanence as a pre-emptive strike. A nice chap the Dalai Lama may be, but he doesn't have all the answers. He's not winning the Game of Life so much as refusing to spin the wheel.

we sat together at the kitchen table, shared a pot of coffee and chatted. This was the first time we had made any small talk – about the weather (temperature and light conditions), our work, a good place to buy socks (Marks & Spencer, apparently).

'This kind of conversation, is it important, do you think?' he asked me.

'I suppose so. It's not really what you say, it's just . . .'

'The fact that you have taken the trouble to say it. Yes.' He scribbled *phatic function* on the tablecloth with a biro. 'For a long time I ignored conversations about the weather. I thought it was simply English people being inconsequential. Then I realised these exchanges are at the very core of humanity. It is a peculiar skill, to be able to converse without communicating anything at all. To put your conversation partner at ease. I cannot do it. I never learned.' He smiled yellow and I got caught in the crosshair of his halitosis. I had learnt to stand not-quite facing him, at an oblique angle, but this was impossible at the table.

'I'm sure you're not as bad as you think,' I said.

'Yes! That is a great example. Thank you.'

He scribbled some more. I reached for the coffee and put my elbow in a puddle of blue paint.

'I've been meaning to ask, why is there always paint everywhere? I thought you were writing a book.'

'Ah yes, but sometimes I paint instead. I cannot stop working or I will not finish in my lifetime, but sometimes I get tired of words, and as they say, a change is as good as a rest.'

'Maybe that's why I like books with pictures,' I said. We mulled silently over our coffee for a while. 'Oh, I've been meaning to ask – any chance you're an expert on cagoules?'

'I know everything that is useful, and nothing that is not.'

'All right then, try and solve this one –'

'A riddle?'

'I don't know, I haven't solved it yet.'

'I will put on my lateral thinking hat.'

He duly went off and came back to the table wearing a battered bowler.

'What could a cagoule have to do with fascism?'

'A cagoule? Or the cagoule?'

'What do you mean?'

'The cagoule, or *la* cagoule?'

'What, is the Holy Grail disguised as some kind of mystical French raincoat?'

'La Cagoule. With a capital C. Otherwise known as the Comité Social d'Action Révolutionnaire. It is better translated as the Hood.'

'And what was the point of this hood? Did someone wear it, or . . .?'

'It was not about items of clothing. It was a French underground society. Right wing. Terrorists in the French sense, they wanted to create order in society through terror, like Robespierre.'

'It's not an actual cagoule?' I asked.

'No. A secret fascist society. They liked to explode people. They used false flag tactics, meaning that they would kill their own allies to make their enemies the Communists look like unhinged murderers. Truly ironic, to have to commit a crime on behalf of those you wish to be guilty. I have a book somewhere . . .' He got up and wandered over to the bookcase, the Post-its swaying like narcissi on a faint breeze, and walked his fingers along spines. 'It is not alphabetical, I am afraid. Alphabetical is a good system, you know, Dewey is fine, I started to develop my own indexing system based on Boolean, but these . . . it should be here somewhere . . . You see, we have entered an age of fractal specialism, as access to knowledge becomes freely available and new technology is built on the foundations of past specialisms.

More and more we see people who devote whole lives to tiny branches of branches of branches of thought. In some ways it is best to write books on one thing only . . . but that is why my book of life is so necessary . . . no one to turn all the little puddles of knowledge into a reservoir.' He now seemed to be mounting the bookcase, like a randy spider.

'I'll borrow the book later, shall I?' I asked.

'Yes, yes. Quite an interesting case in fact . . .'

False flag tactics. Good thing that sort of thing didn't happen these days. I stared at the toast in my hand, threw it down in disgust and went to the cupboard for a waffle.

15

Tissue of Lies

Lieve texted me: *I want to see you*. I considered playing hard to get while I took out my bike, which had already grown cobwebs, and cycled across town to Lieve's. Everyone on the road seemed very angry with each other – cars with buses and vice versa, pedestrians with everything that was moving and vice versa, cyclists with the world in general, except for those on Boris bikes, who pottered obliviously. By the time I got to Baron's Court I was sweating like a hairy pig, so I decided to dry off in a café.

I found another one of those fake French cafés. It had the same wicker chairs and the same 'Chat Noir' poster in the corner. I had another coffee. I had had a lot of coffee, having already shared a cafetière with the Steppenwolf, and my hand was beginning to shake a little on the cup. After that I went into a perfume shop and made a great pretence of sniffing at a few bottles before liberally applying one of them to my neck and arms. *Eau Sauvage*, apparently. Smelt like a bath bomb to me, but then you could fit what I know about perfumes on the back of a stamp. Lieve answered her door in full soothsayer regalia, floaty clothes and wide hoop earrings.

'Why don't you wait upstairs? I'm just finishing up. You look twitchy.'

'Yes, I am quite. Did you know those coffee chains put two

espressos in each coffee? No one told me.'

She leant in. 'You smell different.'

'It's a new aftershave,' I said.

'I prefer your natural odour.' She smiled to herself and hurried back through to the lounge, where I saw a nondescript-looking man in a grey suit. He was holding up a Tarot card and inspecting it. She shut the door on me just as the man turned round, so that he didn't see me.

I walked up the stairs and decided to relieve myself (often, going to the toilet is no cause for relief, but, after all the coffee, this time I felt it flooding through my bloodstream). I went to the basin to wash my hands, and since there was a wastepaper bin there I decided to throw away an old train ticket and a chewing gum wrapper. In the course of this mundane act, I saw something extraordinary: there was only one thing in the bin, and it was a pregnancy test, wrapped up in tissue paper. I didn't know whether I should unwrap it to find out the results, especially since it had been comprehensively soaked in urine.

In the end I left it, partly because hygiene has always been important to me, and partly because not knowing the answer was almost the same as not knowing the question had been asked.

I padded back through thick carpet to the bedroom, which was decorated plainly in comparison to the bedouin tent below. A small grey stuffed penguin sat over in the corner by a row of perfumes. It could have been there for any number of reasons.

I thought about opening her drawers to look at her things. If she came in now, it would not be easily forgiven. I checked the time. I thought about getting in the bed, but I had only really had two proper dates with her, and wasn't sure if this was a bit presumptuous, so I just sat on the edge.

After a few minutes I decided that I might as well find out the results of the pregnancy test. I crossed the landing again, went into the bathroom, got down on my knees and opened the bin lid. I picked out the damp tissue and began to peel it away from the test. The extreme dampness of the tissue had compromised its structural integrity, and it broke apart as I tried to peel it off; on top of which my hand was shaking from the coffee. Nevertheless, I saw that it said '+' very clearly on the blue display. A cross like the little baby Jesus, perhaps. Or a little tombstone to indicate that another little egg had passed over. Or a plus, meaning that she had tested positive for baby-chemicals. Although, perhaps in our Malthusian modern world, it was considered a plus not to find oneself pregnant, and the sign indicated the all-clear.[54]

I sat there for a minute, holding the pregnancy test and trying to calm myself by recalling the various folk methods of diagnosing pregnancy, such as weeing on toads. It was definitely something like that.

As I got my phone out to look it up, the door opened and the man in the grey suit strode in, having already half-undone his flies. He only noticed my bulk crouched by the cistern as he was undoing the button on his underpants and I made a small noise of alarm. He stood, holding his penis, staring down at me as I stared back up at him, one hand full of wet tissue and a pregnancy test, and the other holding my phone. He was evidently in shock because he seemed rooted to the spot. I decided to take the situation into my own hands.

'Please can you stand outside and wait until I have finished?' I said in a low voice.

'Yes,' he said, 'Yes, of course. Sorry to – didn't mean to bother you.'

'Not at all.'

---

54 DW: The Reverend Malthus is credited with foreseeing the problem of overpopulation; he is less often credited with suggesting that the poor shouldn't breed.

He backed out of the room, shell-shocked, fiddling with his crotch. I locked the door, wrapped the pregnancy test back up and disposed of it again. Then I washed my hands with soap, dried them, washed them again, dried them, and then smelt them. They smelt of soap.

We glanced at each other meaningfully as I exited. I understood the look to mean, *let's keep this between us.* I had exchanged a similar look with my father on the way back from the glass museum as a child. The look that said mother wouldn't understand, nor should we ask her to try. I went back to the bedroom, where I listened patiently to the sound of a flushing loo, and the sound of rushed pleasantries by the front door.

Lieve opened the door to the bedroom as she removed a large hoop earring. She kissed me on the mouth before removing her top and stepping out of her skirts. I felt touched to have been included in this simple intimacy. She put on some jogging bottoms and a T-shirt. It didn't fit with my image of her, but I suppose everyone has to let their hair down, and at least she didn't seem to own jogging bottoms for exercise. I never knew why people went running. It was pointless. Either you ran in a big circle, ending up where you started, or you ran on a treadmill, which was as dystopian a vision as I could imagine. To run without having anywhere to be is depressing enough, but to be made to run by a shifting floor without even moving from the spot was a Sisyphean nightmare.[55]

She sat down on the bed and pulled me to her, putting her arms around my waist. I held her too, and slipped my hand under her T-shirt, beginning to fiddle with her bra clasp. Perhaps if we got nude, we wouldn't have to talk.

55 Sisyphus was a (non-Biblical) king who tried to cheat death and was punished by being made to exercise constantly; truly, a modern parable.

'I have some big news.' She paused while I retracted my hand. 'Are you ready?'

'As I'll ever be.'

She raised her eyebrows in anticipation of my surprise. 'I'm pregnant.'

'Oh! Pregnant, you say?'

'Yes. I just found out.'

'Right. So I guess you must have taken a pregnancy test or something.'

'Yes Günter. That's how people find out.'

'Yes of course. And is it—'

'Don't even think about asking that question.'

I stalled. 'So, well. Obviously I didn't mean to, um . . . So. What shall we do? Can I . . . help? In some way?' I asked eventually.

'I'm just telling you as a courtesy. It's not something for you to worry about. It's my body and I'll take care of it myself. I just thought you should know.'

'Well, yes, of course. Especially after everything you've been through. It can't be easy, you know. So if you want me to be there. When . . .' I trailed off.

'Thank you. God. I've been so worried about telling you. I can't tell you how much it means to know you understand. You're a very special person, Günter. Very special.'

My window of opportunity for nudity seemed to have passed, but I didn't mind. I had found the only woman in the world who was willing to speak openly in a language I could understand, and that was good enough for me.

'I'm going to get you a glass of water,' she said. 'You look like you're on drugs.'

True enough, my hands were still shaking and I had a bit of a cold sweat coming on. I saw now that caffeine was cruel. It enhanced nothing, only contaminated the purity of my senses. Perhaps I should cut it out of my diet altogether.

Lieve brought me a glass of water and I felt it spread down my throat like menthol, clearing out my sticky throat, quelling my bubbling stomach. Pure water. I looked through the bedroom window at the sun sailing through the sky and wanted to be back up there, lifted out of the chaos and noise, scraping at the sky. The air was cast in a cobalt blue of such calibre that my eyes couldn't quite settle on it. I stared into it and saw spots. No clouds – only the endless theatre of the sky.

'What are you watching?' she asked.

'Oh, nothing in particular.'

I tore my eyes from the sky and turned to her. She started to cry. I kissed her softly, my lips a cushion against hers, which had tensed as if forming an 'm'. I brought my hand up to her cheekbone and it was cold.

'I'm sorry. Sorry. It's the' – she waved at her stomach – 'I'm not normally like this.'

'You don't need to apologise.'

She shook her head and pulled away from me. 'Look, thank you for being so honest and straightforward with me' – I thought back to the moment that her client had discovered me with my hand in her toilet bin – 'and for coming round at such short notice, but I have another client coming in ten minutes. I'll see you soon, okay?'

'Okay.'

'I'm glad we could talk about this.' She put her hand on my knee. Was there still some hope of nudity? Probably not.

The hemp-bag lady must have heard me fumbling with my keys, because she came out of her flat as soon as I arrived.

'I just wanted to say that I'm sorry for the other day, unloading on you like that. I hope you don't think I'm awful and desperate!' she laughed nervously. 'You just caught me at a funny time, that's all.'

'Please, don't worry about it. I was happy to listen. And it was nice to meet you properly . . . ?'

'Emma.'

'Glass,' I said. 'Günter Glass.'

We stood in silence and I got the impression that she was testing my surname in her head to see if it sounded nice after 'Emma'.

'Well, I'd better get in,' I said.

'Yes, I've got to get to court,' she said, straightening up.

'Oh dear, what did you do?' I asked.

She laughed and touched me playfully on the arm as if I'd made a joke. 'Really, I should go. See you soon, Günter.'

As I reached the other front door I remembered that she was a lawyer. I never seemed able to remember these things during conversations, only afterwards. It worried me occasionally that I didn't seem to be able to understand events until after they'd occurred. Only when I was up high did the world feel immediate, like it was all really happening to me, there and then. I smiled as I recalled the picture of me clutching the spire of Salisbury Cathedral. Up in the air, I was like a hippo in water. Up there I could really breathe.

I unlocked the front doors, put my keys down and opened the fridge absent-mindedly. There was nothing in it but a book: *Murder in the Metro.*[56] There was a Post-it on the book which said, *No More Eating! You are fat. Here is the book. Do some cleaning.*

I tried calling Dad, but with no luck. It just rang and rang. I doubted somehow that he had left the house, which could mean that he had become so apathetic he was no longer prepared to move. It was still morning, so there was a possibility he was still

56 *Murder in the Métro: Laetitia Toureaux and the Cagoule in 1930s France,* by Gail K. Brunelle and Annette Finley-Croswhite (Louisiana State University Press, 2010).

passed out from the night before. Or he had committed suicide. He probably hadn't committed suicide. But I should try again later.

I lay down on my futon with the book. It would be nice to have some furniture. I opened the book and a little clipping fell out from the middle, where it had bookmarked a certain page. I picked up the clipping – another one of the Steppenwolf's little essays.

Chapter 690a – on the genealogy of racism

That peculiar subcategory of European supremacism is based on the erroneous assumption that women are commodities, and thus misogyny and racism are at root the same problem. As the white Western colonists would have it, the black man is more physically capable and less thoughtful than the white man (because of course, the two are inversely proportional), and therefore, whilst the black man makes a good labourer, he also presents a physical threat to their women. Asian people are seen as less physically capable. Thus the greatest fear for the colonist was that their women might be seized by black men, which would undermine their rule; the keystone of the colonist's power was to sleep with the black women – we saw this dynamic occurring frequently during times of slavery. The cultural perception is still weighted so that Westerners believe a black man can snare a white woman easily, or a white man can seduce an Asian woman – the latter irony being that most people living in Asia don't care enough to contribute to a debate on the matter. To much of Asia, white people are known as 'ghosts', rendering them ironically incorporeal. As is so often the case, the white colonist's carefully constructed self-image has served only to humiliate and emasculate him. On the Jewish people, more presently.

I wondered if he might have lost this section, so I slid it gently under his door. There was a flurry of sound like a burrowing animal and the door flew open, the Steppenwolf before me in rags, incandescent with rage.

'I have a system! Do you mean to bring about my undoing?'

'I – you left it in the book. I thought you might need it,' I mumbled.

'It is there for a reason! And no I do not need it! This is part of draft five!' He glared at me, his eyeballs popping so far that I was sure I could see near enough the whole globe of them; he bared his yellow teeth, snatched the extract from my hand and ingested it, chewing furiously as he stared at me. The over-powering smell of rotting fish emanated from his mouth and I flinched on his behalf as he swallowed.

'I'm sorry,' I said. 'I wasn't thinking.'

He went over to the bookshelf and took down all forty-five volumes of a book by an author called Adolf Wölfli. The books looked much older than me, older perhaps than the Steppenwolf himself. Having piled them high in his room, he shook his head at me superciliously and slammed the door.

Was this just what happened when you got a flatmate? Was this behaviour utterly bizarre, or had I myself been blown off course? My mother would know. My mother, who insisted that we all sit as a family to dinner, and who washed my clothes as soon as I had taken them off, who gave me right and wrong, ambition, love, like these were the only things worth worrying about. She had been a standard against which I had measured others, a wristband to remind me: *what would Mum do?* And yet all the time that I had deferred to her was time I had spent cowering under her wing. Now I had been pushed out of the dizzy heights of the eyrie, and I was picking up speed, and I was only just unsticking my own wings from my side. The ground was coming to meet me, and all this time I had thought I'd known how to flap because she made it look easy, but it turned out there was so much more to it. What if no one noticed that I tried to be good? What if no one saw me hit the rocks? Would there still be something left at the bottom, if I hadn't done anything to weave myself into the story of the world? What if I already had, and it was a boy? Or a girl?

I remembered when Dad was clearing out the loft and he found a little girl's dress. He'd put it in the charity pile and Mum had shouted at him because it was a dress she'd made in her O level class. It was a tiny little yellow polycotton thing, with a white yoke and buttons down the back. On the front was embroidered a cartoonish bunny. She'd made it, and kept it, in wait for the little girl she would one day have, but she never had. She had me, and I didn't fit the bill, and she tried again, and Max had his challenges, and they stopped trying. I tried to imagine her reaction if I told her I was having a baby girl. She wouldn't smile; the feeling ran too deep. It would be like a dream which had stared across at her clifftop nest, unfolded albatross wings and flown off twenty years ago, travelled the world, and finally found its way home again. And if I had a boy . . . She was careful never to seem disappointed. She would smile, and squeeze my arm, and say, 'Another boy? Another Glass. He'd better have a good German name.'

But I was making it up because it comforted me. I didn't know what she would have wanted, or what she might have said.

I lay back down on my futon next to the Cagoule book, and picked it up, staring at the cover. Maybe if I could figure out how the Cagoule fit into Blades' web of words, I might be able to figure out what made him tick, maybe even change his mind. I picked it up, and spent a couple of hours reading up. What I gleaned was this: in the late twenties and early thirties, there was a national recession in France, which was part of a wider global recession. Banks had been failing all over the place. People's faith in the economy had been destroyed. As resources became stretched and people lost jobs, the ruling centre-ground parties disagreed on how to make things better and through disagreement became increasingly polarised. Soon there were parties on the extreme left and right – and the extreme right parties were terrified of the apparent success of communism further east, in Russia. They began to mistrust many of the liberal institutions on which the French state had been founded. When a liberal chap called Blum was voted into power, a fascist called Eugene Deloncle formed a party whose main tenets involved racism and extreme nationalism. President Blum banned Deloncle's party for being fascists, so they went underground and founded the Cagoule. They stockpiled weapons and killed anyone who stood in their way, including a woman called Laetitia Toureaux, who had been acting as a police informant from inside the organisation. On 11 September 1937, the Cagoule blew up a building as an act of patriotic false flag terrorism. They tried to blame the attacks on the extreme left and use the bombings as a call to arms for the far right.

The scariest thing was that the Cagoule seemed to have links to some pretty massive companies: Michelin, the Banque Worms and some French oil company. The founder of L'Oréal had been one of the heads of the Cagoule. I used their shampoo every day. I hadn't realised I was perpetuating a fascist dynasty. All I had wanted was to control my dandruff. If it was hard to be good, it was really, unbelievably, incredibly easy to be bad.

The bombings had come to be known as the 'terrorist attacks' or, more commonly, the Etoile[57] attacks. In a way, I thought, every star was a time bomb. It would go off when it was due. Each star had helped to create the universe, and would help to

57 DW: Lit. 'Star'

end it. Perhaps it mattered less that anything was permanent, and more that there was meaning in its birth, and its death.

I met Blades for a pub lunch in the Glassblower just off Piccadilly. I wouldn't have thought it was the kind of pub that Blades would like, but perhaps it fit in with his man of the people act. The walls were dark and the lights yellowish, and Blades was installed at a large table near the back. I couldn't see Frank, but he must have been nearby. He always was.

Blades got up and shook my hand as I approached the table, and he ordered us pie and chips and a couple of pints. His shirt was unbuttoned to below his chest and I had an urge to reach over and button it.

'I drove past the IMAX the other day,' said Blades by way of conversation.

'Oh yes?'

'It looks good. Really good. We did a stunning job.'

'I agree,' I said. 'By the time we were done I could have mistaken those windows for the sky itself.'

'You're good at what you do, Günter. I haven't seen a natural like you since a young boy called John waxed his father's car all those years ago.' He raised his eyebrows and pointed at a bare patch of his chest. I often got the feeling that he thought I was in some way mentally unsound.

The pie and chips arrived, and I watched those canines cutting through a mouthful of pastry shell like hot knives through butter.

'I didn't have you down as a pie lover,' I said. 'I'd have thought you'd only dine where there were Michelin constellations.'

'You've got me all wrong, Günter. I would say that I enjoy food more than anyone else on the whole planet, and here's why.' He pointed his knife accusingly, in the manner of the self-made man. 'Everything is about scale. These gourmet cooks can't taste how good their food is because they've got nothing to compare it to. To truly appreciate Michelin star food, you have to eat KFC the night before. You walk in, you've still got that feeling in your mouth that's somehow both stringy and powdery at the same time, and someone brings you an asparagus mousse. It's asparagus, but it's a fucking mousse, Günter. It's so light you only know it's there because the flavour hits you like a punch from an angry whore. It's a ball-tease, Günter, I tell you.'

'I see.'

'Anyway, we've got something very exciting coming up, Günter, very exciting.'

'Great. Just say what it is, and I'll do it.'

'I need to know I can trust you,' he said, dousing the pie with a great gulp of beer. I dutifully sipped at mine.

'Of course.'

'There's no room for fuck-ups this time, okay? No badly tied ropes, no fooling around with weird sprays.'

'No,' I said deliberately.

'Because this is the big one. This could put us on the map internationally. I've been waiting for an opportunity like this my whole life.'

'What's the job? Not Canary Wharf?' I asked.

He shook his head.

'The Gherkin?'

'Bigger.' His eyes shone.

There wasn't anything bigger. My mind raced. What did he mean? Something in Russia? Or Manhattan? I tried to look at the photocopied file on the table in front of him, but he closed it when he saw me looking. The front page just said 'Northwoods', which must be the group managing the site.

'What is it?' I asked.

'They want us to do the Shard, Günter.'

He sliced his biggest chip in half and dunked it in blood-red ketchup while he waited for it to sink in. The Shard. The mother of all jobs. We could tickle the gods from there. We could blow on the clouds.

'I can't even tell you the square footage we're looking at. I don't think even the Mace group know. They want us to clean it from top to bottom ahead of the official opening. If we play it right, we might get offers from New York, Dubai.' He caught himself. 'Günter, I want us to make this a spectacular event. A one-off.'

So if Mace were managing the site, what was Northwoods?

My phone rang. I wanted to throw it at the wall, but I didn't want to encourage any suspicion in Blades that I was mentally unsound, so I made a quick apology and stood to answer it.

'Glass Cleaning, how can I help?'

'Am I speaking to Mr Günter Glass?'

'You are. How can I help?'

'We're just calling up about your tax return.'

'I haven't done a tax return.'

'That's a large part of the reason we're calling.'

I held my hand up in apology to Blades and took the call outside. 'What's the problem?' I asked.

'We haven't received any tax from you since you were made redundant over a year ago. But our information indicates you've been earning money since then.'

'Not very much. I'm only just finding my feet. If you call back in a few months—'

'We do need to know how much you've been earning.'

'I haven't really been keeping track.'

'We're going to need your bank statements, for a start.'

'I wasn't putting any of it in the bank.'

I heard a strange sound, a bit like a pencil snapping in half.

'In that case we need to set up an appointment to talk it over in more detail.'

I gave him a day in a couple of weeks' time and went back in to my tepid pie.

'You know, I have a very good accountant who could probably help you avoid most of your tax,' Blades said, quaffing a few fingers of my beer.

'Thank you, but I might as well pay what I owe. I'd much prefer to pay my taxes than to have to start filling in my own potholes and setting my own broken bones.'

'Anyone would think you were a communist,' he replied with distaste. 'Anyway, the offer's there. So: the Shard. It's a landmark project for the city, and I want it to propel us onto the international stage. We can help make this country great again, Günter, I know it.'

'I'll do what I can,' I said. If I was going to get through my next job with Blades, I was going to have to think of a lot of noncommittal replies.

'Good.' He leant forward. 'You know, we've had the labs working overtime to develop a completely new technology. I don't pretend to understand it but if we pull it off, it will be so good it might just put us out of business.'

'What do you mean?'

Blades lowered his voice.

'What if there was a way to clean windows only once – a way to make sure they stayed clean?' he whispered.

'But there can't be, can there? There will always be dirt. It's everywhere, exhaust fumes, dust . . . it's in the air.'

'For a little while people have been testing new kinds of windows. Down in the Eden Project they use ETFE. It's not glass but it's so smooth that dirt just rolls off it when it rains. It's strong, durable, superlight – the only problem is you need to keep pumping air through to keep it taut. Other people are looking at replacing glass with smart materials but they're on the wrong track. What if there was a way to modify existing windows? It's glass, Günter, but it's not glass. There's this chemical which hybridises with the surface and repels dirt

– literally repels it. The windows clean themselves.'

'I don't understand. Why would you want to help create a chemical that will ruin your livelihood?' I asked.

His eyes gleamed like dark stars. 'Because sometimes the only way to make something perfect is to destroy something good. This is a chance to change the way that our corner of the world works; it's a moment in history. This project will be our legacy, it will outlive us.'

'Well – and again, I know I'm probably being really moronic – why didn't we put the magical cleaning serum on the windows first, before they put the windows on the building? Wouldn't that have been easier than putting regular windows all over a thousand-foot building, then spraying the whole thing?'

'Bureaucracy,' said Blades, glaring at me. 'Middle-management games. If we had tried to give them the technology sooner, we might not have got the contract. We'd be new in the business of making windows. But we knew that if we waited, we could get the cleaning contract, because we are long established. And besides, I want to climb that building.'

'Yes,' I said. 'I know what you mean.'

16

Liberty

The Steppenwolf was out of his room. He appeared to have drunk a lot of alcohol, and looked rheumy.

'You know it's a Monday morning?' I asked.

He scowled.

'What's wrong?'

'Truth!' he barked. 'Every time I write down one truth, all the other truths must warp to accommodate it. It is a Rubik's cube. It is the problem of quantum all over again.'

'I don't understand.'

'There must be one truth! There is only one truth! You either find it or you do not, but my evidence changes and I must start again!' He pointed accusingly at my laptop, which I had left out by accident. 'I have just discovered "internet". It is a whole new plane of existence. An informational plane which renders the physical unnecessary. A network comprised of human nodes, emergence, singularity. I thought it would take another hundred years. I have not factored this in. How am I to write the permanent truth when the world changes under my feet? I am writing the ocean while I drown.'

'Perhaps it depends what kind of truth you mean?' I said tentatively.

He eyed me suspiciously. 'Go on.'

'Well. When I was an adult, I found out that glass was a —'

'Yes yes, glass is a liquid, everybody knows.'

'Actually, it's a solid.'

His teeth made a gritty sound. 'Sit. Explain.'

'Well. When I was a little boy, I visited a glass museum. I had always thought that glass was a solid because it was solid to the touch, but a kind old man wanted to tell me a good story, and make me excited about the exhibits, so he told me something that you're supposed to find out when you're older. He told me that glass is a liquid. I had some exams a year later and one of my papers tested me on solids, liquids and gases.'

'What about plasma?'

'Well this is the thing – we were too young to learn about all that. And when they asked what glass was, I wrote that it was a liquid, and they marked my answer wrong. I cried a lot that day because I knew I was right. The exam hadn't been about the real truth. It had been about the version of truth I had been taught.'

'The British curriculum is pitiful, but irrelevant,' he snarled.

'Well – later, when I was in my teens, the teachers officially taught me that glass was a liquid, and I was allowed to write it on my exam paper, and I got the marks. I was very pleased. But I didn't deserve the mark, because I found out on Wikipedia recently that glass really is a solid. It has never been a liquid. It has always been solid, unless you want to wait hundreds of billions of years for it to drip. The only reason anyone ever thought it was a liquid was because the glass is thicker at the bottom in old windows. They used to make windows by melting glass and then spinning it in a circle, so more of the glass would always settle on the edge before they chopped it up into square plates.'

'Centrifugal force?' he asked.

'If you like. It's also conveniently bottom-heavy so it doesn't fall out. But most people still like the idea that it's a liquid, that it's breaking all the rules. They don't care whether it's true, because the lie lights up their lives. Who knows, perhaps we'll have new evidence in ten years' time, and it'll turn out that glass is a liquid after all. Perhaps the lie will make more of an impact than the truth ever did. You can't agonise about these things. People will find out the kind of truth they are ready for. You can't force it on them. If you try, they won't believe you.'

The Steppenwolf looked utterly dejected.

'I'm sorry,' I said. 'That's just what I think. I didn't mean that your book was—'

'Yes you did.'

He looked at the empty wine bottle in his hand as if it were a traitor and threw it with great force at the wall, where it shattered in a cloud of green splinters. I have read that, at the moment glass breaks, its points are just atoms thick. Even as it travels through the air it is blunted, so pristine are the shards.

'Leave now,' he said quietly.

I backed away and went back to my bare room and lay on my futon, waiting.

Sometimes I wished, for his own sake, that the Steppenwolf had been born in a different time. He seemed wrong for the modern world. Though I supposed life felt difficult no matter what time you were living in. Two people could just about keep up with one life, like my mum and dad had done. One life had too much to organise, too many bills to pay and washing to do and meals to cook. I'll admit that I hadn't been feeding myself very well up in London, but it seemed a waste to buy vegetables for one. They'd only rot before I'd used them. Steppenwolf hardly seemed to be a fan of the veg, either. He must have been taking some kind of supplement because he only ever seemed to eat fish. Mother had never touched shellfish because she said that they were unhygienic. She used to say she didn't like the smell. She was partial to white fish, sometimes. Monkfish, seabass, you know. She used to say they were safer. Less chance of food poisoning.

I crept to the bathroom to move my bowels and found Archimedes in the bath, his water having drained away. He looked sad – as sad as a turtle can look, bearing in mind that he didn't have lips or eyebrows. I turned on the tap and bent down to stroke him. As my hand came about level with his head he bit me with his weird little jaw. He didn't have any teeth but it bloody hurt. Little bastard. I was only trying to help.

When the coast was clear, I left my room and stepped on a foil yoghurt lid. I looked up and it was as if a veil had fallen from my eyes. The place was a sty. There were mugs containing a kind of gloopy culture, which had furred up out of the cup; crumbs over every surface; a rat was nonchalantly exploring a stack of plates, with its forepaws up on the top, nibbling at a piece of forgotten toast; the pans were piled higher in the sink than the tap which was meant to clean them; the once-cream wall next to the hob was spattered with grease spots like a Jackson Pollock.[58] I rolled up my dressing gown sleeves and went to my room for my cleaning belt. I was about to earn my keep.

Several hours later, I came back from the shops with bags full of new, fresh vegetables and a whole plaice for the Steppenwolf. I'd had the deli man fillet the thing first, so there wouldn't be any bones. I put the food away, and glanced around the place, surveying my work. It looked good. Satisfied, I picked up my copy of *Professional Window Cleaner* and sunk into the sofa. I opened the magazine and was about to delve into an interesting-looking article on water-fed poles when I heard laughter coming from the Steppenwolf's room. There were two distinct pitches:

58 DW: A painter whose work has recently been singled out for unfavourable comparison on the internet with that of an elephant who is capable of self-portraiture. The young reverend showed me and I must admit I was swayed. In Pollock's defence, the elephant really is very good.

one was low and sounded almost like a cough, the other long and drawn out like a donkey braying.

I put the magazine down, got up slowly and edged towards the Steppenwolf's door, which was slightly ajar. As I pushed it open, allowing the redolence of fish to flow over me like a wave, I saw the Steppenwolf sitting in the midst of a pile of bottles, facing my father, who was apparently trying to balance three wine bottles, in a pyramid, on the shell of a distressed Archimedes. Dad looked up as I walked in and the bottles fell just as Archimedes jammed himself back into his shell, causing the two of them to erupt in another bout of coughing and braying.

'Dad? What the hell are you doing here? How did you get in?'

'The nice lady showed me how to use the little . . .' He grappled for words as he mimed aiming the white rod through the hole in the first front door.

'It's okay, I get it. But what are you doing here?'

'I'm just getting to know your landlord. What a feller.'

I turned to the Steppenwolf. 'But it's not your day of contact!'

The Steppenwolf bared his teeth at me, a new savagery in his eyes. 'I have returned to nihilism. We must all return in the end. Your father has shown me the way. His world view is complete, all-encompassing.'

'He's not religious, he's depressed!'

'What is religion but a coping mechanism?'

'What's his coping mechanism?' I asked, jabbing a finger accusingly at my father. 'Drinking?' I turned back to my father. 'Why are you here?'

'House got repossessed.'

'Right. Great.' Archimedes peeked out and, sensing that the coast was temporarily clear, flapped under the bed. 'You've brought your own supply, I see.'

'It's all I've got,' he said, suddenly serious, wiping his wet lips with his palm. 'What did you want me to do with it? Eh? It's all

I've got. I'm a 68-year-old widower, not a penny to my name. Though I might try and cheer myself up a bit, and drinking cheers me up. So there you are. It's bloody sad, but what can you do?' We all took a moment to reflect. 'I tell you what, though,' he said. 'Bailiffs wouldn't touch your mum. I said to Max, we should have kept the ashes in a Tupperware and hidden the good stuff in the urn.' Then he giggled. Giggling is unbecoming to old men. I felt sick, and I am not a man who regrets his food.

I had to get out of the flat, so I went to see Lieve. I decided to walk the long way from her tube stop, through an old church-yard. The city calmed as I entered, the hum of traffic muted by the trees. An old woman was brushing leaves off a new white headstone and I wanted to say something as I passed, offer a few words of condolence, but they would have sounded hollow from a stranger. I had heard those sincere condolences and deepest sympathies before. Someone should be mourning for all these lost lives, I supposed, but we were so few and they were so many.

As I continued on the footpath, I found there was a section of the graveyard devoted to cot deaths. Many had plastic toys where you would expect flowers. They wouldn't degrade for ten thousand years. I wondered whether someone would dis-cover these toys when they had long been buried under layers of rubble, and use them as proof that twenty-first-century humanity believed in the afterlife. I imagined an academic showing slides of a bucket and spade – *they believed that the child would need these when he passed over* – never suspecting that the toys had been left there because the parents didn't want them in the house any more and couldn't bear to give them away. These plastic toys were not sacred objects. They were just painful reminders that needed burying too.

Beyond the children's graves was a patch which had been left for many decades. It was a shame that these people had died in the city, since they'd soon be exhumed to make space for more bodies, their bones packed into a storeroom like a tube carriage at rush hour. Too many bodies, not enough space. Overlooking these graves was a weeping willow, its tendrils propped up on the boundary railings like a sad drunk.

I found my way out the other side of the churchyard and was welcomed back to the din of the city. I tried to tuck in my T-shirt – the largest I had – as I approached the house but, to my dismay, it wouldn't fit under my stomach, so I was doomed to walk around sporting a pre-natal look. I needed to cut down on the waffles. Or cycle to work, perhaps. It was hard to be bothered.

Lieve opened the door.

'Guess what?' I said.

'You have a rare illness?' she asked, straight-faced.

'No.'

'You've brought me a present.'

'No . . . I can go and get one if you like?'

'Don't be silly. Come in. What were you going to say?'

'I have all day to see you.'

'Do you ever work?'

'Sometimes.'

I followed her through to the lounge, watching the muscles on her back rippling under her floaty purple top. You'd need good back muscles, with a chest like hers. Every time we met, her breasts seemed to be getting bigger.

'Do you want some?' she said, indicating a shisha on the low table.

I opened my mouth to speak.

'I probably shouldn't either,' she said, patting her belly. I didn't know shisha made you fat. Still, you learn something every day. She sat on a pouffe and poured out mint tea, adding spoonfuls of sugar to each. She was breathing in and out quite loudly, as if through a paper bag, and looked quite pale.

'Are you all right?'

But she just shook her head as she shot past me and up the stairs.

I sat at another pouffe and sipped at the tea. It was very sweet. I imagined fur growing on my teeth and ran my tongue across them. Every now and again I would hear the noise of vocal chords shunted forwards by a torrent of vomit. Sounded like she'd caught one of those nasty twenty-four-hour bugs that were going around. I shifted on the pouffe, trying to get comfortable. I heard sounds of brushing teeth and then a lock turning. Lieve reappeared, her face shining and newly washed.

'Sorry,' she said, sweeping through to the kitchen. She brought back a bowl piled high with kiwis and two teaspoons. 'Would you like one?'

I opened my mouth to speak.

'You don't like them? I keep getting cravings . . . Look, Günter. I know we've spoken about this already, but I think we need to talk seriously about the commitment we're making.'

We need to talk? It felt like ice-cold water was being poured down my spinal column. Every time I thought I knew how things were, she turned everything on its head. It was like dating a sand clock.

'We're already talking,' I said.

'Günter, I like you a lot. I'm a bit taken aback, because when I first met you, I didn't think this would be a big thing. You're a bit lacking, socially. And you're always squinting into your glasses like a little mole. But against all the odds, you're actually charming, and somehow I've tripped over and fallen in love with you.' I opened my mouth and closed it again, like a fish out of water. 'And if we're both realistic, you're not going to do any better than me.' I smiled sheepishly. She grabbed my hand. 'What I'm saying is, I want you to feel – to be – involved.'

'What do you mean?' I asked.

'You know what I'm talking about, Günter. I want you to be *involved*.' She put my hand on her stomach. Everything went so still that I wasn't even sure my heart was beating.

'A baby?' I asked.

'Don't look so shocked!' she said. I took my hand away.

'I thought you wanted to. Um.'

'Günter, I said I wanted to take care of it.'

'Take care of it?'

'I was hoping you might too.'

'Oh.'

'Oh?'

'That's quite, sort of, different. To what I was expecting. Actually, really very different. It's a . . . well. It's a big decision. Having a baby. Raising a child.'

'What decision? There's nothing to decide,' she said.

'Well. Not nothing,' I replied. 'We're all adults, aren't we, so I need to give my . . . consent.'

She looked at me as if I was stupid. 'I don't need your consent.'

'Yes, well, no, but . . .' I trailed off.

'But what?'

'But that's not fair. You didn't even ask me.'

'You knew how much it meant to me,' she replied indignantly.

'But you – you tricked me. You said we didn't need . . . You said you were on the pill.'

'No I didn't.'

'You – ?'

Unfortunately, I found myself unable to press home my rhetorical advantage. Hyperventilating might look silly, but it doesn't feel great, let me tell you. It felt a bit like I was being assassinated by the mafia, who had wrapped cling film over my mouth. The difference being that the person sitting opposite was looking at me as if I was vaguely pathetic – no more than if, for instance, I had been used as target practice by a pigeon. It's very hard to battle for control of any situation when you are hyper-ventilating, and sadly that only makes you hyperventilate more.

In order to retain my dignity, I waited until she had gone to the kitchen to get me a glass of water, before scuttling out on my hands and knees, gulping down fresh air as I made for the graveyard.

I had to get off the tube after a few stops. I didn't know where I was going, nor did I care. I went where there were crowds to lose myself in. Piccadilly Circus, Regent Street. Everywhere people stopped, shopped, wandered. No one looked at me. I went into a Swarovski shop and stared at the world through crystal shapes. Through their clean, decisive cuts, the light was refracted and geometrical, rolled out like a measuring tape of tailored rain-bow. The world was ordered, here. Distilled. You put in all the chaos and confusion and it came out sparkling in white light.

A noise like a school bell began to emanate from my crotch, and I realised that my phone was ringing. A number I didn't recognise.

'Hello?'

'Oh hello there,' said a shaky voice. 'Do you do greenhouses?'

'What?'

'Greenhouses,' came the voice, louder. 'Do you clean greenhouses?'

'What? No. Who is this?'

'I was recommended to you by Mrs O'Hallahan. She said you did a wonderful job on her conservatory.'

'I think you're getting me confused with someone else.'

'No, you're Günter Glass, from the papers.'

'I don't even live in Salisbury!'

There was a pause.

'I never said you did.'

'Just piss off, will you?'

I cancelled the call and saw a text from Lieve: *Running away is not very fucking mature.* Bloody phone. If only there was some way I could use it to talk to someone I actually liked. If only there was someone I could turn to, who would really listen. I wandered through the store, rebuffing offers of help with that catch-all, 'I'm just browsing.' I didn't even really know what browsing was. A browse didn't involve any real inspection, nor trying anything on, nor could the assistant sincerely believe that browsing ever led to buying. Perhaps that was why they left you alone.

Yes, if only there was someone I could talk to who gave clear advice. I stared at a crystal goblet. The light swam through it in perfect ellipses, following an infinite, prescribed loop. It was, in many ways, the perfect goblet. If I bought that, I'd never have to replace it. It would be my life's goblet. Unless I broke it. I pulled out my wallet to inspect the money in there, which was scant, but spotted a Samaritans card nestled in among receipts. I pulled it out. *Dean Angela Winterbottom.* 01722 335161. I took out my phone and dialled.

'Hello?'

'Hello. It's Günter. I don't know if you'll remember me, I changed your aeroplane warning light.'

'Ah Günter! How could I forget you? Our visitor numbers have shot up since your escapade. How are you getting on? Would you like to come in for a cup of tea? Everyone here is so very dull. Nothing in the Bible about being po-faced, but His believers are nothing if not revisionist.'

'I'd love to, but I'm afraid I've moved to London.'

'Not to get away from us dreadful churchgoers, I hope? I heard you had a bit of a run-in with our choir.'

'Oh God – gosh – yes, sorry about that. I wasn't quite myself that day.'

'What I worry about, Günter, is that you have been claiming

not to be yourself for as long as I've known you. It's becoming quite an untenable position.'

'I suppose so. I'm starting to figure some things out. I have a good job and I have recently met a woman I like very much.'

'But you're phoning me.'

I imagined her hands curling into question marks. Perhaps she was on hands-free.[59]

'Well, yes. I suppose I just wanted some honest advice, and I don't know anyone else who is equipped to provide it.'

'All right. I'm hardly a woman of the world but I shall do my best.'

'Okay, you know how I said I've been seeing someone?'

'I wouldn't worry about the whole spilling semen business too much. Leviticus 15 tends to take the view that everything will be fine by the evening, as long as you wash.'

'Well actually, it's gone rather too far the other way. This woman that I'm seeing, she's got a bun in the oven.'

'Oh my. That's wonderful news, my dear boy! Shotgun wedding, is it? We'd love to have you here. Wouldn't worry what the neighbours say. It was ever thus. The men of Salisbury tend to buy rings and prams in package deals.'

'But I'm not sure that I'm ready to be a father.'

'Ah, the other thing.' I heard a door clicking shut as Dean Winterbottom lowered her voice. 'I'm afraid I can't help you there. The papers would have a field day if they caught me and I really don't have the expertise; you're much better off going to Marie Stopes.'

'No no no, I didn't mean— I suppose I just wanted to know what you think of the idea. Is the little thing sacred or something? Is it wrong to bring it into the world if I can't take care of it?'

---

59 DW: It's a landline with a curly cord like a pig's tail. We might be a cathedral, but we're not made of money.

'Mmm,' she said ponderously. 'It's always hard to do the right thing. Especially in this day and age, don't you think?'

'I quite agree.' I felt a tug of affection inside me then. If only Dean Winterbottom were a little younger, I'd want her to be my mother. Or perhaps if she were a lot younger . . .[60]

'The Bible doesn't really stretch to this debate, I'm afraid. There's no word for abortion, as I'm sure you'd expect. I think at one point someone asks God to inflict miscarriage on a population,[61] but there are a lot of spiteful people in the Bible. I'm not sure people have ever really understood the meaning of infinite love. As for Jesus, he said that it's not what happens to your body that defiles you; you are defiled by what comes from your heart.[62] He was mainly talking about bacon but I think the point stands. The material aspect is not nearly so important as your reasons. It is a good book, I must say. You might consider reading it one day.'

'I don't know what to do. She wants to keep it, but I don't.'

'Perhaps this pregnancy is her own little corner of permanence.'

'But a baby should have two parents, and I'm not going to be there.'

'Why not?'

'Because I didn't choose it. It's as if someone has just showed me a photo of a sports car and then told me I've bought the car and I owe them hundreds of thousands of pounds. I didn't ask for the car, I can't afford to pay for it, I don't even have my own parking space. I just don't want it to happen. If they'd told me what was going to happen, I wouldn't have wanted to . . . you know? Look at the photo.'

60 DW: I was quite the belle in my day, but I'm happy to say there's only one man in my life. Well, two, if you count The Father. Note the capitals.

61 Hosea 9:14 – 'Give them, O LORD: what wilt thou give? give them a miscarrying womb and dry breasts.'

62 Matthew 15:11–20.

'You mustn't dehumanise the baby by pretending it's a car.'

'But . . .'

'You need to talk to your partner, Günter. You could try to persuade her that it's the right thing, but you can't always make all your own choices. What would be the point in living, if you knew how you were going to do it in advance?'

I furrowed my brow and pursed my lips as if willing my face to implode as I walked out onto the street. Two men were washing windows from a bucket at the shop opposite, its front-of-store displays gleaming in their mock Tudor housing. Above the door where two staff arranged exotic flowers ran a single word in two-foot-high letters: LIBERTY. Above that, a weathervane in the shape of a golden ship changed its course slightly, glinting in the midday sun. The summer had arrived, and with it a renewed promise. Soap trickled down across the concrete. These things – glass, water, sunlight, liberty – were bright things, clear and open. Uncomplicated. Pure.

'Are you still there Günter?'

'I am.'

'Be good.'

I took in a deep breath. The air was crisp.

'I'll try.'

17

Wolfish Frenzy

'Long-life okay?'

'Well, yes all right.'

Emma the Hemp Bag Lady came through to the sitting room carrying two mugs.

'It's a lovely place you have here,' I said. 'Really.'

Emma cast her eye around the room coyly.

'I've tried to make it cosy. I know there's a lot of residential round London but it's hard to find somewhere that really feels homely.'

'I had the same problem when I was looking,' I said.

'I used to do his shopping for him, you know. I have a car, so it's no bother. You should see the amount of fish he gets through. Sometimes I wonder if he's not keeping a porpoise in there.'

'He does have a turtle.'

She smiled and rolled her eyes. She knew he wasn't crazy. Or at least not violent. He just lacked social mores.

'So,' she said, looking into my eyes as she sipped.

'Um. How's the law going? Are people still breaking the law? You know, yobs and oiks and that lot?' I asked.

'I wouldn't know. Not my sort of thing,' she said.

'What's your sort of thing?' I asked. It came out sounding a little suggestive, and she laughed nervously.

'Family law. It's mostly divorces, to be honest; hardly a day goes by when I don't hear the word divorce, it's enough to make anyone not want to get married, but occasionally you do see a yummy-looking divorcee and wonder how soon is too soon.' She sniffed. 'You get all sorts, really. Domestic abuse. Pre-nup. Children, custody, that sort of thing.'

'Must be hard to have faith in relationships from where you're sitting.'

'It is. You have to remind yourself that you're only seeing the problems. I imagine there are hundreds of happy couples out there who don't even know what a family lawyer is. Millions. Does colour how you see the world, though. I've always thought, if you worked for the emergency services, you'd think everyone was an arsonist or something. Whereas in reality fires rarely happen. I don't know a single person who's ever set their house on fire.'

'Neither do I.'

We touched the edge of a vast silence, like an unknown forest.

'Do you ever do cases about pregnancy?' I asked, hoping that I'd reached the appropriate quotient of small talk.

'What do you mean?'

'Well, for example, if a woman got pregnant and one of them wanted to keep it but the other one didn't.'

'The law's quite clear on that, fortunately.'

'But would you fight a case in principle? On moral grounds?'

'I don't see why not. Money for old rope.'

'And how much do you charge? Do you do that no win no fee thing?'

'Only crooks do that. A proper lawyer will charge you properly.'

'Ah.'

I thought back to my bank balance. Maybe it would be easier to deal with this all next month. Although that said, time was rather of the essence if I wanted to stop Lieve. I wondered how easy it was to get a credit card.

'Emma, do you think you might represent me? I need a lawyer. My girlfriend tricked me into getting her pregnant.'

'Are you joking?'

'No.'

'What do you mean, tricked you? After the first few minutes, did you not begin to suspect that you were having sex with her?'

'She said she was using contraception, but she wasn't.'

'So you didn't know she wanted to get pregnant?'

'Well, she did say she wanted a child. But she specifically told me she was on the pill.'

'What if she was? Contraception isn't fool proof.'

'*Fool proof?* What are you trying to – look, the point is I know she lied.'

'It's not illegal to lie.'

'Why not?' She laughed in my face, then, and all at once I realised we were both standing, and I saw how absurd it would be to make lying illegal, and I saw how desperately unfair it was that we had laws for everything – where you can leave your car, minimum-clothing requirements, how loud you can be – but no law for basic honesty.[63]

'Emma,' I said. 'Please try to understand. I'll have to pay to take care of it and if I'm not a terrible person I'll end up looking after it as well, but that's going to change my whole life, probably more significantly than anything else that's ever happened to me, and I don't even get a say. I want a child at some point but it's not a good idea now, for me or for the baby. A child has the right to two loving parents.'

---

63 DW: It does, however, crop up in Leviticus 19:11. It is at such a moment that a thinking person might come to think that the fabric of society itself must fray and tear unless we are ultimately answerable for our private actions. How can we hold any belief in absolutes, without a God to justify them? Humanism may be a noble house, but it is destined to subside in the sands of its foundations.

Emma stuck her bottom jaw out. 'If we're talking about rights, a woman has a right to bear children,' she said.

'But bears would make terrible children,' I replied.

She didn't laugh.

'Women have had the short end of the stick for all of history. The one thing that you can't take away is a woman's right to be a mother.'

'But it's not fair. What about equality?'

'I'm not talking about equality. Feminism isn't just about equality, it's about evening out our terrible odds.'

A car alarm went off somewhere and kept going.

'But I've never oppressed a woman in my life.'

'It's not about you!'

'Yes it is, it's my bloody child!'

I was leaning across the table now, anger burning in my crown. The car alarm might in fact have been a smoke alarm, since it was now accompanied by the smell of smoke, which seemed to be emanating from the smoke which had started seeping under the door.

'Come on!' I said.

We flung the door open and bolted out into the hallway. I pressed the lift button but Emma dragged me by the arm down the stairs. We ran down and out onto the little patch of green at the front. She phoned the fire brigade, who had already received a call and were on their way.

As I stood on the grass it occurred to me that the smoke had been issuing from my first front door. What if my dad had tried to cook? It was a Wednesday. I had to go back in.

I shoved the door open and sprinted back up the stairs. I got to the first front door, opened it to find smoke billowing from the second front door and fumbled in its moving shadow. I opened the second and more smoke issued forth in thick plumes, getting thicker. The smoke was coming, without a doubt, from the Steppenwolf's room. I shouted out for anyone who might be there and heard a muffled shout back – my dad's voice. It was loud, the crackling, and I couldn't see through the smoke. I edged closer to the Steppenwolf's room and saw my dad through the smoke, apparently confused, having just woken, covered in his own sick.

'Bad day at the office, son.'

'The fucking flat's on fire!'

He put up a hand as if to say, 'hold on a tic, I'll just get my coat.' Then he picked up his wallet and tucked a newspaper under his arm, gave me a thumbs up and wandered out with me in tow, coughing.

'So the Steppenwolf isn't in there?' I asked as we reached the bottom.

'Oh, shit it!' he said, 'Hang on.' He ambled off back up the stairs. I could hardly let Dad go on his own, since he couldn't lift anything much heavier than a bottle, so I started up after him. By now I could feel the smoke settling in my lungs, each breath like a packet of cigarettes, or inhaling a drink instead of swallowing it, and I felt dread spreading through my chest, not knowing what we would find, or how we would get out again. As Dad receded into the smoke up the stairs I was overtaken by what looked like a dirty alien. He stopped as he passed me, turned and shouted an order to leave the building, pointing back the way I had come, his great moon suit blocking the way ahead. I obeyed the fireman even though, as absurd as it might sound, I resented the glory that would follow him. No one had seen me leave with my dad. It would look as if I had gone into the building, wandered around for five minutes and been rescued by the firemen. I was better than that. I wanted people to know. I suppose, if I'm honest, I'd envisioned a news headline. That's what Blades had said, wasn't it? That I was the kind of person who made the headlines?

But then I remembered that Dad and the Steppenwolf were still in danger. I went back out to the patch of green, where Emma glared at me and others milled about in dressing gowns or towels, and I felt awful.

'Did you find anyone?' Emma asked through gritted teeth.

'Yeah, my dad.'

'Why didn't he come down with you? Did you abort him?'

I pursed my lips and tried not to think of comebacks. Instead, I thought about the Steppenwolf and the flat. My phone, wallet, laptop, clothes, pouches, bike, magazines, my sidekick holster, my grappling hook . . . Oh dear, the GOMORRAH. I hoped the fire didn't get anywhere near that.

My dad was dragged down and taken to a paramedic, the fireman assuming the vomit on his shirt was something to do with the smoke. It was a good thing he hadn't been too near the fire, or he'd have gone up like a whisky-sodden guy. They tried to lie him down but he kept trying to sit up, crying, 'The bloody wolf's still in there!'

Others left the building as more firemen turned up and started to unspool a powerful hose. And then the Steppenwolf was carried out on a single fireman's shoulder. He hung limp and seemed curiously small out here in the world, as if a spell had broken. I rushed up to him as the fireman laid him down and a paramedic tried to strap an oxygen mask on him.

'Archimedes!' he spluttered.

'Is there someone else in there?' the fireman asked urgently.

'It's a turtle,' I explained.

The fireman gave the jaded shrug of one who has rescued a thousand cats from a thousand trees, and strode back to the fire engine. He had good karma to spare.

After various tests and checks at the hospital, we were allowed back into the charred, sodden remains of our flat. The

Steppenwolf's bed had gone up, and my magazines were cindered. Curious, how the objects around you can anchor you. I supposed that was why Max was so sold on materialism – it was the comfort of an external definition, a set of signposts to replace the water-cooler chats that most people used to throw their personalities out into the world. It was a bit like being James Bond, who never got much opportunity to cultivate long-term friendship, and tried to say it all with his watch. The most fashion-conscious places were always the ones where people made fleeting connections. Perhaps that was why people in this city were obsessed with 'vintage' – it gave a sense of continuity to balance out the relentless novelty of city life.

I looked around the blackened floor of the kitchen cum living room, rubbing the Steppenwolf on his back, consoling him as if he were a baby that needed to be burped. He was sitting bent over, cradling his turtle, his eyes red with exhaustion, drink, smoke and weeping. He looked like John Hurt in that film I can never remember the name of.

'So what brought all this on?' I said in a tone which, I was not unaware, sounded like my mother.

'My life's work is ruined,' sniffed the Steppenwolf.

'No it isn't.'

'It is. I burned the manuscript. Every draft.'

'But you have it backed up?'

'I have nothing.'

'You didn't email it to yourself? Or burn a CD?'

The Steppenwolf shook his head and patted Archimedes. He looked like he, too, wanted to recede into a protective shell and wait for the world to behave better. I resisted an urge to mention cloud storage.

'You didn't do it on purpose though?'

'Of course I did! The drafts were secreted in a thousand places! I had to find them first, which took me three hours, then get all the vignettes into one pile. It is said that manuscripts don't burn, but I knew how.' He shuddered. 'I knew how.'[64]

Fortunately, the fish oil had helped to create the thick black smoke that had alerted a neighbour to the fire, so the flat wasn't as badly damaged as it could have been. The fireman had told me, before leaving, that they had initially assumed the fire was ten times as big as it really was. No smoke without fire, but you can get a lot of smoke from a little fire.

'But I don't understand. Why did you burn your book? It was your masterpiece.'

'I was beaten.' He got up with effort and took a book from inside a shopping bag on the counter. He showed it to me. *The Philosopher and the Wolf*. 'This man has written my book.'

I examined the front and back covers. There was a horseshoe of teeth marks about a quarter of the way down, and a few of the pages were crumpled where he had obviously tried and failed to tear the book in two. It seemed to be about a lecturer who had bought a wolf as a pet, and had learned life lessons, become happier, etc.

'But there are loads of guides to life. Yours is completely different.'

'Mine was laid out in geometrical reasoning, but this is the essence.'[65]

'But yours was massive. I saw the manuscript. It was a foot tall.'

'But the best books are a little short. I aimed to condense and distil.'

---

64 DW: Fire is incredibly useful in the Bible, and turns up in all sorts of places: it is a warning; a punishment; a means of purification; fire is God Himself. Just as glass reigns over this volume, one might almost call the Bible *Fire*.

65 DW: Spinoza was one of the first to write all his philosophy using logic (or 'geometric reasoning'), so one couldn't disagree with his conclusions unless one disagreed with his starting point. He was persecuted for preaching tolerance, and was killed by the dust from his day job grinding lenses to help others see clearly.

I sighed. 'How many years were you working on that book?'

He growled and bared his yellow teeth at me.

'How many?' I asked again.

'Thirty-two, not including my extended fellowship at All Souls.'

That was longer than I'd been alive. It was a bit of a loss, I had to say.

'And how old are you now?' I asked.

'Sixty-one this year.'

'Well, most people live till say eighty, so you've got time to write something new. But a little bit shorter.'

He growled a little. 'That is perfectly logical. You rascal.'

'Or you could try and remember what you wrote,' pitched in my dad, 'and if you don't remember it, it can't have been that important.'

The Steppenwolf frowned in the way that people sometimes do when they are delighted, but have so recently been upset that they don't feel they can authentically smile.

'Perhaps I could write a book of aphorisms,' he said with a gleam.

Dad signed, *what's an A-F-O-R-I-Z-M?*

I replied, *no idea.*

The Steppenwolf signed, *it is an idea made into a simple, elegant sentence. Why are we signing?*

We all stayed in after that, talking. There was no alcohol in the flat and my dad didn't go to get any. The late sun gave the asphalt an orange cast, and later still, the tables turned and the city threw its own amber glow at the night, the dark windows of houses mirrored like a lake. I went to my room tired, but pleased to have my father close to me. I hadn't realised how much I missed him until he'd been gone and returned. I wondered if Max would ever come and visit. It seemed unlikely. How would I entertain him? How could I even guarantee that I wouldn't pick a fight? Maybe I was as bad a brother to him as he was to me. Or worse. What if I was worse?[66]

I tried Lieve's number but she didn't answer. I waited a minute, called again and she'd turned it off.

Perhaps I should quit London, go back to Salisbury and leave all this behind. I wouldn't have any money, so I'd have to move back – well, I couldn't move back home, because it wasn't there any more. Or rather, the house was still there, but they'd probably torn off my mum's carefully selected wallpapers and pulled up the carpets to install generic fake-wooden laminate floors. I wondered what would have happened to all my old stuff. I hadn't particularly wanted it, but it had been nice to know it was there. I had some spare pants there, and a Filofax, and a cassette tape of 'Brimful of Asha'. Surely they wouldn't dare auction off my pants?[67]

I had no useful email. One offered me an online loan at 2689% APR, but I declined. Another offered me Viagra, but if anything my extreme sexual prowess was partly to blame for my situation.

The best thing I could do would be to start on the Shard, to pull myself up and out of it all. For a little while, at least, I could be a part of the sky, caught between sun and wind and glass, and leave all the clutter beneath me. Perhaps it was vanity, but I had to go, because I felt that it might be one of the most important experiences in my life; because we had rebuilt Babel, and it hadn't fallen down, and now I wanted to climb it;

66 DW: It is no surprise that the biblical injunction to love thy neighbour takes priority over brotherly love. The kind of love expressed by most biblical siblings hardly acts as an exemplar.

67 DW: Bailiffs aren't generally allowed to take your clothing, bedding, work vehicle or anything belonging to your child, so the best thing to do if you're going bankrupt is to buy a nice car and expensive jewellery for your child.

because I wanted to scrape the sky. People always talked about Manhattan, but if I ever worked there, I would be cleaning with high-rises all around me. The Shard, on the other hand, was brutal and unworldly, sticking out of the ground like a vast pike levelled at God Himself, nothing to touch it in any direction. Not a skyscraper in a sea of skyscrapers, but a stark monolith jutting out beyond the ken of other mortals. An endless field of glass, impossible to read, smooth, hard and cold.

I laid out my clothes and equipment on the floor like a fully dressed person, and it looked like a deflated version of myself. I looked around my bare room. It didn't feel like a home. Not yet, at least. The only place that really felt like home, like a shell, was a house that I couldn't go back to. There was nothing left in the real world that corresponded to my memory of the place. The memory was all I had. A signpost for a lost city. A photo of someone I had loved. I hoped I might find somewhere, one day, that felt like home again. I got under the covers and switched off my sidelight. Lieve's house had a big master bedroom, and a nursery all set up. I was already half asleep, and beginning to dream uneasily that Lieve was shoving my head into the tiny bin in her bathroom, and using her foot to slam the lid over and over and over and over . . .

18

The Shard[68]

I rose in the dark and dressed to tentative birdsong. I felt naughty again, like a milkman, catching out my tiredness and pouncing on it before it could overpower me and drag me back down into the bowels of sleep.

As I approached the Shard, Blades smiled broadly, showing off those pure white canines of his. If I wanted teeth like that, I'd have to lay off the sugar. Waffles . . . Well, I supposed they'd have to go.

We shook hands and looked up. There it was, a ladder to the fading stars, glass and steel tapering out like a long bridge into an indistinct horizon. A veritable palace of glass. The surfaces were smoother and flatter than anything conjured by nature. I could break any of its windows with my insignificant little hand, and yet it stood over us, over everything. It seemed to me that the fragility of the tower was built into its beauty, its perfection held ransom by the whim of an imperfect world. It was a pyramid to dwarf the pyramids, but it was not made of stone; it would not weather over time, rounding or crumbling off, acquiring dunes

68 DW: The London Bridge Tower, as it was called during its planning, was dismissed by Prince Charles as 'an enormous salt cellar' and outright condemned by English Heritage as a 'shard of glass through the heart of historic London'. Unfortunately for them, that turned out to be a very arresting image, and the Mace group co-opted the name long before its completion.

along its base. It would stand perfect, or it would fall utterly.

'Come on,' Blades said. 'The others are up at the top.'

My ears popped in the lift.

'It's going to take us a while, even with a full team, but this is the last touch before inauguration. There's going to be a huge press call for the prime minister of Qatar and Prince Andrew, so we need to look dashing.' He flashed me a PR smile. 'This is the biggest building in Europe. Look.'

The lift doors opened and I felt a current run through me. The roots of my hair buzzed. I had almost reached the peak of a building so high that I wouldn't be able to see the people below me. It was two and a half times taller than Salisbury Cathedral, and that was so high that the wind had nearly carried me off. This time, I was so high I felt I could have jumped and floated off into space. Our view was limited only by the curvature of the Earth. Dawn was breaking – at least, it was from up here – and I could see London spread out before me like a felled, titanic hermaphrodite: the giant Eye; the nurturing breast of St Paul's; the Gherkin, phallus of the City. The Olympic Village was there somewhere, too, barely completed and already scheduled for demolition.[69] I didn't see Big Ben. It was part of an old Britain that had long been superseded. The clock wasn't even considered accurate any more, and the tower was listing. Once, people would have stared at its gothic heights and been impressed at the empire that could have built such a thing. But really it was just sad. Ben was getting old, too, like everything. You could once have set your watch by him, and now he had to have his own pacemakers. And yet, to be old was still to be alive. Every time the fireworks threw pink shadows on his elaborate cornices and curlicues, and his bell chimed twelve, Ben had cheated the

---

69 DW: This was true at the time, of course. You, dear reader, know that the stadium still stands, proud and empty.

natural course of things for another year.

We arrived at what I thought of as 'base camp' and I looked around the room. Pete was there, and the blond man from the football, along with about twenty others, all white men in their late twenties or thirties. Everyone was covering their nervousness by shifting from leg to leg and cracking jokes, though the atmosphere felt tense as I breathed it in. I felt like I needed a tank of oxygen to breathe. Here, there were unknown quantities. Blades stood in the middle of the room and clapped his hands like a motivational speaker.

'Okay everyone, listen up. Most of you know the drill – this is the builders' clean, we've got to make it look pretty before the launch. But I have some bad news and some good news. Bad news is, today will be one of the pinnacles of your professional life. You will, likely as not, never get given an opportunity like this again. You'll go back to cleaning the outsides of crappy office buildings and houses and no one will even notice that you were there.

'The good news is, I'm warning you in advance. We have thousands of square feet of glass to clean, and if we have to, we'll be back again tomorrow, and the next day, and the day after that until it's done. There isn't any heavy wind or rain forecast between now and the opening of the building, so how we make it look is how it's going to end up looking in all the photographs from now until forever.' He winked at me. 'This is your chance to make us look good. Those of you who have been with me for over three years will receive a camera so that you can take photos and video while you're up here, and I'll pair you each off with a newbie.' Someone passed round a few cameras. The men started filming each other and mimed flashing their body parts. The cameras looked unnecessarily bulky, considering that we were going to be lugging them round the outside of the building. Someone fumbled one, and all of the other old hands flinched as he juggled it between his clumsy palms. Blades screamed, 'Don't drop it!' a little louder than was necessary and it plunged floorwards until, with one last desperate swipe, the dropper grabbed at it and saved it from smashing into pieces.

'What are you doing?' shouted Blades. 'This is no time for pissing around.' The other old hands holding cameras looked angry, too. Maybe even a little shaky. Perhaps the cameras were really expensive. They didn't look it.

'Okay, let's zone back in,' he said, clapping his hands again. 'Newbies: don't worry. I wouldn't have picked you if I didn't think you had a safe pair of hands.' He glared at the man who had nearly dropped the camera. 'And we're not heading verti-cally downwards: it'll be more like eighty-six degrees.'

There was some nervous chuckling around the room.

'Now I need you all to sign a release.' The blond man who had passed the cameras around now passed round some sheets.

The release was one side of A4, with one long paragraph mitigating Blades PLC against any accident or injury that might occur in the line of duty, up to but not limited to loss of limb, paralysis, trauma and death. I signed it and filled in the sheet up to the bottom, where there were various tick boxes for ethnic category.

NORTHWOODS: 30/06/12 – 04/07/12

- ☐ British
- ☐ Other Aryan
- ☐ Black (inc. 'African-American')
- ☐ Jew / Jewess
- ☐ Indian (inc. Pakistani)
- ☐ Other Asian
- ☐ Other (please specify) _____

I ticked 'Other' and wrote 'German-Welsh with a British passport.' If I could slip one of these in my pocket, I could definitely build some kind of legal case. The blond man came round and collected them all, snatching mine from me before I could complete the thought.

'You'll now be handed a spray with a karabiner which you need to attach to your belt in case it falls. It's a new fluid we've developed in the lab especially for this building. Titanium dioxide in this one,' said Blades. 'It's hydrophilic so it washes itself. Then we've got another bottle for the inside, to regulate the heat passing in and out.'

'Sounds like hairy bollocks to me,' said Pete.

'Why don't I explain a little more simply. Once we're done with the windows, they're going to look nice and clean and shiny. So keep the bottles safe.' Blades gave Pete his biggest, smarmiest grin.

Next we all put on our regulation gear (I was still wearing my sidekick holster, naturally) and stood together in a circle, singing the national anthem. We were given little sheets to sing from because Blades was adamant that we sing all five verses. I had to bite my lip, though no one else seemed to find it funny. One moment we were singing about everyone in the world being brothers, and the next we were singing about scattering our enemies.

I sidled over to Pete and asked if he wanted to form a pair.

'Sorry guys,' cut in Blades. 'Can't have two from the dominions pairing off; you might try and revolt. Pete, you go with Albie. Glass, you're with me.'

Each pair was given zones or echelons, each echelon covering the same surface area, but since the building was thinnest at the top, these zones were longer, and the zones near the bottom were short and wide. Blades and I were at the very top, not because it was harder – if anything, it was easier, as we didn't have much horizontal ground to cover – but because Blades was the boss and we were going to record the whole event. It suited his ego to place himself above the others, and for my part I was thrilled to be at the summit. Once we had clipped ourselves onto the cradle and climbed out into the cold morning air for our first drop, I caught my breath. The sun had risen high enough to fling shadows across the ground, and the Thames glowed orange, like a lava flow. To my west, I could see the shadow of our building draped across the plaza, other offices, roads, parked cars. My shadow was thousands of feet away, and I was here, perched on a taciturn sundial. In the sunlight, in the air.

'So Günter,' said Blades. I turned and he was holding the camera to my face. 'How does it feel to be a thousand feet up?'

I smiled. 'It feels good. It feels really good.'

Blades panned across to show the whole view as it spread itself out before us in every direction.

'Just being up here makes you feel successful,' he whispered to the camera. 'I feel like a god, and down there' – here I followed the camera downwards and felt a dizzying rush of vertigo – 'that's where all the little office workers do their little jobs. Look at them, running about like ants.'

From on high, it all looked utterly insignificant. Blades put his thumb and forefinger in front of the viewfinder and squashed one. I just managed to pick out Frank's car, but had a sudden urge to sit on the floor of the cradle, to cling to it with my hands. A horrible feeling was spreading across the back of my skull and my testicles lurched up into my body. I tried to breathe. My palms began to sweat. Blades was still smiling and muttering sweet nothings to the camera as he turned and I felt a wave of nausea when I realised that he wasn't clipped on. I was stuck up here on a platform six inches thick with a psychopath and not even the birds could hear me scream.

I had to master myself. I looked at the very tip of the building, and then at the horizon. They were my anchors. It was all a matter of perspective. I tugged on my safety rope for assurance, and it took the strain. I tried not to think about whether I did, in fact, weigh more than a hundred kilos. Below me, I could see an endless field of clear blue glass, glistening like a Mediterranean sea, and I let it calm me. Little windows of simplicity, multiplied along a grid so that each was as the others, following a pattern, knowable always. I looked across at Blades and realised he had been filming me.

'Takes your breath away, doesn't it?' he said, showing a bit of canine. His teeth were a little too white. I wondered if he'd had them whitened. Was there such a thing as artificial purity?

It was beginning to dawn on me quite how big the job was. We'd get it done in a couple of days, because there were so many of us, but there were tens of thousands of square feet to cover.

'How many windows are there?'

'Eleven thousand,' Blades said. 'Here.' He handed me the camera. 'Film this.' Then he grinned, got up onto the safety barrier at the side of the cradle, swung his legs over and sat on the edge holding a metal cable with one hand. He pulled out a sandwich, dangling his legs over the edge. 'You know what they used to call the guys who clean skyscrapers?' he asked the camera. 'Sparrows. We're city birds, and we don't mind being perched up high. Lovely morning for it, eh?' He took a bite and chewed smugly. He always sounded a little bit mockney when there was a camera pointed at him.

'Will you just clip yourself on, please?' I snapped, closing the camera. It was bloody heavy. I thought cameras were supposed to be light these days.

Eventually we had to actually get the windows clean, so

we got out the cleaning sprays and the new lab spray and set
to work.

'So Günter, you speak German?'

'Nope.'

'Great shame, great shame. Beautiful language. I know some
people can't get on with all the Krüppels and Fidschis but it's a
good, solid language. Has a lot in common with English actually, more than you'd think. You know, Hitler was actually quite
fond of the English.'

I gritted my teeth and carried on squeegeeing, trying to main-
tain my concentration. Find the corners. Top left, right, down,
left, down, bottom right, flick. Wax on, wax off.

'Your dad's era was made to feel guilty,' he continued. 'Not
that they had anything to be sorry about. That was part of
putting them down the second time, people were afraid to identify with the losers. Afraid to be patriots. It's the same thing you
get over here, red-blooded Englishmen running scared, afraid to
say anything in case the PC brigade have them thrown in jail.
You know what the two of us have in common?' he said, looking
sidelong at me.

'I honestly have no idea.'

'We're afraid of our own flag. No one wants to see it. But the
thing is, you Germans had a chance at national unity and you
blew it. Now England needs a shot, I reckon. We've got to band
together, send the foreigners all a message. It's all a question of
finding the right moment, and making an event happen, something that will unite the nation. You know, the 9/11 attacks were
a tragedy, but there's nothing like feeling vulnerable to make a
people unite. Can't help feeling we'd benefit from a bit of Blitz
spirit.'

I felt another wave of dizziness.

'Sometimes,' he continued, putting down his squeegee and
levelling the spray at me like a gun, 'I wonder if a bit of direct

action might be in order. I mean, after 9/11, they had every reason they would ever need. They had carte blanche to really fuck the Arabs.' Still pointing the spray at me, he closed one eye like a sharpshooter and quickly spun to face the window, the momentum causing the cradle to shudder. And then he seemed to snap out of it, sprayed evenly and methodically, working his way down the pane. We fell silent.

At the end of the day, my arms and legs were shaking with the long effort of soaping and wiping. The activity might look Zen, but try doing it without touching any of the glass with your hands, spraying and subsequently wiping the whole pane in under eight seconds so that the fluid doesn't dry and stain, and then repeating it a hundred times with your crazy boss watching you.

I unlocked the second front door to find Dad in the kitchen frying three big steaks in beer. He seemed positively energetic compared to the last time I'd seen him. Maybe it was all that sleep. And, notably, he was cooking. At least there was nothing flammable left in the flat.

'All right, Dad?' I asked.

'All right, son. The worker returns,' he chuckled.

'You're a bit drunk, aren't you?'

'Oh, lay off, will you. I've only had a couple of beers. I had to open one for the steaks.'

'They look good. What's it going with?'

'I dunno. We've got some bread in the cupboard, steak sandwich?'

The bread was mouldy.

'That's okay, I'll have it on its own.'

'We've got some ketchup in the fridge.'

'Ketchup doesn't need to be kept in the fridge.'

I wanted to give him a hug, but he'd only burn himself on the pan. Best wait until he was done. He was wearing boxer shorts and I noticed a great purple welt all over the outside of his knee. My coccyx flipped.

'How'd you get that?'

'Oh, it's just a graze.' He didn't seem too bothered, though it looked painful.

'You should have it looked at,' I said.

'Oh, leave off,' he replied.

Let thorns be thorns, I thought absent-mindedly. Stood next to him now, I could see his cheeks sagging like a bloodhound's, a stoop shaping him like an old lamppost, the light at the top friendly but dimming. His remaining hair wisped up like a dust devil at the top of his head. Old age was catching up with him: a tragedy without a hero.

'Glass the Younger returns!' cried the Steppenwolf, stepping through from his room. 'Come, we have much to celebrate.'

He poured me a whisky, which I took reluctantly. As I took a sip, I could feel it killing my cells, poisoning me, corrupting. I looked at how it had ravaged my dad. His skin hung from him like clothes on a washing line, draped as if it might slip to the ground in a stiff wind. Still, the whisky was calming my nerves.

A few minutes later, we sat together round the paint-stricken kitchen table, steaks on plates, all medium rare with a little frozen bit in the middle, which the Steppenwolf and I ate round, but which Dad didn't seem to notice.

'Dad?'

'Yes, son.'

'You know when you were clearing out the back garden, when I was a kid, and I knocked all the thorns off the rose bushes so you wouldn't hurt yourself?'

'What?'

'You remember. In the summer. Mum was sunbathing and you cut your hand and I spent hours knocking all the other thorns off with a hammer to make the branches safe. And Mum said sometimes you have to let thorns be thorns.'

Dad shrugged. 'No idea.'

'Oh.' I had always thought of it as an important chapter in our family history. It had never occurred to me that it could be otherwise.

'She was probably just saying that so you wouldn't cry,' Dad said. 'You were very sensitive, you know? Everything had to have a reason. You wouldn't watch films where bad things happened. Your mum would always sit there covering your eyes and ears. I said to her, It's the world we live in, it's not like he's never going to find out.' He wiped at an eye with the ball of his thumb.

Oh. That's all I could think. Oh. Now that he put it like that. Because . . . If you really believed the world could be a better place, and you could make it so, you wouldn't just let thorns be thorns. You would only be afraid to go near them if you secretly believed in their power to hurt you. If your decisions were hemmed in by that belief. If the best you could hope for in life was to keep the boat from rocking. *Oh.*

'I have started the first of my new projects,' said the Steppenwolf, failing to recognise my seldom worn *utterly crushed* face. 'Enough with the days of contact. My job now is to be in contact always. First I will write a polemical defence of feminism. Then I shall embark on my great opus, a work on mass psychology. It will explain why we are all automata, and why we are doomed to act as if we were not. I am also working on a book of aphorisms. Listen to this.'

Dad seemed grateful for the interruption. We had picked at the scab, and now he wanted to stick it back on. The Steppenwolf took out a leather notebook which looked like it had survived both world wars, and opened it at a random page. 'War is an autoimmune disease, and we shall destroy our host through misplaced efficiency.'

'That's why I like you,' said my dad. 'You're a mad bastard and you don't care who knows it.'

'I feel so liberated by truths, and it was you, Günter, who did it. Nothing is on solid ground. Truth is context. Glass is neither solid nor liquid. Neither and both.'

'If you can knock someone out with it, it's a solid,' said Dad, punctuating his own aphorism with a frothy burp.

'I am always right because I am always writing only with what knowledge I possess, and I do not intentionally tell untruths. Only liars are wrong.'

'Well, you can't always be right . . .' I began.

'Yes! We are all right! Facts do not exist, only interpretations.'

'That wasn't really what I was—'

'Yes! It was what you were saying, only you didn't know it. I have thought on this for a long time. All truth is relative. Apart from that last sentence. Which is. Ah . . .'

He paused, perplexed. He got up, walked over to the charred remains of the bookcase and trailed his fingers along the crumbling spines.

'We've lost him,' said Dad.

'He sometimes does this,' I explained.

'Oh, by the way, I had an email from Max today about—'

'I didn't know you had an email address,' I said.

'Well, Max likes to send me website links every now and then. Oh, don't look at me like that. You never asked, Günter.'

Dad slouched up – being the only man I know who can slouch in any direction – and got out my laptop.

'What could Max possibly have sent you that's of interest? You never do anything except sleep and get pissed.'

'The bloody cheek!'

Furious, he took a swing at me. He had grown old, but I had grown fat, so I couldn't avoid the blow, but it didn't hurt, either. His bony fist was simply quilted by my face.

'There's more where that came from. Bloody nerve.'

Then he picked up the dregs of the bottle of whisky and his phone and stumbled out.

The front doors slammed and the Steppenwolf awoke from his reverie.

'I have reached a logical cul-de-sac.'

I was standing, holding my cheek, my whisky glass knocked to the floor. My dad had never hit me, not even when I was a child.

'Where is your father?' he asked.

'Gone.'

'Where?'

'I don't know.'

'And you are not accompanying him?'

I thought about this. 'No . . .' I said eventually. 'I think I'm going to stay here.'

We sat down side by side, and I picked up my laptop. I thought I might check whether Blades had uploaded any of the day's footage. I typed in 'Northwoods'. First result was Northwoods Property. Just below it was a Wikipedia article: *Operation Northwoods*. The preview contained the words 'false flag'. Oh dear. I clicked.

It was a declassified CIA plan from 1962, to hijack planes, crash them into a US landmark and blame it on Cuba, so that they could start a war on the basis of a credible threat. Luckily, JFK told them they were nuts, and vetoed the plans, and everything was fine again. Not for him, obviously.

'You look worried,' said the Steppenwolf.

'Yes . . . I think my boss might be trying to blow up the Shard.'

The Steppenwolf bared his yellow teeth, and shook his head sadly.

'To build an edifice is human: it is difficult, it takes thought and care. To tear it down again is easy: childish, godlike. The power will always be in the hands of those who refuse to create, those who scatter us across the earth.'[70]

I was used to the Steppenwolf shouting. What I did not like was the eerie calm that had descended on him now. It was a kind of beatific resignation.

'Do you want to come with me tomorrow? Help stop him?'

But he just shook his head. 'It has been too long.'

'You'll have to go outside some time. You know that.'

'No.'

'Maybe I can find someone who you can talk to about your agoraphobia. Figure out how things got like this? I think it would be good for you.'

The Steppenwolf put his hand lightly on my shoulder. 'Günter. It is thoughtful. I know some people like to draw from their wells very often and keep the water fresh. But I prefer to

---

70 DW: Genesis 11: 4–9 gives us a troubling insight into God's possible motivations. Though the conventional reading of this passage interprets man's tower-building as an act of hubris, we see in the text that God destroys the tower for the same reason that he confounds our language: a united mankind is capable of achieving anything it can imagine. He seems almost to feel threatened by our collective potential.

'And they said, Go to, let us build us a city and a tower, whose top may reach unto heaven; and let us make us a name, lest we be scattered abroad upon the face of the whole earth. And the Lord came down to see the city and the tower, which the children of men builded. And the Lord said, Behold, the people is one, and they have all one language; and this they begin to do: and now nothing will be restrained from them, which they have imagined to do. Go to, let us go down, and there confound their language, that they may not understand one another's speech. So the Lord scattered them abroad from thence upon the face of all the earth: and they left off to build the city. Therefore is the name of it called Babel; because the LORD did there confound the language of all the earth: and from thence did the LORD scatter them abroad upon the face of all the earth.'

throw in rubble. I am hoping that, if I wait long enough, I may strike oil.'

Dad trudged in penitently later that night, and we apologised to each other. 'Do you want the good news first, or the bad news?' he asked.

'Bad first,' I said. Better to sugar a pill than ruin a perfectly good sweet.

'Well, the bailiffs have already sold some of our things, your mum's included.' I put my hand on his shoulder and led him over to the sofa. 'Max went down to sort things out with them and it seems they've been a bit overeager.'

'Right. Dare I ask what the good news is? Let me guess. Max happened to be going to the foreclosure auction anyway?'

'Well, there were certain things they couldn't sell, and in among your stamps and keyrings and all that useless junk were our life insurance certificates.'

'I didn't know I had life insurance.'

'Neither did I. It seems that your mother must have set them up for us, God rest her soul. It's not a nice way to get hold of it, not a nice way at all, but it turns out we've come into a lot of money. We can hopefully get the house back eventually . . . and, uh . . .' He looked back at the door nervously. 'Well, good news. So I'd probably better . . .'

'Where are you going at this time of night?'

'Max is waiting in the car. He was going to take me back to Salisbury. Didn't want me to tell you he was here.'

'What? Max is outside? Oh, for goodness sake. Tell him to come in and stop being such a child.'

Dad looked down.

'You are both my sons, Günter. Which, incidentally, means you are brothers. It wouldn't kill either of you to act like it every now and then. I'm not saying he can't be a bit of a nob sometimes, but let's be honest, so can you. You need to cut each other some slack, because one day I'm not going to be around and I don't want the two of you to end up communicating solely through the small claims court. Now,' he risked a sidelong glance at me. 'If I bring him up, I don't want any squabbling. I will ask him not to act like a bloody lout, and I am asking you now not to be . . .' He tilted his head in lieu of a sensitive wording.

'What?' I said. 'What did I do?'

'Just . . . Tone down that whole eco-warrior, know-it-all, lord-on-high thing you do.' He went down to get Max and I heard nothing at all while they argued. Then car doors, and two sets of footsteps. The Steppenwolf raised his eyebrows at me. I supposed this was probably a house-party, by his standards.

Dad and Max were installed on the sofa, and I sat on an empty crate.

Tea? I signed (in the universal language: miming the act of tipping a cup all over my front). Max sighed.

I don't expect an apology, he signed.

What for? I asked.

For anything.

I haven't done anything, I protested.

That's why I don't ever expect an apology. I think you honestly don't believe you've ever done anything wrong, ever. You know, puppies only remember their behaviour for about three seconds, so you can't punish them when you come home and find out they've shat all over the house. They won't make any link at all, they'll just get upset. That's basically you.

I looked at Dad, but he hadn't been keeping up.

I'm an incontinent puppy? I signed.

See, even now you're getting upset. You're just not very good at taking criticism on board, and that's okay. He gave me his Counsellor Max smile and held my hands. He might have meant it in a comforting way, but it felt more like he'd put his hand over my mouth. No response required. He broke away.

I took care of everything with the house. I looked through all the paperwork trying to find something that we might have missed and I found the life insurance certificates. They were difficult at first, asking why we didn't claim straight away, but I'm sorting it out, and I've made sure that no more of our stuff will be auctioned off until we can clear the debt and get things back to normal.

He held his hands palm out. This was his magician's punchline.

Okay, I signed. *Glad that it's cleared up.* His eyes went wide. *What?* I asked. *Do you want a round of applause? What else am I supposed to say?*

First he started trembling, then he jumped up and drummed on my chest with the blade of his fists as if he were a wind-blown traveller beating upon the door of a forbidding castle.

Just once in your whole life, I wish you would say, well done, you did the right thing. No, not that. That's not the problem. I wish that you would pay me your full attention. I can't just swan around meeting people everywhere I go, no one ever speaks sign so I have to vocalise and they look at me as if I'm diseased. There were three people in the whole world that I cared about, and now there are only two. One of them is always asleep, and the other one will only deign to look at me if I challenge him to a battle of wits, or if I tell him something interesting. Do you know how exhausting it is to have to try and be interesting all the time, just to hold your attention?

I didn't say anything for a little while. Mostly because I was surprised. It hadn't even occurred to me that our fights had had an emotional impact on Max.

Say you're sorry, signed Max. *It will be good for you.*

I lifted my hands.

Sorry, I signed.

Good.

I am, I signed.

Good.

Thank you for finding out what was going on. You are a good brother, I signed. *I'm glad to have you as my family.*

You wouldn't be saying that if Mum was still alive, Max replied, *so don't start now.*

I got up, nodded. *It's late.*

I should go, he signed, standing.

I didn't mean that. Stay, I signed. *Please. We can talk more tomorrow.*

I got Max a blanket for the sofa and said goodnight to the Steppenwolf, who had been regaling Dad with the colourful history of the urinal in the corner of the room.

As I undressed and brushed my teeth, I tried to picture what my life would be like if my mother had lived. Dad would be sober. I might never have visited the Cathedral. Perhaps I wouldn't have met Dean Winterbottom, Blades, or the Steppenwolf, or Lieve. I wouldn't be approaching fatherhood, or climbing the tallest building in the country. I would be a different person. Happier, perhaps. Or perhaps just different.

But the world had fallen together in this way, as it was bound to do, because the gradual unfolding of our selves over time was a condition of our existence. I had to be here, now. I had to go back to the Shard in just a few hours and look for ways to stop Blades, just as Blades had to do what he could to convince the world that foreigners were plotting against us. Lieve had to try and have her baby, just as I had to feel that she had broken my trust. But if Blades blew up the Shard tomorrow, with us on it, I'd never see her again. I looked at my watch. 10 p.m. I was due to be picked up at 6 a.m. If I cycled to Lieve's house I could still get a few hours' sleep. I siphoned off some of the GOMORRAH into a smaller spray bottle and slotted it into the sidekick holster, the escaped fumes as corrosive as a thousand onions. When I could see again, I picked up the grappling hook and the titanium scraper, which could serve as a blunt instrument if things got hairy. Tomorrow was going to be a big day.

19

Absent Without Lieve

I cycled as fast as I could to Lieve's house. My thighs felt like
they were disintegrating with heat. I cycled and cycled for what
seemed like an age, switching down gears until I didn't feel I was
travelling any faster than if I had walked. It felt as though I was
cycling uphill, though London was flat. Really, no more waffles.
I'd have to find a healthier source of energy in the mornings.
Cheese on toast or something.

I parked my bike and fumbled around in the dark with the
chain lock, which rattled in protest. I was panting and clammy
with sweat. More than clammy, in fact – I was sopping, my
T-shirt several shades darker than when I had left. I stood by
Lieve's door trying to catch my breath, hands on hips like a folk
dancer, and heard the rustle of key in lock. Lieve appeared, tow-
ering over the threshold, wearing her silk gown. She didn't seem
especially pleased to see me.

'Did you predict my arrival?' I panted.

'Go away,' she said.

'No,' I replied.

'What are you doing here?' she asked.

'I was just locking my—'

'At my house?'

'I need to talk to you,' I said.

'No, Günter, I can't have this. Do you even know what time

it is? I need to sleep, and so does the baby.'

She made to close the door but I put my hand against the cool frosted glass. She was a powerful woman and could make sure it shut if she really wanted.

'Please. Let me inside. It's cold out here and I'm all sweaty.'

'You always know the right thing to say,' she sneered and backed off down the hallway.

I followed and she threw me a towel before clicking the kettle on.

'I have something important to tell you.'

'So important that you had to keep me up in the middle of the night?'

'Yes.'

She glanced over, dropping her guard, poured out mint tea and came to sit with me.

'What?' she asked.

'I wanted to talk to you about the baby issue, tonight, in case . . . In case . . .'

'I don't think this baby is an issue,' she said authoritatively.

'Well they always say the first step is denial.'

She put her hand on my cheek and kissed me. 'When you see its little face, you'll change your mind.'

'I'm not saying I hate babies' faces. Of course it'll look loveable. And I think I might be a really good dad, one day. But I don't think I'm going to be a very good dad in eight months' time.'

'Then you don't have to be involved.'

'What kind of a person would I be if I didn't want to be involved?'

She hugged me tightly. 'I knew you'd change your mind.'

'No!' I said, wriggling free. 'I haven't changed my mind. I still don't think it's a good idea for us to have a baby now. Why didn't you ask me?'

'But you'll be there for it.'

'If you decide to have this baby, I can't turn my back on it, because a child needs love and stability, but I'd rather we weren't having one right now, which doesn't mean I wouldn't love it. I'm not saying you can't be a single mother because there are lots of good single mothers but if you want the best for the kid then it's preferable for it to have a mum and a dad. It's not about just having a child to have one, it's about having a child that feels loved and grows up happy. What if it grows up miserable and weird because I'm such a bad father?'

I thought I'd come off sounding quite reasonable, but rather than appreciating the soundness of my argument, she started to cry.

'You don't want to have a baby with me. You don't want me to be the mother of your child.'

'I think you'd be a brilliant mother,' I cooed. 'It's just the situation. I'm not ready.'

'I thought you'd come round, if I just waited. I thought you might actually want to have a baby with me. Here I am in this big, dusty house; half the rooms I don't even use, and you're still sleeping on the floor in some horrid shag pad—'

'It's really not a shag pad.'

'—and I thought that you might eventually want to move in, maybe not now but soon, and we'd have a baby, and my life might be back on track again. But no, I'll just kill it then, shall I?'

'Well, it's not alive yet but . . .' I let the end of the sentence trail along, like wind under a falling leaf. 'I suppose it just worries me a little that this might not be about us. That I might just be interchangeable. You want a family, but not necessarily with me. I just happened to come along. Should we really have a baby together just because our meeting was neatly timed?'

She wiped a forearm across her face like a builder on a hot day and her cheek shined with smudged tears. Her mouth hung slightly open and I could see the tip of her tongue. Something stirred in my trousers and I silently chided myself for losing focus. We were having a proper talk. We never had a proper talk. It was very important that I did not think about sex. Lovely, lovely sex.

'So you really believe that love is unique?' she asked me. 'Doesn't it seem odd to you that, all through history, people have been fucking whoever is next to them, falling in love in tiny villages where they don't meet anyone new? People just see who's around them and pick. If two people get stuck on a desert island they still pair off. I mean, for fuck's sake, you stick a load of men in prison together, even they pair off. What were you waiting for? This is what happens, Günter. You don't know how you're going to find someone, and then someone comes along, and if you're sensible you make the best of it.'

I sat sullen.

'Not very romantic,' I mumbled.

'No, Günter, it's not. Maybe it's different for you with your big ideas but life isn't very romantic for me. To be perfectly honest it's pretty laughable, what I've had to put up with. Everyone starts off believing in fairytale love. And you get over it, too.'

I tried not to sulk. 'Can I put my hand on your stomach?' I heard myself say.

'What?'

'Can I, um? Feel your stomach?'

'Why?' she asked.

'I don't know.'

She softened a little. 'Fine.'

She undid her dressing gown. Her breasts had grown even bigger, and through her sturdy frame, I could see the beginnings of a swelling just above her pelvis. Perhaps I was imagining it. I reached out and tentatively put my fingers on her.

'Cold hands,' she said.

'Well, I've been cycling.'

'You have poor circulation. You need to do more exercise.'

I didn't know why I was doing this. I knew I didn't want to have a baby, not any time soon. I suspected that I was acting out of morbid curiosity, or masochism. I had seen fatherhood. It made people grumpy and boring and exhausted.

'What is that?' asked Lieve, sitting up.

'It's a grappling hook.'

'What possible use could you have for a grappling hook?' she asked.

'Well, it . . . I don't know. For climbing things.'

'Were you going to break in?'

'Oh no – don't worry, nothing like that. No, it's just that I think your ex-husband is going to try to blow up the Shard tomorrow.'

'What?'

'I think he's going to try—'

'What in God's name makes you think that?'

'Well, the racism was my first clue. He keeps talking about fascism.'

'He reads a lot of history.'

'Exactly. On his white board upstairs there are all these references to secret right-wing societies like the Cagoule—'

'That's my white board,' she said.

'I don't understand.'

'A year or two ago I helped some American academics solve the murder of my grandmother, Laetitia Toureaux.[71] John didn't care what I was up to then and I very much doubt he's started to since.'

'Okay, so that wasn't him. But I have other evidence. He's said things—'

---

71 DW: Of course, Günter had, by now, read *Murder in the Metro*, but as far as we know he never saw how it fitted in.

'Günter, you don't know him like I do.' My gut burned with jealousy. 'He likes to provoke people. He doesn't believe half the stuff he says, he just enjoys baiting liberals. It's one of his less endearing habits. He likes the idea that people talk about him all the time; it's as if he really believes that any publicity is good publicity.'

'I can't think of a better talking point than blowing up a building,' I said.

'He's not a violent man,' she said.

'Maybe he's changed.'

She picked up the grappling hook and put it in the cupboard under the stairs, next to the hoover. 'You're not having that back until after you've finished all those windows.'

'What if he's really planning something awful?'

'I just don't think he is,' she replied.

'Well, it can't hurt to be vigilant, can it?'

I followed her eyes to the clock. I had about three hours until work. This was the danger zone. If I slept now, I'd probably be more tired, or even omit to wake at all. No, I had to stay awake at all costs.

'I think I have to go,' I said, taking my hand away.

'What are we going to do about us?' she asked.

'Are you absolutely sure you're going to have this baby?'

'Yes.'

I nodded. 'Then there is no point in us arguing. You are having the baby, so I'll be there. I might be bad at it, but I will be there. I never know how to do the right thing. But I do know that I couldn't bear to have a child that didn't know me, or couldn't call on me. Life is hard enough without losing a parent before you have begun. It is like trying to live with a chunk carved out of your innards. You don't know how much damage it is doing, no one does. Nothing can take its place.'

'Not until you have someone of your own to look after,' she replied.

We stood up.

'I wish I didn't have to go,' I said.

'It's okay. I'll see you tomorrow night.'

'Maybe.'

'Definitely.'

I opened the front door to the chill winds and Lieve pulled her gown tightly around her. I kissed her soft lips passionately – the last kiss I ever gave her – and stepped out into the dark.

In the End

I became aware of Archimedes nipping at my ankle, the little bastard, and hot rain falling on my head. I realised I was naked and vertical. I had fallen asleep in the shower. I stumbled out, taking out a couple of the shower's curtain rings, and found my phone. Seven missed calls. I was very, very late.

I threw on my clothes, gathered up my equipment, strapped myself into my pouches and holsters and ran outside. Frank was outside, reading his little book.

'Frank, I'm so sorry.'

'That's all right,' he squeaked. 'I've been doing some reading.'

'What is that book you're always reading?' I asked.

'New one every week. Police procedurals.'

'Oh. Any good?'

'Yeah. Reckon I could get away with a murder if I done one now.'

He opened the door and I sat inside. The seat hugged me, but my quads and bottom ached. Frank got in the other side and we took off, the acceleration forcing my head back onto the headrest. I let the orchestra wash over me as we sped down alleys and up one-way streets, just inches from skips and the sleeping homeless. I still found it amazing that he'd never hit anyone.

'Have you been working with Blades for a while?' I asked as

we passed Monument.[72]

'Years.'

'Would you say you know him pretty well?'

'Better than he thinks. I overhear a lot. He doesn't take much notice of me because I'm black. He's a bit of a prick like that.'

'Oh.' I let the thought hang for a moment. 'Has he ever talked about, ah, fascism? Getting rid of foreigners, that sort of thing?'

'Yeah, it's his favourite party piece. Mostly when he's drunk.'

'And it doesn't bother you? Working for a guy like that?'

'Why would it bother me? I'll take as much of his money as he wants to give me.'

'You know what I like about you, Frank? You're imperturbable.'

He nodded appreciatively, and we said no more.

When I arrived at the Shard, the sun was already up and I could see the platforms out like little magnets stuck to the side of the building. There were almost no clouds and, even through my glasses, the world seemed drawn in crisp lines, the angles and shadows of the building sharp and clear.

I went in on my own to see the site manager, who gave me a pass. It was a long and lonely lift to base camp, where everyone's bags and lunch boxes sat in heaps on the floor. There was no point in trying to get out there now, I could hardly shimmy down a cable and commence work. I looked around the newly furnished floors, watching people sweep up dust and fit mirrors behind drinks bars.

---

72 DW: This is the particular monument whose name is Monument, dedicated to those who suffered in the Great Fire of London. From 1681 to 1830, the plaque blamed the incident on Catholics, claiming that 'On the third day, when it had now altogether vanquished all human counsel and resource, at the bidding, as we may well believe, of heaven, the fatal fire stayed its course and everywhere died out. But Popish frenzy, which wrought such horrors, is not yet quenched.' I suppose they felt they may as well put the tragedy to good use.

One of the gondolas was stationed where I was, so I decided to go out. I waved my pass at a nosy cleaning lady and wandered up to the sixty-sixth-floor maintenance deck. It was the second day that we'd had no wind, and I could see the steel mesh cables that were holding the cradle below, taut and near vertical. It was a beautiful day. From here, the higher part of the building mirrored the sky, a cool blue with one lone lamb of a cloud drifting in to meet its reflection. The sun was really up now, and soothed my goosebumps. I took a great breath, and soaked it all up. Perhaps I would go and get a glass of water.

I was just on my way back in when I spotted one of the video cameras, lying on its back, as if sunbathing. Someone had obviously forgotten to take it with them and left it there. I picked it up and looked at the screen. The video timer was running down, and not up, as I would have expected. And why would they have been recording the sky?

It was really heavy. And there would be tens of other cameras, all the same, stationed around the whole building. All of them heavy. All counting down. Ticking down towards zero. Heavy, ticking electronics, all over the building. Ticking.

My first instinct, when I realised that the camera was a bomb, was to throw it over the side, but I obviously couldn't do that. I ran back in, grabbed a spare sheet of cardboard and wrote, OUT OF ORDER. I taped the sign to the inside of one of the lifts and put the camera inside. Then I gathered any others I could see, and took the lift up as far as it would go, to the highest level where there were offices. Above it, there were only stairs up to what was once supposed to be a radiator system, but had already been repurposed. I went up to the roof and found another camera there. There were a couple more on what would become the tourists' viewing platform, and a few in the service lift. I took the cameras I'd found and rode to the ground floor. I explained what I could to Frank. We carried the cameras out together, leaving them in his car boot.

'What are we going to do with all the bombs?' I asked frantically.

'Loads of time before they go off. You go back up there and keep him distracted,' said Frank, waving his little book. 'He might have some kind of remote control trigger. He'll be going on his break now. I'll phone the muck once you're back out on the cradles, he'll be helpless by then.'

I looked back up at the summit, and true enough, it looked like they were all coming in for lunch. I went back inside and made for the lift.

At base camp, the people were just coming in, chatting excitably. I didn't know who was in on the plot, so I thought it best to steer clear of the cameras-are-bombs issue entirely. People ate sandwiches and drank tea from thermal flasks. Generally the mood was upbeat, but I kept looking out for signs that one of them might be preparing their last rites. Someone handed me a coffee which I gulped down. I'd had almost no sleep and hadn't eaten since the previous night. Come to think of it, all I'd had then was a whisky and half a steak.

Blades found me and split me off from a cluster.

'What happened this morning? I thought you were a team player.'

'I'm sorry, I . . .' I couldn't believe I was apologising to the man.

'Forget it. So,' he said, slapping me hard on the back, 'did you see the Palace game last night?'

'Oh. Um, yes. Yeah. It was good. A good match.'

Blades smiled, showing off his canines. 'There wasn't a Palace game last night, you kiss-ass. Don't think I can't see through you.'

He moved off to talk to others, and I was left alone.

'You all right mate? You look a bit white.' Pete was getting a bottle of Lucozade from his holdall by my foot. He looked up at me with a childlike concern.

'Yes. Yes, I'm fine thanks. How about you? Have you got anything fun planned over the weekend?'

'Nah, nothing much mate. Gotta live in the moment. Anyways, after today I'll probably be out for the count. You?'

'Might catch up with relatives,' I said. *Out for the count*, eh? I'd had him down as a good guy.

I got a text from Frank, telling me he was taking the cameras out of range of Blades and whatever happened, we should rendezvous at 3 p.m. Where should he meet me?

People packed up their stuff. The break was ending. Blades took me with him into a lift, and we took the remaining stairs to the very top. I had become aware of every twitch he made beside me. He had rolled his uniform down to his waist, tying the arms, with only a vest underneath. I could see pools of shadow grow and disappear as he flexed and unflexed his arms. He wasn't a big man, but his hands looked as strong as clamps, and he had that nervous tension I sometimes saw in drug addicts on the street, as if at any moment he might just lunge forward and sink those canines into my nose.

We got out onto the maintenance deck, set the gondola and he climbed into the cradle. I noted with a certain satisfaction that he hadn't clipped himself on. But then really, what was I going to do – hoist him over the side?

We were just preparing to drop, and I hadn't yet heard any sirens. The cradle ran on an automated reel that would take forty-odd minutes to come back up once it was fully extended. If Blades didn't know we'd taken the cameras, he'd continue washing the windows in blissful ignorance. If he did find out, he wouldn't suspect me, because I'd be up here with him. I climbed into the cradle after him, feeling very clever.

We got our equipment ready. I clipped myself securely on,

twice. I had my standard spray, squeegee, suction cup, scraper, titanium scraper, GOMORRAH. Check. Glasses pushed up to bridge of nose. Check. T-shirt still too small, possibly still too heavy, but the cradle felt pretty solid. I doubted any human could break the steel mesh cables. You could hang a wrecking ball off one of these.

We pressed the green button to start the programmed descent. Our pace was pre-determined, our rhythm absolute. Here was our crow's nest, there the horizon. All around us, the curved earth. If only we had been able to look out from this vantage point hundreds of years ago. You could see things more clearly up here. People were put in their proper proportion. Red ants, black ants.

'Günter, have you moved the camera?' I froze. Blades pointed over near the stairs. 'The camera. Did you move it?'

'What makes you think I moved it? I only just got here.'

'Did you or didn't you?' he asked.

' . . . '

'Why did you move it? Are you stupid? We spent hours finding the right positions.'

'I don't care how long you spent. I wasn't going to let you get away with it.'

He took a step towards my end of the platform. 'I'm not in the mood for practical jokes, Günter. Where is the camera?'

'I don't know.'

'You do.'

'They're hidden. All of them. You'll never find them.'

Blades took another step towards me. The platform shuddered.

'This is the last straw.' His voice rose. 'This is the last. Fucking. Straw. I brought you up here, I gave you a job. You were nothing when I found you, just some local yokel. People in Salisbury didn't respect you, you were a circus act to them. Don't you understand? You were a joke, a fat man flying like a wind sock. I mean, look at yourself. Really look. I constantly have to send Frank to pick you up because you refuse to own a car. The other cleaners don't respect you either, I have to step in for you every time your back's turned. They say you're too fat, you talk nonsense, your methods are eccentric. I've been defending you, because I thought you might be grateful. I thought you might go far.' He took another step forward, now only inches from my face. 'And this is how you repay me.' He put his hands on my shoulders and looked me deep in the eye, like a drill sergeant. 'So what is this? Some kind of fucking hidden camera show? What?' I said nothing. 'Why have you hidden my fucking cameras?'

He started to shake me hard and the cradle wobbled.

'Take your hands off me,' I said, my voice cracking. I grabbed his arms and tried to pull them off me but he was shaking me more violently now. The cradle began to bounce gently.

'Give me the cameras you bloody hun! I've had enough of your fun and games, tell me where they are!'

He was gripping me so hard that I couldn't pry even a single finger off my shoulders – he was just too strong – and now the cradle bounced and swung in towards the windows, smashing against the glass, which fractured at the point of impact.[73] I stamped on his foot and his hands moved from my shoulders to my neck and he started to push me backwards, bending me over the side.

I panicked. I had a safety rope, but instinct took over. Before I knew what I was doing I had taken the GOMORRAH out of my sidekick holster and sprayed it into his face. He let out a shriek like a man possessed and clutched at his eyes, stumbled backwards, tripped on a metal strut and fell back over the side, one hand trying to snatch at a cable. I reached out to grab his arm but pulled back. It was too late.

73 'There's a window cleaner's cradle swinging wildly.' Call to London Fire Brigade ('Shard Worker Struck on 72nd Floor', *BBC Magazine,* 2 July 2012).

It wasn't quite a freefall. As one foot caught a window frame it threw him into a spin, so that he seemed to be cartwheeling erratically down the building. He must have lost consciousness at around the thirtieth floor, when his head hit and cracked a window, slowing the cartwheels. From that point on he was a rag doll, lifeless arms like streamers on a kite. He barely bounced when he hit the concrete, though his body broke up a bit, stuck bull's-eye in a cloud of dust.

My ears rang. I felt as if I was underwater. I looked at my watch and saw that it was just gone half past two; I unclipped myself, wiped my sweaty palms on my trousers, climbed a couple of feet of cable and hoisted myself back onto the deck; I took the lift to the ground floor; I walked out quickly past the crowd that had gathered around the body; I entered London Bridge underground station; I texted Frank to meet me at Liberty's. Somewhere crowded. We could get anywhere from there. I heard sirens dipping in pitch as I walked down the escalator; I changed at Bank and ended up at Oxford Circus, where I began the short walk to our meeting point; I looked at my watch: 2.58.

I had saved the day. I had definitely saved the day. Blades was evil. Everyone knew it. It had been me or him. It was self-defence. He had attacked me first, he was trying to strangle me or throw me over the side. I had done what anyone would do. Burned his face and sent him on a thousand-foot flight. It was the right thing to do.

I had to think of other things. That was something to think about later.

I turned onto Great Marlborough Street and saw the sun cleaving the road into light and dark. It was so obvious, so clear-cut. I saw the LIBERTY sign, the beautiful exotic flowers by the entrance. Along the shop front, from floor to ceiling, was plate after plate of cool, pristine glass. I stepped out into the road to get into the sunlight and saw the golden weathervane, in the shape of a ship, sailing on air towards some land of hope, the sunlight caught in its intricacies as if charging it with energy. I walked out further into the middle of the crossroads, and stopped. This was the moment that everything had been building up to. This moment. Now, here. The sun blazing like a furnace, the clear light, liberty, purity. This is it. I feel a blistering rush as if I am being lifted from the ground, hear a screech as of shuddering tyres, the split of metal and the fracturing of glass.

In this moment, I see God's teardrop start to form: the universe is flung outwards, matter grabs on with its fingertips and waltzes with its nearest partner; stars form, stars waltz, combine; and then whole groups of stars, waltzing and combining. Some of these huge bodies start to collapse under their own weight; I am born and die; life is born and dies; and still the teardrop wells, gathering weight, becoming rounder, pregnant. More stars collapse to become so dense that the light itself is waltzing around them, gathering itself into a compressed black mass, finding other darknesses, feeding. The teardrop has formed. It ripples ever so slightly. The darknesses begin their last waltz around the unseen centre of everything, God, antimatter, all worlds. They waltz closer, faster, like water down a plughole. The teardrop falls, and when it lands, all worlds collide, and there is a monstrous splash. The universe is flung outwards.

'You have to get him to hospital,' someone cried in distress.

'No!' I croaked. I couldn't feel my body.

'You're pretty mashed up,' said another voice, speaking softly from the throat. 'You're losing a lot of blood.'

'No,' I heard myself reply. 'I want to go home. I want to go home. I want to go home.' I repeated it like a mantra, like a spell. I must have blacked out, because the next thing I knew I was lying in a bed.

'You're awake,' he said.

'Yes.'

'I thought you might be dead.'

'No.'

'Don't be alarmed,' said Frank.

'I'm not.'

'Good. But try not to be alarmed when you see your chest. And don't try and pull it out. That might make you die.'

I looked down at my body. There was nothing obviously untoward, except that I could see something out of reach in the very bottom of my vision. I craned my neck, trying to pull my head upwards, and saw a thin but discernible sliver of glass, lodged in my chest like an award.

'How far in is it?' I asked.

'Far enough that taking it out is worse than leaving it in. They want you to speak to your family before they operate.'

In the face of this injury, which was so obviously mortal, I became calmer than, perhaps, I have ever been. I was to die. It was decided. There was not a thing I could do about it; to struggle against it would only bring death closer. I imagined the edges, just atoms thick, cleaving my cells like a knife through hot butter on a scale so minute that it almost didn't matter which side they were on.

'What happened?' I asked. It hurt to talk, or breathe.

'I tipped off the muck from a phone box and then got your text and realised I was late to meet you, so I was driving a little over the agreed speed limits and I caught you as I came out of a side road. You really took out my bumper. Half a shop front too.'

'Is Blades okay?' I asked, somehow unable to believe any of it.

'He's not going to get any worse.'

'Have they diffused the bombs?'

'Don't know. Spoke to one of the lads who'd come down to see the body and he seemed to think the cameras were all filming the sky to do a time lapse video.'

'That's probably just what Blades told him.'

Frank didn't say anything.

'But he really was planning to blow up the Shard, wasn't he?'

'Wouldn't rule it out. Either way, you've relieved the world of a prick.'

'I didn't kill him.'

'Course not. He fell.' Frank cracked a good-natured grin. 'You get some rest. Your family will be here soon.'

He looked anxiously at the door. I closed my eyes. I tried to shift in the bed but it hurt too much. I should do more exercise, I thought. Here I am, alive, a miracle of muscle and joint, unused.

My mind lapped gently at the shores of consciousness. I thought of the seaside. It was so vivid, the ocean so impenetrably deep. I could almost smell fish.

A hand took my hand. A strong hand. An expressive hand.

I couldn't muster the breath to speak, but my hands still worked.

I'm sorry, I signed.

You're just saying that because you think you're dying, Max signed back miserably.

I really am sorry. I'm sorry that you'll only have one person left to care about.

You're sorry for your behaviour? he signed.

No. You are my brother. It is your job to put up with me. And tell Lieve—

Lieve was real? No way! So you finally got laid? he replied.

Yes. Tell her she will be a good mother. Important.

He nodded. We could not say anything else. I could not say *love* without disturbing my wound, and wouldn't have known how to say it to Max. I hoped he knew.

Sometimes it is hard to tell whether you are crying without touching your face. My temples felt hot. There could have been tears running down them, I supposed, but my hands were heavy now. As the late afternoon sun fell, it shot in through the window and filled my eyes with light. I didn't close them. I wanted the image of that light burned onto my retinas. The sheets around me were soft and hot.

For a long time I have been looking for something simple to reach for, something that stays the same always, that is not subject to conditions. Something pure and clear as light through glass.

When it comes down to it, though, I suppose I don't know what that is. You can't rise up out of the world. Nothing that exists can be pure. Purity can't feel, or interact; it might as well not have been. I have tried to live by ideals, to find something after my mother that might carry me over the rocks. I wonder what she would say. 'You tried your best, and that's what counts.' I did. I did try my very best. But I suppose I wasn't up to the job. I suppose, if anyone's up there counting the scores, they might concede that they have made it too hard to be good.

Still, I suppose a lot of things.

Dad was trying to show me a text message.

'Your friend the Dean is on her way.'

Too late, I signed. I imagined her sitting on a train, her hands curled up into each other like a Grecian key, and tried to smile. *Any messages for Mum?* I signed.

'Tell her I broke one of the plates from our nice set but I've found a wholesaler who can replace it.' Dad chuckled through his bleary eyes. He never knew what to say when it mattered. But that was for the best too. 'Tell her I love her, and I hope it's bikini weather up there. She always had a cracking pair of legs.' He shook his head, choked up, and covered his face with his hand.

It's okay, I signed. *Get some rest. I think we could all do with a rest.* I don't know if he saw me. I don't know if anyone did.